First paperback edition July 2022

Cover Design by Liana Phan

ISBN 979-8-9865156-0-1 (paperback)
ISBN 979-8-9865156-1-8 (ebook)

Acknowledgments

The making of this story has been an incredibly challenging and personally transformative endeavor. This is my first novel and quite honestly, I was terrified of falling on my face and making a fool of myself throughout most of the writing process. The first draft was definitely something I shuddered at the thought of seeing the light of day. Yet the final product is at the very least, something I can be proud to say is mine.

However, there are many people to whom I owe credit for helping me with this project. I cannot thank Zack Rollins, Ava Giacomozzi, Isaiah Britt, and Maverick Larkin enough for taking the time to proofread the final draft for me. Your advice and insight were invaluable in smoothing out the story and making me feel confident about this project. I cannot express enough gratitude for my family for being a steady source of support for me throughout my life, as well as during this process. My mother and father, Rachel and Matthew; my siblings, Taylor, Devin, Emma, and Madison. All of you are very dear to my heart and I wouldn't have been able to get anywhere without you. Lastly, I would like to thank my cover designer and partner Liana Phan. I appreciate you more than words can say.

WINNER

TAKES

ALL

PART ONE

April 24th, 2159

Aamil

Aamil's feet slid across the smooth canvas inside of the cage. He circled his opponent, a gangly young man with gloved fists raised before the snarl on his face. *So much fire in his eyes, he reminds me of Rahim,* Aamil thought to himself.

A jab snapped out to graze his cheek, forcing Aamil to abandon his musing and focus on the task at hand. Thus far the match had been quite explosive, the young man started the opening round hot by launching forward like a sprinter off starting blocks. Furiously, he had thrown a wild combination of strikes at Aamil. Blows that arrived with such frequency and intensity that they would have overwhelmed a lesser man. To no avail, however, as Aamil kept his feet busy, meticulously slipping out of range for every potential hit.

Not attempting any offensive maneuvers of his own, the more experienced fighter resigned himself to studying his opponents' movements before engaging further. These tactics were quickly growing stale though, testified by the glancing blow that had just been dealt him.

The oscillating sounds of "ooh" and "ahh" accompanied the performance of the two men as they clashed, with the occasional "boo" being hurled in dissatisfaction at Aamil's passivity. Loge seating loomed overhead, clusters of sumptuously dressed people leaned over balconies to observe the two.

Still more extravagantly dressed individuals peered from massive screens lining the walls. People who did not desire to appear in person, but still craved the exclusivity of having their faces displayed at such an event. A smokey gray insect-like creation hovered over the event, the

FilmBot streaming the fight to millions of absorbed viewers across the globe.

The pompous atmosphere of these affairs always left a sour taste in Aamil's mouth, but more urgent matters prevented him from dwelling on his distaste. Although fatigue had caused him to slow down, the young man still pressed forward relentlessly. Taking note of his opponent's impetuous decision-making, Aamil analyzed the other man's movements and prepared to seize his opportunity. Just as he was about to strike, a bell pealed through the air signaling the end of the first round.

Lamenting his poor timing, Aamil strode over to his corner to await the next round. Upon his approach, an opening formed in the canvas near the edge of the cage. A faucet ascended from the opening to about chest level. Leaning forward he pressed a button on the back of the faucet and took a single long swig. Having quenched his thirst, he motioned to dismiss the spigot which promptly descended, followed by a closing of the opening in the floor.

Turning around, he eyed the young man who was still greedily sucking water in his own corner. Breaking his lips away, the man finished his drinking to straighten himself up, still shakily gasping to regain his breath. *He's definitely a fighter more than he is a true martial artist. Although I suppose the latter is a rare find these days. In a healthy environment with proper training, he could really become something spec- , no shut up Aamil. No point in dwelling on things you can't change, just focus on taking care of you and yours.*

Aamil fought to rid his mind of these distracting thoughts, managing to focus shortly before the bell announced the second round. The young man came darting in again, evidently intending to continue his barrage against Aamil.

To his surprise though, Aamil chose that moment to go on the offensive. Having gotten a full measure of what he should expect from his opponents' unvarying approach, Aamil expectantly waited for the man to overextend as he threw his leading right jab. Stepping to the outside of the striking arm, Aamil level changed to drop his hips. Exploding up and forward with his other foot, Aamil clasped his arms around the neck and leading arm of his opponent. Yanking him to the side to change his leading leg and further unbalance the man, Aamil swept his foot between the legs of his opponent and jerked his upper body as if he were throwing a baseball.

The man slammed into the canvas and wheezed like a dog toy as Aamil landed atop him. Reaffirming his grip and flexing, Aamil strained to cut off his opponents' air supply. After a few moments, he was rewarded by the sound of the man's hand frantically slapping against the ground in submission.

Relinquishing his hold, Aamil rolled away and rose to his feet. Bending over, he extended a hand to help the other man up. His beaten opponent gave him a bitter look and slapped Aamil's hand out of his face. "Don't be like that. You fought well, I'm proud to have had you as my opponent tonight. With a few more years of experience, you could have really given me a run for my money," Aamil commended.

The man shook his head, rolling his eyes, "and tonight you cost me money of my own. Your false flattery isn't going to put food on my family's table when I go home. Drop the nice guy act, at the end of the day we're each just obstacles for the other to overcome."

With that, their short exchange ended, and they stood in the center of the cage waiting for their results to be announced to the spectators. For lower ranked events, fights were ordinarily announced by a RefBot, a Narrow AI software system that analyzes the flow of fights and determines the outcome. However, for high-profile events such as this, celebrity guests were brought in to enhance the spectacle of the performance. Aamil was rather peculiar in that he declined to keep himself up to date with the latest celebrities in the spotlight. As such, he failed to recognize the petite spritely-looking lady who crossed the entrance of the cage to join them in the center of the ring.

Her bubblegum pink hair was pulled up into bunches on either side of her head. Wideset eyes sparkling at Aamil, she squeaked out, "congratulations." Aamil was cut off before he could thank her, she had already pulled out a microphone and was delivering her lines to the audience. "This match has concluded. With a second-round submission over Marcello Suha, the winner tonight is Aamil Jackson!"

Aamil politely nodded as the crowd began their applause. Turning, he reached to try and shake the hand of Marcello, only to see his ankle crossing through the door as he left. Sighing, Aamil followed suit and made his way out of the cage.

Approaching the top of the steps leading out of the cage, he was confronted by a smokey gray cylinder stationed outside of the doorway. Standing chest high to Aamil, the device was made of an almost seamless metallic material, broken up only by a smooth glass screen set into its face. He leaned over to bring his eyes across from the screen, the machine emitted a quiet hum while it scanned his retina. Confirming his identity, the DistribuBot displayed an assembly of information on its screen.

In a cordial tone, a voice emanated from the DistribuBot, vocalizing the information found on its screen. "Your victory has been processed and recorded in Quell's database. Three thousand credits have been transferred to your personal account; your PQ has been adjusted to sixty-one. You will now advance to the All-West competition pool, the bouts for which will take place in Los Angeles. You are allowed one month of inactivity before your status will be reverted, at which time you will be forced to rejoin the Northwest competition pool. Although, you may schedule your next fight any time before that month has expired. What date would you like to designate for your next fight?"

At this point, Aamil was quite antsy to leave and ended up choosing the first date that popped into his head, "May first."

"Confirmed. Your bout will be on May first, one week from today. This session has concluded." As it dismissed him, the Bot powered down, the screen dimming back to darkness.

Aamil hopped down the steps, blanching as realization struck him, "shit the first is Rahim's birthday," he said aloud. *Linh is going to kill me.* Aamil shuddered at the thought of the talking to waiting for him when he got home.

He walked out of the room, entering a long corridor lined with doors identical to the one swinging shut behind him. Striding down the hallway, he passed by several individuals waiting in anticipation of their own fights to come. Many of these poor souls appeared in no condition to be on the verge of participating in a fight. From their choppy movements and pained expressions, it was evident they were nursing injuries from previous clashes. The sight elicited a grimace from Aamil, internally cursing the fact that so many were being forced onto this path of pain and conflict out of desperation.

Reaching the end of the hallway, he stood before an elevator stained with the familiar smokey gray color that characterized the Bots he had seen. A moment after pressing a button set into the wall, the doors opened, and he stepped inside. The walls of the elevator were glass, providing him a sweeping view of the Seattle skyline. Elevated 500 meters in the air, the city unfolded spectacularly before his eyes.

Skyscrapers of equivalent size were planted adjacent to the building he stood within, dozens more in the distance disappearing out of sight as he descended. Bots with a variety of shapes and purposes zipped through the air, and along the city streets where they were indistinguishable from the human occupants that dwelled below. The sun stood high in the sky, its brilliant rays illuminating the pristine exterior that defined all the buildings within the city. Aamil did not have long to admire the view, soon arriving at the base floor of the Tower.

Traveling through the lobby his feet soon found pavement as he walked out onto the city streets. Like the structures that towered above them, the sidewalk and streets were immaculately well kept. The nature of this urban sprawl was akin to how almost all the major cities in the world were maintained. Aamil began the long walk to the train that would transport him home.

Strolling along, he observed the passerby wandering about around him. Unlike the inorganic machines and structures surrounding them, most of the people who inhabited the city were worse for wear. Tattered clothing aplenty adorned many of the pedestrians walking by, draped over emaciated and battered figures. Nary an individual passed Aamil who was not burdened with a limp or wince, not displaying some sort of bruising or scar.

As it always did, the sight of these toiling masses struck a painful chord in Aamil's heart. While most were dressed in rather drab clothing, flashes of color stood out here and there amongst the people. Several different shades of blue were worn by people who walked about.

Distracting from the gloomy sight dominating the crowds, drifting in and out of buildings as well as sitting in their vehicles on the road, was a cast of intriguing individuals. Far fewer in number than their compatriots around them, these individuals were lavishly dressed, and most were escorted by a detail of SecurityBots who hovered close to their persons.

These bots roamed on swiveling spheres, coasting over the ground with ease, their upper halves vaguely humanoid. Though their reputation alone was enough to deter any would-be assailants, SecurityBots emitted an imposing glare from their heads sufficient to spook all but the most determined of harassers. The presence of these Bots assured such protection, that the individuals they guarded walked with confidence and lightness of heart seldom to be found in most ordinary people.

After about twenty minutes, Aamil got to his destination The Sounder, a RailBot with a name from a forgotten time. Paying one hundred and seventy credits, he quickly boarded. While still significantly cheaper than alternative modes of transportation, the sum was still enough to make him inwardly cringe.

A few moments later, the train raced down the tracks. The outside scenery quickly passed by through the view of Aamil's window. Gargantuan metropolis soon gave way to a more modest suburban landscape as he left Seattle. A few more minutes of this and Aamil was once again looking upon another impressive, albeit much smaller skyline.

Exiting the train into the station, Aamil entered the city of Tacoma. From there he began the walk to his home a few miles away. On his trip, he spotted an apartment complex in the midst of being built by a crew of ConstructaBots. Standing tall outside of the development was a digital billboard that said 'Quell' in large silver letters. A message underneath it read, 'We put the power in your hands, so you can seize the life you've always wanted'.

A cluster of particularly ragged-looking people sat on the sidewalk under the billboard, each had a crimson DW emblazoned on their foreheads. Abashedly, Aamil averted his gaze and quickened his pace to walk by. *There's nothing you can do for them, just focus on yourself.*

Several minutes later, he caught sight of his home, a squat two-story house dwarfed by the humongous structures surrounding it. Looking at the property always gave him a swell of pride and a speck of hope, often absent in his day-to-day life. Aamil had managed to utilize his success to save and become the owner of this land, a rare accomplishment for those not born to illustrious heritage, as most other people were renters.

Though not nearly as glamorous as the other structures that were almost all possessed by Quell, the quaint home gave him a sense of security. The house was defined by wide open windows wrapping around most of the bottom level and a wooden staircase leading up to the top level of the home. A woman and a young boy tended to a large garden bed along the side of the home.

Rahim

Rahim bent over in a squat, fuming impatiently as he jammed his fingers into the soft rich brown earth. He scoured the dirt to rip out any unfortunate weed that fell under his gaze. Discontent with this monotonous work, a single mantra ran through his mind. *I hate this, I hate this, I hate this.* The repetition eventually became unbearable to the point he groaned in protest, "I don't understand why I have to do this; this is YOUR garden mom! If you want it so bad, why can't you just do this?"

A flash of irritation shone in Linh's eyes, turning from her watering, she narrowed them in her son's direction. "Why does everything have to be such a battle with you Rahim? Can't you just do it because I asked you to, and you want to make your mother happy?" Rahim rolled his eyes, grumbling under his breath in response.

Linh began to snap at him before reminding herself of her own strong-spirited personality as a youth. She thought for a moment before retorting, "has it ever occurred to you that perhaps I'm trying to teach you something here? And I'm not just trying to work you to death?" Linh gripped her throat with one hand while melodramatically reaching for the sky with the other, "the horror," she rasped.

Rahim pouted, "you just think you're hilarious, huh mom?"

"Well, aren't I?" Linh said with a wink. Walking over to Rahim's side, she lowered herself, raven black hair falling forward before her face. Bunching her khaki shorts higher up her thighs, she knelt in the soil beside him. "There's a lot of lessons to be had here." Gently smiling, she leaned and brushed her finger against the petal of a tulip rooted near where they sat. "Flowers are a lot like people. Their outcome largely depends on the quality of care they receive. You must learn to put in consistent time and effort to nurture their growth. You need to have a balanced hand, if you are overbearing, they can flounder and drown under your thumb. If you are neglectful, they will wilt and wither. An incompetent gardener can squander the plant's potential. If planted in poor soil and left at the mercy of weeds and insects, it will have little opportunity to reach what it might have been capable of. At the same time, not every flower requires the same touch. Some may need more attention and some less, the wallflower does not need the same care as the rose. Secondly, this is to teach you..." Linh scowled mid-sentence as she noticed her son's attention drifting.

"OW!" Rahim whined after his mother rapped him on the head.

"PATIENCE! I am trying to teach you patience, Rahim. Something you apparently need since you can't be bothered to hear out what your mother is trying to tell you. It is important to be able to sit with one's thoughts, to be fully present in the body. We must be vigilant and reflective of our internal states of mind, as well as aware of what others are going through."

"I couldn't agree more," replied Aamil.

Linh and Rahim jumped like toads in a thunderstorm upon the unexpected intrusion, "AH!" they both yelped. Their features transformed, realizing who had walked in on their conversation. "DAD!" Rahim hooted excitedly, a grin stretching across his face. Happily, he looked up at his father who appeared every bit a superhero in Rahim's eyes: tall, broad-shouldered, square-set jaw with a moderate layer of stubble.

Aamil stepped forward and tousled Rahim's tightly curled hair, "hey tiger." Placing a hand on her back, he looked at Linh, "sorry for the wait, work was kicking my ass."

A loving smile graced Linh's face, rising, she greeted her partner, "no bruises? Well, that's something I don't see all the time." Affectionately, she placed her hand on Aamil's chest. Raising herself onto the balls of her feet, she pecked him on the lips, "I love you," she whispered.

"I love you too," Aamil mouthed back, pressing his forehead against hers. Looking back to Rahim, he asked, "so have you been good for mom while I was away?"

"Yeah, I've been helping her garden," Rahim answered.

Linh made quotation marks with her fingers as she repeated, "helping." She rolled her eyes, "what he's really been doing is chewing my ear off with complaints. It seems he's a bit too full of energy to weed, maybe you can tire him out for me?"

A wicked look crossed over Aamil's face, "is that so? Well, I think I just might be able to get that done. He won't be bothering you when I'm through with him." Dread sunk into Rahim's mind as he had an inkling of what his father meant to do with him. He knew protesting would only bring a harsher sentence onto him, so he voicelessly followed his father through the front door of their home.

Aamil fumbled with the light switch until the room was fully illuminated. The light revealed a cushy maroon mat covering the entirety of the floor, along with various pieces of training equipment scattered around the edges of the room. "Get those feet moving," Aamil ordered Rahim. Reluctantly, Rahim obeyed and began running around the white circle that ran around the circumference of the mat.

Rahim's limbs initially protested at being forced into exertion but soon acclimated to the situation. While he ran in circles, Aamil walked over to the corner and unfolded a chair, taking a seat to observe Rahim warming up. A few minutes in, beads of sweat began to form at Rahim's temples. "So, what are we going to work on today?" inquired Rahim.

Aamil chuckled, "that's for me to know and you to find out. How about you get some sprints in for me, then we can stretch and get started." Rahim lined up at the base of the mat without complaint. Jolting back and forth, he zoomed across the surface of the mat like a hare running for its life. "FASTER, come on Rahim, I know you can do better than that! I need to see you breathing harder, let's work up a sweat here!" Aamil laced his fingers behind his head, leaning back in his chair as he watched his son frantically pick up the pace. Aamil enjoyed a feeling of amusement as Rahim tried to meet his demands.

Once Rahim was thoroughly out of breath, clothes clinging to the sweat on his skin, Aamil directed him to go stretch, getting out of his chair to go join him. They strained every inch of their bodies till the stiffness left their limbs. Bouncing up and down, they shook their arms and legs, driving the vigor back into their extremities.

Finishing this, Aamil directed Rahim to stand before him and shake his hand in a ritualistic fashion as they always did. Accompanying this gesture, Aamil guided Rahim into repeating the lessons he had drilled into his head for years now, "why do we do this?"

Rahim responded like clockwork, "to honor and respect our opponent."

"Why should we honor them?"

"They are doing us a service. As iron sharpens iron, their spirit helps strengthen our own. Even in the heat of competition, they are giving us an opportunity to learn, a chance to improve ourselves."

"Why should we respect them?"

"When we respect our opponents, we respect ourselves. It is an acknowledgment of our common humanity. Regardless of ability or skill, everybody is going through their own struggles to get where they are. Because everyone is born with different advantages and disadvantages, their success or lack of does not matter. We do not respect the respective destinations people may arrive at; we respect the journey we all must take to get there. It takes courage for anyone to continue moving through life in the face of pain and hardship. It is important to respect our opponents for this, and by extension to respect ourselves and the journey we have taken to get where we are."

Aamil smiled, feeling proud of how well he had taught Rahim. Before he could get choked up, he moved along in their lesson, "ok," Aamil said with a grunt. "I have a two-part lesson for you today, son. We're going to work on positioning and timing." Rahim furrowed his bushy brows annoyedly, *this is gonna be so boring,* he thought to himself. Nonetheless, however, he positioned himself in a defensible stance; legs staggered and squat, back straight, core tight, and elbows tucked in, waiting for his father's directions. "Alright first we are going to drill footwork," announced Aamil.

"Lovely," remarked Rahim in a sarcastic tone.

Aamil waved him off, "alright wise guy, save the attitude for another time." Coughing he proceeded into his lesson, "the name of the game here is action and reaction. You move, I move, and vice versa. Just maintain a good stance and keep me in front of you." Lowering himself, elbows tucked in, and hands arrayed before him defensively, Aamil and Rahim began to engage each other.

Prowling forward, Aamil approached Rahim. Each foot placed forward with the constrained elegance of a natural predator. Rahim hopped backward, prompting a scolding from Aamil, "get off those heels, you mustn't cede any ground to your opponent. If you have to create space, then circle around me. Keep those feet close to the ground and don't let them cross, balance is everything!"

Aamil began to quicken the pace, cutting back and forth as he randomly and suddenly switched directions while circling. Rahim struggled to keep up, thighs burning with the burden of carrying his weight in a stance for so long. Two minutes passed, his breath started to come in gasps, struggling to keep up with the pace his father was setting.

Noticing Rahim's fatigue, Aamil took mercy and let him rest for a moment. After two more rounds of this, Aamil took the opportunity to introduce the next part of the days' lesson. "This next drill is going to be like the last one, except we are going to be initiating the first step of our attack. Come at me however you like, just remember we are only drilling, don't be an asshole about it. I'll show you the same courtesy."

Rahim exhaled sharply and nodded, the two once more began to circle each other. Looking for his chance, Rahim threw a wide hook at his father. Aamil casually blocked the blow and tugged Rahim's elbow forward. Stepping outside, he fell to a knee and pulled Rahim to slump over his shoulder like a sack of potatoes. "You overcommitted, remember balance is everything."

They trained together in this manner for a few more minutes. Rahim repeatedly attempted to strike his father, trying a handful of takedown attempts, before he grew disheartened and stopped. Fuming with frustration, Rahim snapped at Aamil, "this is stupid, how am I supposed to do anything if you know so many more moves than me? What am I learning? Can you please just teach me a new move or something and we can drill that?"

Aamil rudely tapped his index finger on Rahim's forehead, "look I am telling you it doesn't matter WHAT you know. I can teach you any strike combination, any takedown, any throw, any submission technique...but if you don't know HOW and WHEN to use them, then it would be worthless. Knowledge is only useful if you have the ability and the will to make it reality. Not just for fighting but for life, simply knowing something is possible and wanting to achieve it isn't enough. You have to master the how and the when, if you don't know where to start, you won't get anywhere."

Rahim began to argue again but was cut off by Aamil tutting and wagging his finger. Recognizing his father was in no mood to tolerate backtalk, Rahim begrudgingly nodded his head. Despite his reticence, Rahim's expression betrayed the dissent he still felt inside. He resumed practicing, only to find his dissatisfaction swelling as he continued struggling to land anything successful against Aamil's seemingly effortless counterattacks.

Rahim's legs soon began to fail him, buckling under the constant stress he was putting them through. He was saved by the echo of metal incessantly being slapped from the doorway at the top of the stairs. "DINNER!" was the lone word shouted before Linh disappeared back into the house, letting the door close.

A mischievous grin manifested on Aamil's broad face. In one motion he pushed Rahim's right shoulder while sweeping his leg between Rahim's, driving him flat on his back. "DIBS ON THE SHOWER," Aamil jeered, sprinting up the stairs into the house.

Peeved, Rahim slowly got up and began walking upstairs. *How can he just go from lecturing me a little bit ago to acting like such a child?* Rahim shook his head and smiled before making the trek upstairs to clean himself off.

Feeling refreshed a short while later, Rahim salivated as he smelled the Doro Wat simmering atop a scoop of white rice within his bowl. Dipping his spoon into the bowl and thoroughly mixing the dish, he brought a spoonful to his mouth. He breathed deeply, enjoying the plethora of flavors dancing across his palette, spicy berbere tingled in his mouth. With a mouth still full of food he garbled, "so good mom, thank you!"

Linh sat in a slouch over her bowl of food, blissfully consuming bite after bite. Looking up at her son while still chewing, she said, "I'm glad you like it, thank you." Turning her eyes back down to her bowl, she spotted an unwelcome additional spoon diving towards her food. "NO!" she exclaimed, thwacking Aamil's thieving spoon with her own resulting in a loud CLINK. "What the hell dude?"

"I'm sorry it just tastes better when it's yours," Aamil apologized sheepishly. Making kissy faces he attempted to appease his feisty partner, "I mentioned how much I like your cooking right? You're so talented, baby."

"Alright alright I get it, I am kind of the best. Just don't be getting any more funny ideas, that's strike one mister," she said with a smirk.

Rahim internally gagged at the open displays of affection between his parents, *make it stop,* he groaned in his mind.

The dining table they ate at was tucked into the corner of their kitchen; the sounds of the television audible from the living room just through the doorway. A news broadcast could be heard, 'skirmishes between Reds and Blues left Portland, Oregon reeling last night. DetectiBots have reported 4 dead and 7 wounded, with no leads on potential suspects behind this clash. The survivors of the incident have been taken into custody and are undergoing interrogation, no further updates. In other news, one of Quells Towers was the target of a recent attempted terrorist attack, several pounds of explosives being found...'

The latter portion of the broadcast seemed to spark a thought in Linh, turning to Aamil, she asked, "by the way, I forgot earlier. When is your next fight supposed to be?"

Aamil nervously dissembled, realizing he had yet to break the news to them. "Yeah, uh...um, it's funny you ask. I, uh, actually am supposed to be fighting next week."

Linh glared at Aamil suspiciously, "when next week exactly?"

Aamil smiled apologetically, "the first."

Linh punched Aamil on the shoulder, "asshole! What were you thinking? You know that's Rahim's birthday! Well, you better apologize to him!"

Rahim sheepishly excused his father, "it's ok mom, really." He looked towards Aamil, "I understand you have other commitments, its ok, dad. I enjoy watching you fight anyway, so it's enough for me to just root for you from home."

Aamil placed his hand between Rahim's shoulder blades paternalistically, "thank you for understanding. I promise I'll make it up to you." Linh still didn't seem happy with the situation, but she let it slide for now.

After they finished eating, Rahim excused himself and grabbed his phone. Clicking a button, the device lit up to display several options on the screen. Interacting with the device, Rahim scrolled past the live Tower feeds of the fights and the various social media applications, to his contacts. Finding the person he was looking for, he dialed and waited for a response. The image of a boy about Rahim's age appeared on the screen as the call connected. Bleary-eyed, the boy rubbed his face, tiredly answering, "hello?"

"Lyall get ready, I'm headed over to your place."

The other boy protested, "come on man I was sleeping...can you at least bring me food if you're going to make me come out?"

Rahim shot finger guns at his friend, "easy peasy, I'll see you there." He wrapped up some leftovers from his family's meal and headed out of the house. Trotting down the wooden steps outside of his home, Rahim headed over to the apartment complex directly across the street. Pacing outside of the building, he perked up when he noticed his friend approaching.

Lyall stood about a head taller than Rahim, with a very wide girth about him. The much larger boy wore basketball shorts and flip flops that slapped the cement as he walked up, "what's up uce," he said while dapping up Rahim.

Rahim smiled, greeting his friend and presenting a box filled with leftover food, "sorry it's a bit cold, I'm sure you could just heat it up later though."

Lyall eagerly grabbed the box and snapped open the lid, digging into the food voraciously. "It's ok, I'll just eat it here. The folks were only able to make enough for rent this month, so ya boy is HUNGRY!" He made sounds of immense satisfaction as he dug in.

Rahim nodded sympathetically, "I'm sorry to hear that man, well there's always more at my house if you need something to eat. You know mom and dad think of you like family."

Lyall patted his friend on the back, "I appreciate it!" he said gratefully between mouthfuls of food. Once he had finished, the two boys wandered down the street aimlessly, lost in conversations about life.

Eventually, talk turned to Rahim's birthday next week, "yeah, my old man is going to be busy fighting down in Los Angeles, so I'll probably just be spending it watching him. Would you want to come over and watch with me and mom?"

"Of course bro, I wouldn't miss it! It always makes me so amped seeing your old man fight. My folks lose more often than not, so it's a nice change being able to watch him. He really carries the pride of the whole neighborhood on his back!" Rahim hummed at hearing his dad's praise from his best friend. The two carried on their conversation for a few more minutes.

They were interrupted by yelping around a nearby street corner, followed by a thumping sound. Drawn to investigate what was going on, Rahim and Lyall walked over and were dismayed by the spectacle that awaited them. What appeared to be a tent, along with several articles of clothing, were strewn all over the sidewalk. Being dragged aggressively by the arms were a couple with crimson DW's on their foreheads. Pulling them along was a SecurityBot, 'QUELL' written across its chest.

The couple yelled and screamed for the Bot to leave them be, protesting that they were not doing anything wrong. The SecurityBot in a dispassionate voice proclaimed they were on private property and could not sleep there, tossing them off the sidewalk onto the street. Rahim and Lyall shook with anxiety, processing the tragedy playing out before them, unable to make sense of their emotions in the moment.

Too engrossed to mind his surroundings, Rahim's shoe knocked into a rock, sending it skittering down the pavement. Alerted by the noise, the Bot turned its glare in the direction of the boys, scaring them so badly that they nearly jumped out of their shoes. Turning tail, they ran back the way they came, not stopping until they reached home.

Out of breath, they bent over, heaving for air, trying to consider what they had just witnessed. DW's were a normalized sight for them, poor souls who slept in the elements with little to their name. All Rahim knew of them was that they had gained their status from being unable to participate in fights or find other sources of income. So, they were labeled and received small stipends for survival.

Though Rahim was used to seeing them tucked away in odd spots throughout the city, witnessing them being subjected to such treatment was a novel sight. Desiring to return to the safety and comfort of their homes, the boys said their goodbyes. Rahim walked home with a troubled mind.

Linh's face twisted with concern when Rahim came home and told her what he witnessed that night. "Are you ok? You aren't hurt or anything right?" she fretted.

His eyes were glued on his shoes, "yeah I'm ok, it's just...why do those people deserve to be treated like that?"

A pain grew in Linh's heart, helplessly watching a part of her son's innocence wilt away. "They don't deserve to be treated like that; nobody does."

Those words only served to fuel the indignation that Rahim was experiencing, "then why do we let it happen? Why doesn't anybody do anything about it?"

Linh struggled with that for a moment, "well, people are too absorbed dealing with their own problems. When you're fighting week in and week out to put food on the table and keep a roof over your head, it's hard to find the energy to care about what other people are going through."

"But if everyone looked out for each other, then we would all have enough help to make it so our problems weren't too hard to carry. Isn't that what you and dad always say to get me to help you around the house, many hands make light work?"

Rahim's use of one of her frequent idioms was adorable enough to make Linh smile in the midst of this serious conversation. "You have a point there, but the system we live in makes that pretty hard to achieve. That might work, but the problem is getting other people to see the bigger picture and agree to go along with it. To get people to work together, first, you have to convince them that it's in their best interest to do so."

Rahim concentrated, processing her words, before lighting up. "That's kind of like what dad was saying to me earlier today; the how and when of things is more important than the what."

"So, you've actually been listening to us this whole time? That's good to know." Linh winked at Rahim, "you might have a point though. Who knows, maybe you'll be the one to figure this out someday." Their conversation ended there, and Linh sent Rahim to bed, or rather the couch since the living room also doubled as his bedroom.

The rest of the week proceeded rather tamely, Rahim spent most of his time training with Aamil and the rest sneaking off to hang out with Lyall. Eventually, the night before Rahim's twelfth birthday and Aamil's big fight came around. While Linh was in the other room entertaining herself, the two sat across from each other engaged in a friendly game of chess. "Dad it's your move," Rahim reminded Aamil, stirring him from the trance he was lost in.

"Ah yes," Aamil grumbled, moving a chipped white knight to the top right of the board. This move took advantage of the gaps in his son's sloppy pawn movement, forcing him to decide between sacrificing his rook or his queen. Aamil jokingly tsked to jab at his son's ego as Rahim woefully swooped his queen out of harm's way, relinquishing his rook in the process.

"Do you remember what we discussed the other day? About thinking about martial arts as a process of action and reaction? Well, chess is a lot like that. If you ever hope to beat me, you are going to have to start anticipating my moves. Think to yourself, if I do this, what are the possible moves he can make? And how will you respond to any one of those moves, and so forth. You must learn to carefully consider the consequences of your actions."

Rahim furrowed his brow, absentmindedly brushing his hand through his thick curly hair as he absorbed Aamil's lesson. Leaning forward he scrutinized the board until a plan of action manifested itself in his mind. Cautiously, he moved his bishop across the board to threaten Aamil's rook. Deftly, Aamil reacted by moving forward a pawn to block his son's advances, leaving an opening for Rahim to utilize his queen. "Check," he said proudly.

"Is that so?" replied Aamil, appearing to have all the confidence in the world. Smugly, he picked up a bishop that had escaped Rahim's notice, dragging it to usurp the queen's position. The game went quickly after that,

Aamil calmly dismantled his son's defenses until the inevitable "checkmate," slid off Aamil's tongue.

Despite his loss, the corner of Rahim's mouth twinged with the hint of a smile. He had never once put his father in check before, in fact, most games often ended in less than 10 moves. *I guess the old man isn't unbeatable after all.*

Aamil

Aamil impatiently tapped his foot as he signed in with the CheckBot before his fight. No matter how many times he went through this process, he was always wracked with nervous energy before he competed. A few seconds after verifying his identity, the machine informed him of the opponent he would be facing that day. "Your bout in the one-hundred-eighty-five-pound All-West competition pool will be against Kolby Balgair."

The name sounded strangely familiar to Aamil until he realized why, *he's one of Quell's plants, isn't he?* Quell had its own batch of fighters on call that they slipped into bouts from time to time. These individuals were ill-regarded, but as Quell ran the fights and most everything else, people had little room to complain.

Aamil had heard whispers about Kolby, suffice it to say, the man did not have a glowing reputation. The idea of facing a Quell plant troubled Aamil. *Coincidence?* He pondered to himself, but was resigned to the idea that he couldn't change the path that lay before him.

These thoughts weighed heavy on Aamil's mind as he took the elevator to the upper floors of the building. Stepping off, it was a short walk to find the room that he would be fighting in. Arriving, all he had to do was wait in the corridor with the other combatants awaiting their own trials. Two clusters had formed among the people awaiting their fights. One made up of individuals wearing blue outfits, each a different shade. The other group composed of people all wearing vermillion getups. Suspicious glares shot across the divide between both groups, their gazes containing barely constrained hostility. As he usually did, Aamil chose not to get involved in the group identity warfare and instead relegated himself near the wall on his own.

"It's pathetic, isn't it? They spend so much time pointing fingers and squabbling amongst themselves that they didn't even notice they were trapped in this cesspool of misery together."

Aamil was startled by the unexpected voice that spoke beside him. Although after looking at the figure, it was hard to piece together how he hadn't noticed him. A man of imposing stature leaned against the wall next to Aamil. Lanky and appearing to stand at about six and a half feet, close to a head taller than Aamil. Dressed up in a dazzling white tracksuit, a mop of ivory hair to match, the man cut quite the intriguing figure.

Aamil curiously appraised the man, responding, "it's hard to blame them, everything about this world is designed to keep us at each other's throats."

The man flashed a set of pearl whites at Aamil, grinning ear to ear. "I suppose you're right about that, but one could say they're responsible for keeping it that way, no?"

"I think you're ascribing entirely too much agency to the average person; how can they even realize what's being done to them when everyone is buried in a day-to-day battle for survival? The mouse does not realize it is in a maze, it just knows that it's hungry and it smells cheese."

The man raised an eyebrow, "so is that how you think of these people, as mice?"

Aamil shrugged, "it might not be the most flattering way to think of others, but I can't help but believe it. People tend to look for the easiest explanation. It is much easier to believe your problems are due to the failings of yourself and those around you; rather than pointing the finger at somebody you have never seen or met. Someone operating comfortably in the shadows. And thus, they spend their time fighting each other rather than bothering to ask the larger questions."

The man gave Aamil a look of admiration, "you are quite perceptive, Aamil. It's a shame really, in another lifetime perhaps you could have been something great, but instead you're destined to squalor in this miserable world."

His words rang alarm bells in Aamil's mind, "who are you and how do you know me?"

The man shook his head and wagged his finger, "maybe I was too hasty in offering you praise. Really now, I think that should be obvious. Your skills have made you quite the notorious man, as for me...you can call me Kolby."

At that, Aamil squared his shoulders to face Kolby head-on, "what do you want from me?"

Kolby nonchalantly shrugged, "me? Absolutely nothing. I'm just another mouse in the maze, a pawn to be moved about in the grander schemes of others. In fact, I think I like you Aamil. You should go home to that wife and son of yours, I'd hate for you to get hurt."

Aamil clenched his fists, growling, "how do you know all of this about me?"

Kolby chuckled darkly, "Quell sees everything, don't you know?" He walked away without another word, leaving Aamil to sit with his now frenzied thoughts.

Minutes turned into an hour until finally the time of reckoning came due. Aamil warmed up and stretched thoroughly in preparation until his dark skin was coated with a fine sheen of sweat. Squatting low to the ground, he meticulously wrapped straps of cloth over his hands to stabilize his wrists and protect his fists, before sheathing them in padded fingerless gloves.

Entering the door into the room he was meant to fight in, Aamil kept his eyes to the ground, ridding himself of all distractions. His feet carried him to the stairsteps of the cage. Going up them, he walked onto the gray canvas within. Aamil nimbly moved about, getting his measure of the space he would soon be competing in. Lightly, his feet hopped and slid over the semi cushioned surface.

Unnaturally soft footsteps heralded the arrival of Kolby as he meandered into the ring. His face was cool calm and collected in contrast to his earlier humorous affect. Dressed down now, his physique was truly menacing. Long of limb and coated in dense wiry muscle that had previously been concealed. A faintly visible white fox was tattooed across Kolby's chest, its teeth bared in a permanent snarl. The audience seated in the rafters above the cage began to clap politely.

The applause increased in volume as the celebrity announcer entered the cage. He was an older man in a black and white tuxedo, heavy jowls hung from his face. In a rather unanimated voice, he announced, "this will be a five-round bout, each round will be five minutes, all other rules remain standard per Quell fight regulations. Rounds will begin and end with the ringing of a bell." Just like that, the man left as quickly as he had entered.

* * *

Rahim, Lyall, and Linh sat glued to the television screen with bated breath, they waited for Aamil to begin his fight. "Jeez that guy is yolked!" exclaimed Rahim as he saw Kolby enter the cage. Lyall nodded in agreement, "dude must live at the gym."

"SHHHH" snapped Linh, hushing the both of them. Before the fight could begin, Aamil walked over and extended a hand out to Kolby. The other man gave Rahim's father an odd look before tentatively accepting his hand. Just as Aamil returned to his side of the cage, the peal of a bell rang loudly, signaling the beginning of the fight. As it did so, Linh nervously reached over and squeezed her son's hand.

The two men circled each other on-screen, appearing to be sizing each other up. With almost nothing telegraphing his intentions, Kolby abruptly launched a head kick, which Aamil somehow managed to perfectly react to and circle out of range. Fluidly Kolby resumed his posture and circled away, appearing to waste almost no energy as he scrutinized Aamil.

Aamil remained stone-faced, however, deploying a less efficient but more unpredictable style. Bouncing on the balls of his feet, frequently switching his lead leg. However, he remained mostly on the defensive, allowing Kolby to continue to throw out testing blows.

Noticeably growing impatient, Kolby attempted to take advantage of the reach difference and stepped forward, throwing a straight right jab. Aamil lowered himself and slipped inside, rotating to counter with an uppercut connecting right on the soft spot of Kolby's chin. Stunned by the unexpected impact, Kolby's legs wobbled beneath him, stumbling backward he fell on his butt.

"YESSSSSS!" cheered Linh, jumping off the couch jubilantly. Rolling in the last second, Kolby avoided a flying hammer fist from Aamil, who appeared to be Zeus himself throwing a thunderbolt. Not sparing any time, Aamil angled himself right back to smother Kolby. Here he was stymied by Kolby assuming a full-guard position, his legs on either side of Aamil.

Good luck with that, you're in dad's wheelhouse now, thought Rahim. Although his confidence in his father was belied by the nervous chewing of his lip. Compulsively he twitched and leaned, anticipating Aamil's moves through the screen, envisioning himself in Aamil's place.

* * *

Aamil traced his hands along the ankles of Kolby, then rapidly gyrated his knees side to side to throw off Kolby's timing and pass his guard. Hooking his right leg in-between his opponents, Aamil assumed half mount and began throwing a ballistic assault of elbows and overhead punches.

Right as Kolby's defense began to falter, Aamil slunk downward and shot back up to catch his rival's arm by his head into a shoulder lock. Just as he began to twist the joint for a submission attempt, the sound of a bell cut through the air.

Aamil moved away from his opponent as the bell rang. Kolby brushed the back of his hand against his mouth, wiping away a smear of blood. Glancing at it he raised his eyebrows provocatively at Aamil, "ouch," he said.

Aamil chose not to indulge him and silently walked to a corner of the ring where a spigot waited for him. Taking a long gulp of water, he swished the cold liquid around in his mouth before letting it slide down his gullet. Feeling refreshed now, Aamil jumped up and down, shaking the built-up lactic acid from his limbs.

The second round began suddenly with the toll of the bell. Aamil once again took up a mostly defensive posture across from his opponent. Kolby appeared to be developing a large lump over his left eye, where many of Aamil's blows had landed. Kolby feinted a left cross. When Aamil hopped away out of range, his opponent deftly pivoted on his lead leg, driving his right heel into Aamil's gut. Gasping for air, Aamil struggled to remain composed as he continued with the wind knocked out of him. *I guess those muscles aren't just for show*, Aamil joked to himself.

He forced himself to rouse his spirit, forging ahead into the fight. Circling, he allowed himself to eat a series of body blows from Kolby, waiting for the perfect opportunity. Soon seeing his chance, he struck, slamming home a hard left elbow into Kolby's cheek, slicing the corner of his face. The rest of the round passed in this back-and-forth manner, until they found themselves once again resting in the corner of the ring, waiting for the midpoint of the fight to be underway.

Starting the third round, Aamil felt bruised but invigorated. Thus far, this had been the most nail-biting match he had ever taken part in. The thrill of the competition coursed through his veins. Looking across the cage he nodded at Kolby, receiving a wink in response. *What does this fox have up his sleeve?*

Similar to the first round, Kolby opened up with a kick. This time though, he chose to go in for a low calf kick. Ready for the move, Aamil went in for a double leg and blasted Kolby to the ground. Kolby's defense was such that he was able to stall Aamil in his submission attempts. The two tangled together on the ground like this for the duration of the round.

At the end of the third round, they both got up shakily. Both of them were experiencing significant fatigue from their lengthy exchange on the ground. If the third round was a battle on the ground, the fourth round was a war on their feet.

The two men went shot for shot, landing vicious blows on one another. By the time this round ended, both of them were dripping blood profusely from the head. Tomato red welts swelled rapidly all over their bodies. Battered but not broken, Aamil fought an internal battle just as fierce. *Dig deep Aamil, dig deep.*

* * *

Lyall reassured Rahim, "he's got this, Aamil has him on the ropes for sure."

Linh enthusiastically agreed, "if that lug is going to spend so much of his time training, he knows better than to let himself be beaten. Don't you think so Rahim?"

Always the stoic type, Rahim simply nodded without saying anything. The others didn't notice the mask concealing his true emotions slip. A slight quiver ran through his frame as he worried for Aamil. His foot tapped the floor in anticipation, watching his father appear on the screen to begin the fifth and final round.

Forcing himself to breathe slowly through the nose, Aamil retained his composure, preparing for the round to start. He was disappointed to look over and see that Kolby similarly was not showing significant fatigue, but did not let that discourage him. The bell rang to start the round, departing from his more signature defensive style, Aamil shot forward with intensity. *This is the last round; I need to put my foot on the gas pedal.*

He came in hot with a spinning hook kick, pivoting to throw his back leg towards Kolby's head. Having become accustomed to the earlier flow of Aamil's movements, Kolby was caught off guard and only managed to partially recoil from the impact. Aamil's foot slapped the cheek of his opponent, sending spittle flying out of Kolby's mouth. Aamil followed up on the attack to immediately launch a series of jabs and crosses, switching up to target the head and body. Kolby was wheeling backward at this point, allowing him to shake off the brunt of the potential damage.

Slamming his back into the cage, Kolby managed to snare them into a clinch as Aamil pressed forward. Momentarily stymied by his opponent's much lengthier limbs, Aamil focused on trying to maneuver Kolby to the ground. Meanwhile, Kolby kept himself busy landing hammer fists about Aamil's side and back. It was when he tried to throw in a knee to Aamil's gut that he went too far. Aamil caught the leg and dragged Kolby to the ground.

Landing on top, Aamil assumed side control and started fighting for control over his opponent's far arm in order to establish a kimura lock. Kolby squirmed to get out of danger but was unable to fend off Aamil's advances. Aamil finally got a firm grip and stepped around the head to wrench the arm, eliciting a pained gasp from Kolby. Aamil worried he was going to have to break the arm, Kolby was resisting fervently. Kolby gritted his teeth and growled through the agony wracking his arm. Seeing that Kolby had no plans of relenting, Aamil ruefully uttered, "I'm sorry," before twisting the arm further.

He was greeted with an unsettling popping sound as the rotator cuff in Kolby's shoulder was torn to shreds. Kolby yowled and punched the mat over and over in distress. Aamil took this as a sign of submission, but just to be safe, waited until a horn blew, signaling the end of the match. An awful feeling lingered in Aamil's chest, he berated himself for needing to resort to such drastic measures. He held no ill will towards his opponents and loathed having to do something that would negatively impact their lives in such a way.

Remorsefully he helped Kolby to his feet and grabbed his hand to shake it. Dazed from his injury, Kolby relented at first but then with a sullen expression, ripped his hand away. Understanding the sentiment, Aamil made one last attempt to make peace before leaving him be. "You're the best fighter I've ever had the honor of competing against, you should be proud. I'm sorry things ended the way they did here, I hope I have the good fortune to face you again one day."

Letting those be his last words to the man, Aamil patiently waited for the results to be announced. After the announcer finished speaking, Aamil took advantage of the cameras to make a statement of his own. *Hopefully, this can make up for me not being there today,* "I don't want to take up too much time, I just want to send a message." His lips morphed into a big goofy grin, "happy birthday Rahim, I'll see you at home." Having gotten those words out, he exited the cage.

He stopped briefly to interact with the DistribuBot, "Your victory has been processed and recorded in Quell's database. four thousand credits have been transferred to your personal account and your PQ has been adjusted to sixty-four. You must win nine more fights before you are eligible to advance to the national competition pool, would you like to schedule your next fight now?"

Laughing, Aamil declined, "I've learned my lesson, I think I'll save that chore for another day soon after I talk with my partner." Hopping down the steps of the cage, he stumbled to the door out of the room. He had accumulated a considerable amount of damage during the fight and could tell that moving would be troublesome for days to come.

Opening the door, Aamil was startled to see a SecurityBot waiting for him in the corridor, its glare firmly affixed on him. The usual combatants who lingered in the hallway had all migrated far to the edges of the space to avoid the menacing machine. In a grating voice, it stated simply, "come with me," not seeming to leave any room for objections.

Perplexed as to what could be going on, Aamil followed behind the Bot. It made a rolling noise, its spherical base rotating smoothly and efficiently over the floor. His previous exertions having thoroughly worn Aamil out, he struggled to keep pace with the implacable Bot. *I'm going to sleep for the next hundred years once I get home*, he whined internally. Arriving at the end of the hallway, the elevator opened to allow the SecurityBot and Aamil entry.

A dry silence hovered uncomfortably in the air of the elevator. In an attempt to ease the tension he felt, Aamil jokingly asked, "so how's this job treating you? I'm sure the hours must be killer, but the benefits are comprehensive right?" The Bot declined to acknowledge Aamil's words, resulting in him awkwardly looking away. *Note to self, Bots aren't very good for audience feedback.*

The Tower they were in was one of the tallest in the world. All the same, Aamil's eyes widened in disbelief when he saw they had reached the one hundred and ninety-third floor. The doors opened up to another hallway, different from the ones that characterized the floors below. This one was devoid of all people, and instead of doors lining the walls along the hallway, there was a singular door at the very end.

The empty space echoed with the clacking of Aamil's feet and the rolling of the Bot as they walked to the end of the hall. Questions ran rapidly through Aamil's mind as he tried to figure out for what reason he had been summoned. The door they approached was quite opulent, made of black teak wood with ornate gold handles molded into the shape of tiger heads.

The Bot opened the doors, allowing Aamil inside. If he thought the door was extravagant, the interior was positively decadent. From the Persian rugs that lined the floor, to the lavishly upholstered couches, the entire room was visibly dripping with wealth. *Rather tacky if you ask me*, was the first thought that entered Aamil's mind. Though, the sybaritic appearance of the room was undercut by the pungent smell of sauerkraut that filled the air.

Wrinkling his nose, Aamil noticed a liver-spotted head facing away from him upon one of the couches. Presuming that this was his host, Aamil walked over to greet the person. Coming about to face him, Aamil saw a decrepit old man dressed in a pinstriped suit. His pale skin hung loosely from his face, jiggling lightly as the old man looked up at Aamil with a gleam in his eye. "So, who do I have the pleasure of speaking to today?" Aamil asked.

Without answering the question, the man motioned to a couch across from him, "have a seat," he said in a monotonous tone. Awkwardly Aamil listened and went to sit, the SecurityBot rolled to position itself behind him. "You may refer to me as President Rommel, or just Rommel if you prefer."

The name sounded very familiar to Aamil until it hit him, *wait...the head of Quell?* The realization stunned Aamil, he never expected to be standing before such a high-profile figure. "What can I do for you, Rommel?"

Rommel folded his hands in his lap, "It's been fifty years since I built this system, give or take. I was a young man, younger than yourself when I inherited the controlling interest in this company from my father. A company he inherited from my grandfather. The-"

Aamil interjected, "I'm sorry but is this going to take too long? I'm rather tired and would like to get on out of here soon if I can."

A long silence was his response, Rommel looked at him icily. "You will sit there and listen to me as long as I would like you to."

Aamil looked up at the SecurityBot poised behind him. Sighing, he slouched on the couch lacing his fingers behind his head. *I wonder if this is what Rahim feels like,* "fine then, carry on."

Rommel nodded, "the world was a very different place before I came along; everyone was so very preoccupied with demanding their 'rights'" putting up physical air quotes as he said so, "and not at all worried about what they deserved, what they had earned. My grandfather built Quell up from a small tech company operating out of Silicon Valley. A company that my father, and I in turn, grew and maintained. Yet there were those envious of our success, who wanted to point their fingers at us to blame for what they did not have. The technology Quell built was revolutionary, it eliminated the need for human hands to be involved in most sectors of the economy. As unemployment rose and rose, one would have thought that a new golden age of entrepreneurship would arise as the masses had more time on their hands. Yet instead of innovating, instead of buckling down to work hard as I and my family had, they turned to laziness and jealousy. Mass protests arose, people complaining about what they did not have, instead of working hard to take it. Yet rather than abandon them, as young and idealistic as I was, I could not blame them for not being as smart or not having the same kind of vision that I had. After all, there is a natural order to things and I could not blame them for being lesser than I, it was just fate. So, I decided that if they did not have the vision to find a way to make do themselves, I would show them the path. Which resulted in the fighting system I created, a chance for people to seize the American dream for themselves. The path was laid out right before them, if they were willing to work hard enough, they could pick themselves up by the bootstraps and realize it for themselves."

Waiting a beat and a half to see if Rommel had anything else to say, Aamil then responded, "so what does all of this have to do with me?"

Rommel stretched his thin lips into a smirk, "you're a very talented fighter, I'm sure you must have worked very hard to get where you are. I don't deign to focus my attention on any but the most elite competitors. I would like to extend to you, the honor of working for Quell, for me."

Aamil laughed in disbelief, "an honor? Oh, I'm sure you think it would be. Unfortunately for you though, I can't be bought. I think I'll pass, no thank you but no thank you."

Rommel put his hand to his temple, barely concealed irritation on his face, "I don't take kindly to anyone who affects my bottom-line, Mr. Jackson, I do hope you will reconsider."

Aamil had had enough at this point, no longer caring about the consequences of angering Rommel. He stood up, "I don't really care what you will or won't take kindly to. I've had just about enough of this conversation, good day." Stomping over to the door, he flung it open and walked down the hall to the elevator.

The encounter left a host of unpleasant thoughts swirling through his mind as he descended to the base of the building. Getting to the lobby, Aamil exited the building, almost running into a metal frame before he stopped himself.

Looking up, he saw two SecurityBots standing side by side in front of him, 'Quell' inscribed across their chests. They looked upon him with their menacing glares, making his skin crawl. He tried to walk around them but was stopped by a four-pronged metal hand clamping around his arm, "what the hell?" he started to say, but was grabbed by the other arm by the second Bot. They picked him up with ease and carried him off of the street into a nearby alley.

A man in a white tracksuit leaned against the alley wall, taking a long drag off of a cigarette. The smoke pluming in the air around him, he bent over and picked up an aluminum baseball bat leaning on the wall next to him. Turning, Kolby faced Aamil, one arm in a sling, the other holding the bat loosely. Kolby contorted his lip to keep the cigarette in his mouth while he spoke, "so you turned the old man down, huh?"

Aamil spoke angrily, "now what? So you lost and now you're going to ambush me?"

The smell of tobacco wafted off of him as he continued to puff on his stogey, "you would think so little of me? I'm hurt, pal."

Confused, Aamil asked, "so what then, what is this about?"

Kolby shrugged apologetically, "orders are orders, I have to think about myself after all. If you had done the same, then maybe you wouldn't be in this situation."

Those words concerned Aamil, "and what situation is that?"

A harsh laugh caused the cigarette to tumble to the ground, Kolby cursed and put it out with his foot. "Telling you would only make things worse, just close your eyes and maybe it will all be over soon. Then again, maybe not, having one arm might slow me down." As Aamil protested, Kolby motioned for the Bots to spin Aamil to have his back facing Kolby.

"Bastard," Aamil seethed.

"I know you won't believe me when I say this, but this really isn't personal. I hold a lot of respect for you. If you're going to hold a grudge, hold one against the million-year-old creep upstairs." Aamil heard the bat scrape against the ground as Kolby picked it up. He had no time for any more words before a heavy impact on his lower back caused pain to shoot up his spine.

Gritting his teeth, Aamil flopped the way a fish might, struggling to get out of the Bots grasp, to no avail. A sigh came from behind him, "don't make this harder than it has to be, just relax." Aamil was struck again in the same area. Again. Again. Again.

Aamil heaved for air, the pain driving the wind out of him, tears involuntarily rolling down his cheeks. Helplessly, his mind did the only thing it could think of and sent him into a numbing dark place far from the pain. A few hits later, and he fully drifted into unconsciousness.

Time passed incoherently for Aamil from there; he blinked and he was laying on the side of the road, another blink and sirens were blaring around him, another blink and he was with a MedBot in what seemed to be a van, another and he was laying in a soft bed surrounded by white walls. *Am I dead?* he wondered. The movement of a MedBot in the corner of his eye told him no.

A twitch of his arms pulled at IV tubes attached to him, affirming that he was just in the hospital. A soft sobbing sound from a few feet away drew his attention, craning his neck he felt a swirl of emotions. He saw Linh with her face buried in her hands and Rahim, arm around her offering comfort.

Calling out to them, Aamil's voice slipped weakly from his lips. Their heads snapped up in rapt attention, Linh's lip trembled, approaching Aamil's bedside. His heart ached as he noticed the streaks on her cheeks where tears had been rolling down. Rahim stood a distance behind her, appearing distressed, his hands were at his sides shaking almost imperceptibly. "Are you guys ok?" Aamil asked.

"Shut up," Linh said softly, "you don't get to be the one hurt and then act worried about us. How are you feeling?"

Aamil smiled, it was just like Linh to scold him even in a time like this. "I'm a bit woozy but other than that I feel alright. How long have I been out?"

"Three days," she said while chewing her lip.

"What?!" he said in alarm. Aamil attempted to sit up in the bed, only to feel something was off. *That's weird, I can't feel my...*

Linh's voice cracked trying to explain what happened to him. "The MedBots told us you suffered severe damage to your spinal cord. They said that you...you might not be able to...you can't," she struggled to deliver the rest of the news, breaking down, tears flowing freely now.

"I can't feel my legs," he said numbly, still not quite absorbing the gravity of what had happened to him. Wide-eyed, he grabbed Linh's hand, "but they can fix me, right?" He looked over at one of the MedBots busying itself in the corner of the room, "You guys can fix me, right?" he yelled across the room.

Rahim stepped forward to comfort his father, but Linh stuck her hand out, signaling to wait. "There is a procedure they can do to fix your spine, but...it would cost eight-hundred-thousand credits, not including the costs for physical therapy, among other things. For this visit alone we're at seventy-five thousand credits already. I don't know how but I'm willing to do whatever it takes to make you well again."

"I'll do my part too dad, just tell me what to do to make the money and I'll do it," Rahim said.

Linh held up her hand again, closing her eyes sorrowfully. "I don't know how much it will get us, but we can sell the house. I can go into the cages and start fighting, I'll do whatever I can to make the money you need."

Her words sent the reality of the situation crashing onto Aamil's shoulders. He knew even with all of that, it wouldn't be enough. "The house won't get us close enough to where we need to be. We'll have to rent out a unit if we do that, and then we'll just be running in place between you earning money fighting and then making payments. I can't put you and Rahim through that, just for me."

Linh nodded, sensing the truth in her partner's words. She had been sincere with her earlier offer but knew it would ultimately be a futile gesture.

Somberly Aamil looked at Rahim then back at Linh, he knew what had to be done but struggled to find the strength to suggest it. His body slumped with a sigh, "my savings should cover most of the costs I've already accrued from this visit...but you might need to fight to keep us afloat for the time being. For our son. I will work as fast as I can to figure something out so you don't have to put yourself in harm's way for too long, I'm going to fix this."

Linh punched his shoulder, "what did I tell you? Stop worrying about us when you're the one whose hurt, you lug." Aamil gave a slight smile at that, but internally his heart was wilting at the thought of the hardships ahead of his family.

Nia

Nia stood in rank and file among the other children in her age cohort, the first generation produced by the designer program and trained at Camp Crisp. Their instructor, Han Liu, was a member of the last generation of the spartan program. A short muscular man with a widow's peak and well-defined cheekbones, he was dressed in a black sleeveless Gi.

In the midst of loudly lecturing the class, he asked, "why are you here?" Sensing the rhetorical nature of the question, the class remained silent. "You are here to win. Nothing else matters. You are soldiers for Quell, each a cog in a machine, meant to crush the competition on the field of battle. Compassion and mercy are meaningless, empathy a hindrance, only victory has meaning. The matter of superiority is decided by who wins, if you lose you are inherently inferior, having been born either weak of mind, of body, or spirit. I don't care if you must use deceit, exploitation, or cruelty to get there, if it gets results and helps you win, do it." The children stood quietly, absorbing the instructor's words. "Now, I want you to get into pairs and begin sparring. I and the assistant trainers will be walking around to keep an eye on you and offer...guidance."

All the children smoothly found a partner and searched for a place on the mat where they wouldn't run into any of the other pairs. Han and the assistant trainers roamed around the room, examining as everyone got busy. Nia ended up paired with a little blonde boy named Brandon, who was close to her size. They quickly found a spot to train as there was ample room to spar due to the room's massive size.

Nia and the boy went back and forth for a few minutes. One taking turns drilling their punches and kicks, with the other keeping a firm posture to be a good partner. Eventually, they began to freely compete against one another, each giving partial effort to avoid injuring the other.

Sensing a window of opportunity, Nia spun around and planted a back heel kick in the boy's gut, knocking him to the ground. "Oh sorry," she exclaimed, "I didn't mean to go that hard." Reaching out a hand she went to help the boy off of the ground, as she did so her collar was yanked backward and she was thrown to the ground.

Grabbing at her throat she struggled to find her breath. Looking up, she spotted instructor Han standing above her, his brows furrowed in discontent. "What were you just about to do?"

Confused, she replied honestly, "I was just about to help him up is all."

"You were going to help him? As in you were going to show an act of kindness towards him. Do you not remember my words at the beginning of class?"

Frantically trying to get out of trouble, Nia struggled to answer, "...yes"

Kneeling, Han looked her straight in her eyes, "he got knocked down, he's a loser, and he's going to remain a loser if you try to help him. Your kindness does him a disservice and it exposes your own weakness."

Tears began to well in Nia's eyes, "...I'm sorry."

Roughly grabbing her by the arm, Han began to drag her along, "You need to be taught a lesson, come with me." Lugging her to the front of the class, Han threw her at his feet, "ATTENTION!" On command, the whole class jumped into formation, looking straight ahead at their instructor. "Nia here has chosen to deny my instruction and has shown weakness by trying to help her opponent. All of you shall stand there and watch while she receives her punishment, let this be a lesson to you all." Han said, his frown causing his widows peak to dip near the middle of his eyebrows.

He stuck out his hand expectantly, receiving a light wooden rod. In a testing motion, he swung the rod rapidly up and down, the air emitting a high-pitched whistle around it as it snapped to and fro.

Several of the children winced, recalling their own punishment at the hands of that rod. Han was known for having an especially cruel streak, Nia herself had been on the punishing end of that weapon many times. Closing her eyes to remove some of the anticipation for what was to come, Nia steeled herself for her punishment.

She was surprised when she received a blow to the face, slicing open her cheek. Bending over and covering her head with her hands, she tried to protect her face from more damage. "Stop moving or else your punishment will be even more severe!" shouted Han. Her eyelids twitched as the stinging slap of the rod began to slam into her sides.

The feeling evolved from a sting, to pain, to searing agony as he struck the same spot over and over. He hit her until her composure completely vanished and she writhed on the ground sobbing and begging for it to stop. Right when she expected him to hit her again, she heard him make an angry indignant noise.

Turning her head, she saw Kolby, another fighter from the spartan program. Wearing a white Gi with the robes open, exposing the white fox on his chest, he held the rod to prevent it from moving. Han struggled to pull it back to himself. Holding out his index he wagged it in Han's face, "tsk tsk tsk," he tutted at Han mockingly, "you know we can't have you damaging the merchandise. Old man Rommel would be furious, do you know how much Quell has spent on these children?"

Han finally yanked the rod back out of Kolby's hands, "that is not your concern Kolby, it was not your place to interfere with me disciplining one of my pupils."

"Calm your tits Han, your widow's peak is going to fly off. I just didn't want you to injure the girl is all, look at her she doesn't even seem like she can get up." Kolby responded flippantly. Casting his gaze down at Nia, he nudged her with his foot, "hey girly, can you get up?" Tears running down her face, she looked up and nodded slowly. "Well, your class or not, I think I'm going to escort this one to the medical bay, maybe she can rejoin the others for PT."

Before Han could argue further, Kolby bent over and swung Nia into his arms, carrying her off like she weighed nothing. Striding out of the room, they walked down a modest dimly lit carpeted hallway for several moments. Nia leaned against Kolby's chest in a pained daze.

* * *

As Kolby walked, he looked at Nia's distressed face and felt an unfamiliar twinge in his chest. Paternalistically he patted her back and turned the corner into the medical bay. Warm light permeated the room, illuminating the state-of-the-art medical equipment scattered throughout the area. An assortment of machines with various purposes were neatly lined up in their intended places. Made up of a collection of wires and beeping lights performing functions that neither Nia nor Kolby had any clue about.

A Nurse with expressive blue eyes walked up to Kolby. The Nurse gently placed her hand on Nia's back, "what happened?" she asked in a concerned tone.

"One of the instructors became a little too enthusiastic in their lessons, I think the little one may have taken injury as a result."

Pursing her lips, the nurse questioned Kolby, "Han?" she asked as if she had to deal with the fallout from his actions before.

Not wishing to dig himself into a bigger vendetta with Han, Kolby abstained from giving a straightforward answer. "You know I really couldn't say, she was in this state when I got to the room, I couldn't tell you who hit her."

The nurse scrunched her nose, "fine, go lay her down over there and we'll take care of her." Seeing the soft white hospital bed she was referring to, he walked Nia over and gently laid her down over the cotton covers.

Scanning the room, he walked away and grabbed a chair to drag over to her bedside.

The Nurse moved to dismiss Kolby, "you may leave now."

Kolby shrugged and put his hands behind his head, "I think I'll stay till I know she's going to make a full recovery."

The nurse smirked, "worried about her? It seems the fox is just a puppy dog after all. Well, you can stay here as long as you like, but we'll be taking her to another room to conduct some scans on her to make sure there is no internal damage."

"I'll be here," he said without breaking his gaze from the nurses' eyes. She nodded and began to adjust the bed to wheel it into the other room. While she busied herself, Kolby asked, "so what's your name?"

The nurse brushed back a strand of blond hair, looking towards Kolby, "Veronica."

"Veronica," he repeated, letting the name simmer in the air. Looking around at the Bots that were going about their work at the edges of the room, then back to Veronica in her nurse's scrubs, a question entered his mind. "So, if you don't mind me asking...why are you here? Why does Quell keep you on staff?"

Veronica seemed unfazed by the question, "well," she said, raising her finger to her lips thoughtfully. "I suppose you're justified in thinking that my being here doesn't make much sense. After all, Quell doesn't employ any humans in its hospitals and health clinics around the world so why here in its own facility? Operations that would be difficult and painstaking work for any human surgeon are an easy matter for machines. Bots can file and distribute medical information far more efficiently than any person, they can make diagnoses and prescribe medication with far more fidelity and accuracy. So why have a human nurse in charge of these children's care? Or, for that matter, why have people like Han and yourself help supervise their tutelage? I guess it's just a testament that when it comes to their assets, even Quell has to acknowledge the power of human connection."

Kolby frowned, perplexed by what he had just heard. "What do you mean by that?"

"Did you know the touch of another human being is proven to boost the immune system, reduce pain, and help the growth of undeveloped children? It is not just a physically beneficial connection but an emotional and spiritual one as well. When it comes to molding the minds of young children, such impressionable creatures, nothing is quite as sufficient as having another human being to look up to. Despite Quell's bluster about the merits of competition; they rely on the power of cooperation to teach these children, and on me to take care of them when they are unwell. The spark that binds human beings together is so tremendously powerful."

Veronica became embarrassed when she realized how openly she had been speaking to a man she hardly knew. Blushing, she demurely bowed her head, "anyways I think it's time to take this one over for her scans, I'll be right back."

She rolled the bed carrying Nia over to the other room. As she walked away, Kolby smiled at her back. He couldn't quite place it, but something about her words warmed his spirit. Ordinarily, he had trouble bridging the emotional distance between him and others, but something about her...fascinated him.

* * *

Nia stirred from her daze due to the mild hum of the MRI scanner she was ensconced within. Opening her eyes, she was alarmed to see herself laying within a white gray tube. The nurse peered in through a window outside the room. Although Nia had been here before, it was concerning to have such little recollection as to how she got here. Then it hit her, *Han,* she thought to herself, remembering how she had gotten hurt. *I must have passed out from the pain after Kolby picked me up,* Nia thought to herself.

Nia found herself outside speaking to the Nurse several minutes later, "we found two fractured ribs in your scan. You'll have to come with me to get some stem cell treatment and have your ribs wrapped. You should experience some significant bruising over the next few days, but after about a week you should be all healed up and feel good as new."

Sighing, Nia indicated that she understood, "thank you." Heading back to the main room to be treated by the Nurse, Nia was surprised to see Kolby there waiting for her. "What are you doing here?" she asked.

"That's no way to greet the man who saved you, I was even nice enough to wait along for you." He said, feigning offense.

"You were the one who helped me with Han?" she asked.

"Didn't you see me there? I spoke to you?"

"The pain must have made me forget, thank you I appreciate it."

"Don't mention it, I'm going to stick around a little longer to escort you to PT, let me know when you're all finished here."

Nia was perplexed, adults never took time out of their day to speak to her unless she was being punished for something, let alone having them try and help her. *Why me?* She wondered. Putting her speculations aside, she laid still as the Nurse went about her treatment. After the procedure was finished and the bandages were all wrapped around her side, Nia trotted over to Kolby, "ready to go?"

"I thought you'd never ask." They walked together toward the PT area in silence. Nia looked up to Kolby several times, thinking maybe she would break the quiet and ask him something, but hesitated and decided against it. It seemed as though he was mulling something over in his mind, so she figured it was for the best that she preserved the quietude on this stroll.

At last, he spoke to her, "you know Han is a piece of work, but he was right about something." Nia looked up at Kolby to see what he had to say.

"You can't afford to show kindness to others. Just look at the way Han was treating you, the way this whole place is run, softness has no place here. The only person you should look after is yourself. Caring for others is only going to weigh you down and hinder you from getting where you need to go."

They neared the location where the rest of her class was undergoing Physical Training. Turning, Kolby knelt to look at Nia, a ferocious determination in his eyes. "You must harden your heart, Nia. Turn yourself to stone, hide your humanity deep inside yourself, and don't let it out, it will only slow you down. This is a world made by machines Nia, and you must turn yourself into one as well if you hope to survive." Giving her one long last look he stood up and placed his hand on her head for a beat before turning and leaving for his next excursion. Nia watched him leave, the top of her hair ruffled from his palm resting there.

His words weighed heavy on her mind as she rejoined the other kids. Nia was quickly accounted for by the TrainBots supervising the exercises. Having received notice of her visit to the medical bay, they sent her over for a full physical examination before participating. Nia numbly allowed the TrainBots to measure her vitals and take full body measurements. She remained withdrawn throughout the whole process. After they were concluded with their check-up, they sent her to join the other children in Physical Training.

Brandon, the blonde boy Nia had been training with before, perked up upon seeing Nia rejoin the group. Carefully looking around to not get reprimanded, he snuck out of the line they were doing exercises in to go speak to her. "I'm sorry you got in trouble for helping me, I was worried it took you so long to come back. Are you ok?!"

Nia looked at him dispassionately, seemingly unmoved by his apology. "I'm fine, worry about yourself," she said coolly before brushing by him to take her spot in the group. Her heart screamed at her as she did so, but her mind stifled those qualms, repeating to herself over and over, *you are a machine, you don't need anyone else.*

Manfred

'Ius Divinum Reges' these words engraved on a gold plaque set in the door of his father's study, stared Manfred in the face every time he was summoned here. *The old man does love his Latin*, Manfred thought to himself. Doing his best to appear dignified, as his father was always so exacting of how one should carry themselves, Manfred knocked on the door.

The door automatically swung open, revealing his father sitting behind a desk made of rich dark brown wood. Partially blocking Manfred's view of his father was a head of black hair slicked back with too much gel. The two were conversing quite intently until Manfred stepped into the room, whereupon the man stopped speaking.

The man looked back at Manfred, showing him that the man was wearing a black suit, white undershirt, and a red tie. Flashing an awkward smile, the man looked questioningly at Manfred's father, "should I go?"

Manfred's father waved his hand, "no, no. It's important to me that he is here for this, someone has to take over once I'm gone after all." Looking up at Manfred, he spoke authoritatively, "have a seat and listen, Manfred, I'll speak to you after this business is finished." Manfred instinctively complied without question and lowered himself into a supple leather chair.

The man coughed awkwardly, "as I was saying, Mathias, overall, your company is still riding the popularity surge caused by your efforts over the last two decades. Particularly, you are still receiving widespread acknowledgment for mainstreaming nuclear fusion, and solving the energy and climate crises plaguing the globe. However, in the last year and a half, your approval rating has dropped about a dozen points."

Mathias steepled his fingers under his chin, "of course that's to be expected, is it not? Recency bias has always been a critical factor in public approval, I'm sure our ratings will bounce up again when we release our next line of products."

"Respectfully sir, I don't think it's that simple. The survey data we have collected indicates that several other eminent tech firms including yours are suffering the same dip. From what we can see, this trend is highly correlated to recent spikes in unemployment related to automation. Additionally, these spikes have been tied to bouts of civil unrest that have begun to brew throughout the nation. As your brand is the most notable, you've garnered the most disapproval. Among...other reasons."

Manfred's father raised an eyebrow, "other reasons?"

"For starters, the public is rather riled up about recent reports that your company hasn't paid any taxes. Also, you have a leak somewhere in your ranks. News was released to the press that your organization is affiliated with the election security bill that recently hit the senate floor. They're calling it voter suppression."

Manfred's father shot out a guttural laugh, "as if I'd let one penny of my earnings go to the buffoons running the government. No offense, Senator."

The Senator cracked a yellow-stained smile, "none taken."

"I suppose the simpletons may have a keener eye than I thought, to catch onto the nature of the bill we're pushing through. No matter, with a majority of the senate in my pocket, this bill is certain to pass. Then I'll have carte blanche to do as I please." Mathias had a look of satisfaction cross his face after that remark.

The man leaned forward in his chair, "if you don't have any further need for me then, I'll be on my way." Standing, he waited for Manfred's father to respond.

Mathias waved his hand to dismiss the Senator. "That is all I need from you, for now." The man turned to walk to the door, but just as his hand touched the doorknob, Mathias spoke once more, "one last comment, however. When you return to speak to the others, you would be wise to impress on them how imperative it is that this bill gets passed without a hitch. This is simply the first step in a grander plan. If anything were to go awry, let's just say the lot of you would not come out unscathed. Carry on now."

The man paused for a long moment, shakily he turned the handle and exited the room. Manfred's father stood without a word and walked over to the window of the study. Rays of light shone through the window onto his stern face. Manfred was used to being kept in suspense by his father, he had a way of demanding attention even when he wasn't speaking.

A few seconds passed until Mathias spoke, "what are the odds, do you think, that I, out of the billions of toiling masses, would be the one to stand in this position today? That I would have had such a hand to play in redefining the future of this world. For decades society was threatened to be upended by problems of its own making, greed and short-sightedness consumed most all the world. Nobody was capable of stepping up to the plate and doing what needed to be done, not until I came along."

Manfred was unsure how his father wanted him to answer, "um, I'm not sure, sir. I suppose that they just didn't possess the intellect that you have."

Mathias pensively pushed the large ring he was wearing in a circle around his finger, "that is one explanation that had crossed my mind. While that might be true, I think that there is a grander truth at play here. I very well might be blessed with ability far surpassing that of most people, certainly, that must have a part to play. But the life I have led seems too coincidental for ability alone to have carried me this far, it must be fate."

These ravings confused Manfred immensely, "what do you mean?" he asked.

Mathias walked over to the front of his desk and sat against it, staring directly into Manfred's eyes from a few feet away. "I mean that the universe has conspired to bring me to this point. The path to salvation is too arduous to leave for the complacent masses to decipher amongst their multitudes. It must be left in the hands of the capable few who know better, who can make the necessary choices to guide the herd to their betterment. I know best what is beneficial for the world, it is my destiny to remove all obstacles from me being in the position to do so, and by extension your destiny."

Manfred looked wide-eyed into his father's intense gaze, "my destiny?" he mumbled uncomprehendingly.

Mathias placed his son's head between his hands, "yes my son. As my seed, my destiny is yours. It is our divine birthright. The work that is required is too great to count on completing in one lifetime. My plans extend far from now, when I am gone you will carry on my legacy. More than likely your children will have to be groomed to carry on that legacy as well, such is our natural place." *Divine birthright...natural place,* the words pleasantly stroked Manfred's ego as they swirled around his head.

Rahim

Rahim tapped his foot impatiently, listening to the chest-high silver cube before him chatter. "…therefore, as you will of your own free will and volition agree to register with Quell Inc, you shall assume the status of an independent contractor and waive all rights to claims or benefits beyond those listed in this contractual agreement," stated the RegisterBot.

Patronizing bastards, yeah some choice that is, thought Rahim to himself bitterly. "Yes yes I agree ok, let's just get this over with."

"Before we proceed, I must review the credit award system with you. Your compensation will be determined by your Power Quotient; this score will be determined by a combination of your win percentage, current standing within national rankings, as well as a consideration of the dominance of each of your wins. If you advance in the rankings, your position will increasingly become a larger factor in your PQ score. You will be paired against other fighters according to weight and sex. Fighters will begin in their local municipal competition pool, where they must win twenty fights in a row to advance. Then they will move on to the county competition pool, where they must also win twenty fights in a row. The state competition pool requires fighters to win fifteen in a row to move on to the regional pool, which also requires fifteen consecutive wins. From there, fighters must win ten fights in a row to advance from either the All-West or All-East pools to the national pool. A loss will result in relocation to the beginning of your current pool, two losses in a row will result in relocation to the previous pool you advanced from, three consecutive losses will result in relocation back to the municipal competition pool. If you understand everything that has been told to you, lean forward to bring your eye before my scanner. Your retina will be scanned and linked to your personal credit account."

Obliging, Rahim leaned forward, "the process will now begin, please do not move." Searing pain began to concentrate within his left eye, tears squeezing out from the light exposure, only to subside after about a minute. "I am finished," announced the RegisterBot. "You are now eligible to schedule your first competitive entry."

"How about three days from now, on May fourth," he said, picking a day at random.

"Your time has been scheduled and you are slotted to begin at three pm for the men's one-hundred-eighty-five-pound bracket in Tacoma Washington, this concludes our session, have a great day."

"Thanks a Bot," he said as he left, chuckling at his cleverness. Passing by dozens of other individuals interacting with RegisterBots stationed around the building, and dozens more waiting for their time to register with Quell, Rahim exited the building.

Rahim stepped out onto a smooth grey sidewalk, matching the overcast weather looming over the city, waiting for him was Aamil. Waving from his wheelchair, Aamil called out to Rahim, "how did it go?"

Giving an awkward thumbs up, Rahim responded, "as expected, it was a bit surprising to hear about the PQ system though. Why didn't you ever tell me about that?"

Aamil shrugged, "I figured you'd learn easy enough on your own, as you just did. Some people like to lord it over others as a sign of superiority, but it's not all that important. Just take care of business and the rest should sort itself out."

"Makes sense," Rahim said plainly. Grabbing the handles on the back of Aamil's chair, he pushed him down the sidewalk in the direction of their home. Though bringing his father along made the journey take a bit longer, Rahim was glad of the company. He had initially planned on registering with Quell on his own, but Aamil had insisted that he come with. Pushing Aamil along, he noticed the older man was checking his watch every few minutes. "Got somewhere to be?" Rahim prodded.

Aamil surreptitiously put the hand with the watch in his pocket, "oh nothing, just a bit restless is all." He quickly diverted the conversation, "I am feeling hungry though, do you think you could stop and grab me something to eat?"

Rahim politely tried to turn him down, "mom just picked up food a few days ago, that tapped out most of our food budget until I start pitching in when I start-up in the cages. Can you wait till we get home?"

Aamil had nothing to say to that, simply squirming in his chair grumbling in response. About a minute later, he spoke up again, "can we just stop for a moment though? I think I'm getting motion sickness."

Rahim was now growing irritated, "motion sickness? You've been in this chair for six years and you've never once had this problem. What's up with you today, is something going on?"

Noncommittally, Aamil declined to give a straightforward answer. "I don't know, I'm just having an off day. Your old man isn't entitled to having a moment to rest?"

Rahim sighed, "fine, I'll give you a moment." They paused on the sidewalk for a little while, standing in a patch of shade protruding from the side of one of the buildings that stood overhead. Rahim's interest piqued as he once again noticed Aamil checking his watch, this time attempting to do so more discreetly. *Something is afoot here*, he thought to himself. A few minutes later, Aamil indicated that he was fine to continue traveling home now. Rahim kept his questions to himself and in a short while they arrived home.

The stairs prevented Rahim from taking Aamil to the top floor from outside the home, so they walked through the front door. A ramp they had built for Aamil years ago, led up from the training room to the top level of the house. Rahim backed up the ramp, dragging Aamil with him. A benefit of this ramp was it had been good strength training over the years, rolling his father up and down many a time. After years of this, he now pulled Aamil up with ease, not feeling any strain from pulling the weight.

Entering the top floor, they then walked through a doorway into the living room, "SURPRISE!!!" Shouted out several people, leaping up from behind the furniture with big toothy grins. He began laughing, "what is this? What are you guys doing here?"

A long-haired man in flip-flops and basketball shorts that partially concealed the tribal tattoos running up and down his legs, walked over to Rahim. Throwing his thick arm across Rahim's shoulders he assured him, "you didn't think we would forget your birthday did ya uce?"

"I guess I was an idiot for thinking you might Lyall," said Rahim, patting his best friend on the back. In fact, he had assumed that his birthday was forgotten when he got up that day and didn't hear from anyone. Turning to Aamil who sat laughing next to him, Rahim smacked him on the shoulder with the back of his hand. "I knew something was up, you're a terrible liar! You were acting so suspicious."

Aamil put his hands out to act like he was placating Rahim, "I didn't know what to do! You walk so damn fast and I had to stall for time!" Rahim chuckled, having to admit that he had a point.

Linh came over to have her chance to wish Rahim a happy birthday, the others piling behind her. Bruises were randomly splotched in black and purple all over Linh, her left hand hung at her side in a splint. The sight, as always, elicited an internal wince from Rahim.

After Aamil's injury, they had to come up with a way to generate more income to tide them over, so Aamil had started a small school to train people for fights. It was not very profitable because he was reluctant to charge people very much, but it was enough to stabilize them along with Linh's earnings. As it was though, she still had become battered from having to step into the cages to support them.

That morning, Rahim's heart had felt considerably lighter knowing he could do his part to take care of the family now. He had vowed to never let his mother come in harm's way again. She wrapped her arms around him, "happy eighteenth my baby boy, I can't believe you're a man now."

Rahim rubbed his hand on her back in a circle, "me either, it's a crazy feeling. Well overdue though, this means I'll be able to take care of you and dad from now on."

She looked at him with a frown, "honey, that's not your job. We're the parents, it's our job to-" her protestations were cut off by the next person in line coming over to congratulate Rahim.

They trotted over in a cornflower blue sequined dress, gushing over Rahim in their usual bubbly way, "I'm so happy for you, congratulations Rahim. I can't wait for you to show me what you got out there!"

"Thanks, Dani, I appreciate it! I'll do my best to impress!" Rahim said with a laugh, grateful for her kind words. She had joined Aamil's school four years prior, becoming the life of their group ever since. Tall with a square jaw, she exuded a presence that intimidated most, but upon further inspection, she had a positively scintillating personality.

Behind her wearing his signature white hoodie was a mountain of a man, making Lyall look small. He approached Rahim with his typical stoic expression, "happy birthday," he said gruffly.

Knowing he was not one for small talk, Rahim kept it short, "thanks Deandre, I appreciate it!" He extended a hand, which was swallowed up by Deandre's and shaken stiffly.

"When is your first fight?" Deandre asked.

"Three days from now on the fourth!"

"Good, good. Tahmejia and Lyall are fighting that same day, that makes things easier." Deandre broke off from the conversation, appearing to have reached his word count for now.

Deandre then meandered past Rahim to hang out with Aamil, his long-time friend. The two had met when Aamil was still fighting. Having a lot of respect for each other, Deandre had agreed to help run the school even though he himself was still competing.

A strong onion smell wafted into Rahim's nostrils as an old man hobbled in front of him. A walrus mustache and tipped fedora made the man look as if he was from an entirely different era, which from the look of his wrinkles, he might have been. His hand latched onto Rahim's collar the way an eagles talon might, shaking aggressively, he spoke in a southern drawl, "looks like I just gained another drinking buddy eh? Your mother might think you're too young, but she don't need to know."

Linh glared at him from a few feet away where she was now speaking with Dani, "I can hear you, Gavin."

Gavin guffawed and waved her off, leaning conspiratorially towards Rahim he muttered, "maybe we should talk about that another time, out of earshot. In other news, I hear you've registered to begin fighting with Quell soon? I was just a lad when the system began, back then you couldn't find work for nothin unless you were rich, or a creative type lucky enough to break out. You ready to go out there and prove your worth in the heat of combat? I remember relishing the opportunity back when I was a youngin, that's where your nuts and guts will shine."

Gavin's impolite nature was always a source of delight for Rahim, the old man's charm was infectious. He was a brilliant fighter in his youth, though now he couldn't do much more than compete for consolation credits, as he was too brittle to actually win any fights. He had turned on their doorstep a couple of years back and was a regular visitor ever since.

"I'm ready to show what I'm made of, I've been training for this my whole life," Rahim responded confidently. He gave no reason to doubt his words, in the past several years he had developed a mental and physical resiliency that gave quite the potency to his demeanor. It was this potency that daunted the demure middle-aged woman who next approached Rahim.

Despite her timid affect and slight frame, she stood out quite flamboyantly with her orange-colored pixie haircut. A juniper-toned high collar jacket was buttoned up enough to slightly cover her chin, muffling her already softly spoken words, "happy birthday Rahim, I'm very happy for you." Rahim, who was accustomed to her withdrawn personality, nodded thankfully in return. "I appreciate that Tahmejia, I hear you're going to be fighting on the fourth?"

She looked down at her feet and squeaked, "yeah, I'm pretty nervous about it though."

"I can relate, I'm going to be having my first fight that same day! So I'll be there to cheer you on, I'm sure you'll do great!" Rahim meant his words to be a source of encouragement, but from Tahmejia's awkward shifting, they appeared to have only made her more self-conscious about the situation.

"From watching her in the practice room I doubt it, but I'm ready to be proved wrong." The words came from the corner of the room, their source a boy about a year younger than Rahim, on the cusp of leaving adolescence. Dressed in vermillion clothing with a red head of hair to match, the boy stood apart from everyone else, declining to come over and congratulate Rahim.

Not wanting to ruin the gathering by causing a scene, Rahim declined to press him too hard for his comments. Instead, he opted to double down on his faith in Tahmejia, "I think you'll be surprised Elliot, she's been working extraordinarily hard. Just you wait and see."

The boy snorted and rolled his eyes "I'll believe it when I see it," Elliot returned his attention to the phone he had been absorbed in for the entirety of the event so far. His attire and attitude had been cause for concern a few months ago when he joined their school, but Aamil had sensed an aura of desperation about Elliot and took pity on him. However, he was rather cagey about his life outside of their group and prone to callous remarks towards the others. Rahim regularly had to restrain himself from confronting Elliot, following his father's request to play nice.

Dani however, had no such instructions holding her back, and would not have been inclined to agree to them even if she did. She had no tolerance for Elliot's attitude and regularly clashed with him, as she did just then. "What is your problem, why do you have to pick on her like that? Especially when you know she isn't going to defend herself?"

A mortified expression took over Tahmejia's face as she became the center of this dispute. Dani continued, "How about you try to say something like that to me? You might think you're hot stuff honey, but this girl knows how to handle her spice." Elliot shot off a dark expression in Dani's direction, mumbling something inaudibly under his breath. Dani appeared to have made out what the others could not though, narrowing her eyes she seethed, "what did you just say to me?"

Elliot looked around at the others and decided against repeating himself, "nothing," he spat out. The room fell into silence at this point, everyone stopping what they were doing to observe the argument. After a few moments of quiet, Linh chattered, "so, who wants cake?"

Chance

I hate going into the field, Chance thought to herself. She had been sent to a private school in the sunset district in San Francisco. Apparently, a TeachBot was on the fritz, straying from its programmed curriculum and spouting off all sorts of nonsensical phrases. The prestigious institution evoked a sense of nostalgia for her school days. Which was strange, given that she had been miserable for most of her school experience.

She strode through the well-lit halls until she found the room she was seeking. Chance opened the door and walked into a standard classroom with a whiteboard and small desks arranged in neat rows and columns. The room was devoid of students, which wasn't out of the ordinary since it was a Saturday. However, what was peculiar, was the Bot running itself into the window of the classroom over and over, resulting in a PANG every time it struck the window. The malfunctioning machine had descended into muttering incomprehensible gibberish, outside of the ability for anyone to understand.

Chance pulled out a remote transmitter and pointed it at the TeachBot. With a simple flip of a switch, the transmitter sent out a frequency, the Bot coming to a standstill as it deactivated. Chance whistled while she went about her work, opening up a hatch in the back of the Bot's head. Taking a tablet from her pocket, she plugged a cable into it, with the other end plugged into the Bot. The Bots code became visible on the screen, and she stuck her tongue out as she searched for the source of infidelity.

Normally commands could be uploaded to Bots from afar, via the network that connected all of Quell's Bots. However, for Bots that strayed from protocol such as this one, a technician was required to come in person and handle the problem. Being proficient at her work, Chance was soon finished with her task and the Bot was back up and running. It maneuvered behind its desk, where it became motionless, awaiting school to begin that Monday.

Chance left the campus and got into her AutoBot. The day not being yet over, she directed the AutoBot to drive her back to her work. Soon the vehicle dropped her off in Silicon Valley at Quell Park. As she entered the building, she encountered Joe Mahme, the head of AI Solutions at Quell.

Joe waved furiously at her, directing her to come to stand before him. Not wasting any time, he broke his news to her deadpanned. "Chance, just the person I was looking for. I have some news that might excite you. No more fieldwork for you, you're being promoted. The boss upstairs has a special assignment and I'm going to need some extra brainpower to help me get this done. From now on you'll be working with me in AI Solutions, understood?"

The matter of fact manner with which he delivered this news prevented Chance from fully absorbing what she had just heard. Finally, the information sank into her brain. Realizing she had left him waiting for an answer a hair too long, the answer tumbled out of her mouth. "Yes, yes. I understand! Thank you so much for this opportunity! You have no idea how happy this makes me!"

Joe nodded, "I'm sure. Don't let me down."

Chance walked away feeling jittery, *I can't believe this, mom and dad are gonna be so happy. I have to tell them!*

* * *

A lofty wall dominated Chance's view, rising and dipping across the rolling hills in either direction as far as her eyes could see. Her AutoBot drove her towards the head of the road where a gate was set into a stretch of wall before her. Leaning out of the vehicle, Chance allowed the GateBot planted alongside the road to scan her retina. Confirming her identity, the gates swung inward to allow her passage.

Entering through the wall, Chance passed by several sprawling luxurious estates scattered throughout the neighborhood. One particular property, sitting atop a hill in the distance, had such palatial quality to it that it cast the others in a penurious light in comparison.

Chance pulled up to one of the other properties, pausing to secure entry through another gate. Her AutoBot then took her down a long curving private drive. An expansive lush green field dotted with a variety of tall trees, consumed the landscape out the window as she was whisked along.

After a few minutes, the vehicle stopped in front of a wide circular pool with an ornate fountain spewing forth water. The fountain, however, was merely an appetizer for the mammoth mansion looming before it.

Home sweet home, she thought to herself sarcastically. Hopping up the steps she did not bother knocking, instead heaving open the heavy oak doors, letting herself in.

The Macassar ebony flooring flaunted its wide-striped patterns under the even lighting of the immense foyer she entered. Hearing the echo of voices, Chance followed the sound to the left up one of the dual-curved staircases that greeted her after entering the room. From there, it was a short walk down an arched hallway leading her to one of the living rooms where her parents were deep in discussion. They seemed to not notice her as she walked in, she got within a few feet of them and spoke up, "hey."

They jumped, "oh my lord, you scared the daylight out of me," said her mother, clutching the pearls that dangled around her neck.

"So, somebody finally decided to come home and pay their parents a visit." Her father said, wearing a polo with his distended gut bulging through the fabric.

Chance shrugged unapologetically, "sorry I've been busy with work. You're the ones who pushed me to get this job after all, so I figured I'd try and put my best foot forward." Her parents had already dived back into their talk though, seeming to forget their daughter's presence.

Chance's mother seemed to be upset about problems they were encountering with renovation being done on their home. "I just really think that as long as we're rearranging the house, we should have our gym moved upstairs where the studio is now. It's just such a hassle to have to go all the way downstairs to get exercise in, and then I have to go all the way up here to take my shower. Plus, then we can have it close to the billiards room, so most of our recreational activities are close to each other."

"Regina, why don't you just use one of the bathrooms downstairs to shower? Wouldn't that solve the problem?" Responded her father, waving his hands in the air emphatically.

Regina pouted, "but it gets drafty down there. Also, there just isn't enough natural light in those bathrooms, it disturbs my Zen, Mark."

Awkwardly observing them interact, Chance waited for the opportune moment to jump back in to deliver the big news that she wanted to tell them. Clearing her throat, she tried to get their attention, but that effort failed. After a few seconds of this, she stopped attempting to be cordial and loudly interjected, "guys!"

They turned to her, lips curved upward, her father grunted, "is there something you want?"

Yeah, I want you to care about your daughter who took time out of her day to come see you assholes. Chance gave a quiet sigh. "Yes, I had some exciting news that I wanted to tell you guys."

"Oh?" they said.

Now feeling slightly self-conscious due to the lack of enthusiasm shown by her parents, Chance shifted uncomfortably. "I um, well...I got a promotion at work. I'm being moved up from Narrow AI troubleshooting to AI solutions."

Her parents gushed, "how exciting," exclaimed her mom. "You know Karen across the way is having a dinner party on her yacht tonight, you should come with us and break the news there as well! Most of the neighborhood will be there, I'm sure they would be ecstatic to hear our daughter is doing so well!"

Chance was a bit miffed at the suggestion, "no I think I'm ok mom, I just wanted to tell you guys. I'm probably just going to head back to my place in a bit."

Mark rolled his eyes, "you're always off in that cave, come on you have to come! Besides, President Rommel is going to be there, this is the perfect chance for you to introduce us to your boss!"

"Dad I don't even know the guy, I wouldn't feel comfortable approaching him, much less introducing him to you." Her parents continued to pester her. Unsure of how to keep turning them down, Chance relented and agreed to come with them. So, she sat down on the couch and allowed herself to be lost in the tv that played in the background, while her parents reverted to their previous discussion.

Being broadcast to her was the Northwest regional tournament, Quell was showing an up and coming fighter in the one-hundred-eighty-five pound weight class, undefeated and coming out of Tacoma, Washington.

Chance never did care to watch the fights very much. She didn't have much knowledge on the particulars of fighting, so watching the people square off against one another rather bored her. Although, the fighter on the screen right now did catch her interest. He was a dark, muscular, handsome man, though it was not his appearance that caught her attention.

The fight had finished with his victory, and in a rather unusual fashion, he got his defeated opponents' attention to shake their hand and bow his head to them. From the fights she had seen, they generally didn't end with any positive display between the two fighters. "Peculiar," she mumbled to herself.

After some time, she was alerted to the fact that her parents were ready to leave for the party. "So which AutoBot do you think we should take?" her father asked.

"Hmm, well I'd like to take one of the coupes but since Chance is coming with us, maybe we should take one of the sedans?" said Regina.

"You guys don't need to worry about me, I'll be taking my vehicle," Chance assured them.

They shrugged, "well, do you know where to go then?" Mark asked. Chance nodded, and then they went off to the garage to pick out what AutoBot they wanted to take them to the event.

A short while later, Chance could see the lights on the pier shining in the night. They reflected off of the dark surface of the ocean, extending out of sight. Her vehicle dropped her off near a dock stretching out to a porcelain white yacht floating statically in the water.

A gentle light radiated from the deck of the ship, the sounds of people engaged in conversation carried on the breeze towards where Chance stood. Striding up the dock, the talk grew louder in Chance's ears as she approached the vessel and boarded to join the party.

Individuals were strewn around the deck, in pairs and groups. Everyone present wore sumptuous, refined attire. The dulcet tones of educated conversation echoed around the boat, marred by the occasional champagne-induced slur.

Scanning the boat, Chance found her parents who arrived before her. They were chatting with their neighbor Karen who lived across the way from them. Her mother spotted Chance as she approached them. Seeming to perk up, she waved excitedly, "Chance darling come join us! Karen here has been indulging me while I've inundated her with your praise, tell her about your new promotion!"

Never one comfortable bragging about herself, Chance plainly told her, "yeah, I got promoted at Quell to work in AI solutions."

Karen, a middle-aged woman in a flower print blouse with an inverted bob haircut and hoop earrings, congratulated Chance profusely. "Splendid! I'm sure you must be thrilled. It's an honor to work for such a prestigious organization in the first place, let alone being promoted to that kind of position."

Chance smiled politely, "thank you, that means a lot."

Eyes uncomfortably wide, Karen looked back and forth between Chance and her mom, "you know my husband, Philip, you know Philip, right?" Cutting herself off she looked around the deck obnoxiously yelling, "Philip? Phil? Phil? Phil honey?"

A squat man broke away from one of the groups, seeming to have a reluctant expression on his face as he did so. In tow behind him were a young pair of twins, appearing to be his children. As he approached, his wife, who was a half foot taller than him, put her hand on his shoulder possessively.

"As you know, Phil here is a part of Quell's strategy team as a senior executive, remarkable I know. Anyways, Phil managed to pull some strings and get our children, Emily and Joshua here, interviews for Quells Institute of Technology for juniors. They're just so precocious for their age, aren't they lovely? They so impressed the admissions team that they were given ex-ante acceptance for the upcoming year, isn't that marvelous?" Her husband and children gave half-smiles and remained silent after their mothers fawning.

"Oh lord, what a delight! That is absolutely wonderful, I'm sure you must be filled with pride." Chance's mom gushed, although Chance could tell her mother was seething at being shown up.

Karen had begun to seem distracted though. Diverting her attention from the conversation, she was now on her tiptoes scanning the yacht. Turning to her husband she asked, "honey dear, do you know when Mr. Rommel is meant to arrive?"

"It's President Rommel, sweetie." Phil gently corrected her.

"Oh, you know what I mean, you said that he had agreed to come. I'm sure many of our guests are expecting him." Karen then noticed her rudeness and refocused on Chance and Regina, "pardon me for cutting off from the conversation. You knew that President Rommel was coming tonight, right? It is so astounding that Phil has worked his way up to be able to know the man on such a personal level. Then again, you know him, don't you Chance?"

"I'm not quite that far up the ladder yet, though I have seen him walking around HQ once or twice." Chance responded awkwardly, suddenly finding the floor beneath her feet of utmost interest."

Regina took that moment to eject from the conversation, "you know I think we should locate Mark, I'm sure the delectable scent of those hors-d'oeuvres has him in hot pursuit somewhere on deck. I'll have to make the rounds to rejoin you after we find the man." The two of them then left the family to go look for Chance's father. Once she was confident they were out of earshot, Regina began complaining, "can you believe her? Trying to show me up after we tell her about your news. Ugh, I despise that woman."

"Then why do you try so hard to impress her?" Chance snapped at her.

Chance's mom seemed taken aback, "Well, she is the most influential wife in the neighborhood. If I want to keep up appearances I have to try and ingratiate myself with her. Your success is the perfect opportunity to give our family a good image."

A scowl came over Chance's face, "maybe I don't want to go be some trophy for you guys to show off in front of your friends? It makes me feel like I'm just some object and not your daughter. Besides, they don't even know me well enough to care about this anyway, do you think bragging about me will change anything?"

Her mom seemed offended at the implication they were only using their daughter for prestige, "what on earth would give you that idea? Honey, that hurts my feelings, just because I want to brag about you means I can't also be proud of my daughter?"

"Except it's not about you being proud of me mom, nothing in my life has ever been about that. The only reason I got into this job in the first place is because you forced me into it since I was a child, threatening to kick me to the curb if I didn't do what you wanted. You did that for no other reason than to be able to brag to your friends that your daughter is working for Quell. All you have ever done is just use me as another status symbol to make yourself seem superior, you and dad both have."

Her mother grew flustered and indignant, "how dare you!"

Chance rolled her eyes and began to walk away, "I need some air, please just give me my space." Chance walked to the rear of the boat and leaned off the rail, staring out into the murky waters. Her mind began to clear as she looked out into the darkness. Although the light obscured the bulk of them, several stars could be seen dotting the night sky.

Footsteps echoed behind her, assuming her parents had tracked her down to speak with her, Chance sighed, "I told you I just want to be left alone for right now."

Turning around, she was abashed to realize that it was not her parents, an older man looking to be in his eighties was standing there partially concealed by darkness. Two sets of glowing red eyes floated in the shadows on either side of him, which she guessed to be SecurityBots. The pungent smell of sauerkraut drifted through the air over to her.

Unfazed by her words, the man walked forward, revealing himself in the light. Chance did a double-take as she realized who was standing in front of her. "P-p-president Rommel, what are you doing here?" Suddenly regretting her harsh words towards her boss and arguably the most powerful man on the planet.

His eyes traveled up and down her figure with a slightly unsettling expression on his face, "I enjoy taking advantage of the hospitality that sycophants like the people here provide me, do I know you?"

"Yes sir, I work for you, in AI solutions. Sorry for being so rude to you a second ago, I thought you were someone else."

Stepping towards Chance, he leaned on the railing beside her, "and who did you think that I was?"

"...my parent's sir, I just...I came out here to be alone and to get away from them."

"Why is that?" he asked.

Chance did not want to answer, but due to the position of the man she was speaking to, she felt obliged to answer truthfully. "I guess they're among the people you mentioned a second ago. They've just been trying to use me to show off and make themselves look good in front of their friends, it made me uncomfortable."

Rommel laughed, a choppy barking noise that crawled under Chance's skin. "I see. I dislike those kinds of people as well, groveling for attention just for the sake of appearances is rather silly. I never understood why some feel the need to bend over backward to impress others."

Given what she knew about Rommel, the vain and egotistical manner with which he portrayed himself in the media, Chance was rather surprised by this. "You do?" she asked, hoping he would not be insulted by the question.

Rommel looked at her, that faintly unpleasant stench of sauerkraut wafting into Chance's nostrils as he did so. "Certainly. I think it's rather pointless to try and dance around for others to like you as if their validation could change one iota of your life. You see, much like how the tiger does not fret about whether other animals recognize his greatness, great people do not worry about proving themselves."

While he spoke, Chance noticed that Rommel was inching closer to her. "Similarly, sheep know they are sheep and meekly let themselves be herded around in acknowledgment of that fact. They know it in their bones, their worthiness, or lack of it, comes as an unchangeable fact at their birth. Why should I worry about the approval of others? I do not wait for others to tell me what I can and can't have, I TAKE it because I know that it belongs to me. I take what I want because it already belongs to me, it all does."

Alarm bells were firing like crazy in Chance's mind, *creepy monologue, yeah something is not right with this guy.* Every fiber in her being was telling her to get far away from this man. She started to give an excuse to leave when his hand dug into her arm like a set of talons. His fingernails dug painfully into her flesh, Rommel's other hand reached out to grope her in more inappropriate ways.

Chance was frozen, contemplating whether she dared draw the ire of her boss by withdrawing from his advances. Leaning forward, he planted his thin old man lips on hers. She fought off a wave of nausea as he kissed her, no longer caring about the consequences, she had had enough. Shrieking, she shoved him off of her and sprinted away.

Darting past his security detail, she ran past the other guests and off of the boat. A few seconds after her exit, a collective cheer rang from the deck, Rommel had evidently made his arrival known to the other guests. The noise barely registered through her panic; Chance raced down the dock without slowing down until she reached her AutoBot.

What the hell just happened, feeling grateful to be out of that situation she got into her car and gripped her arms around herself. Feeling violated, she shivered uncontrollably as anxiety shook her limbs. Chance fought the tears that threatened to spill from her eyes. Even in her private moments, she did not want to feel like she had given him control over her emotions.

Rahim

Rahim awoke in the early morning hours on the day his first fight was scheduled to begin. Nervous energy tied knots in his stomach, anticipation for the unknown consuming even his unconscious thoughts. Gently pulling the covers off, he got off the couch and trotted through the living room to see light spilling out of the small kitchen across the hall.

Peeking his head in the doorway, he saw his father sitting before the window near the kitchen table. Linh knelt in front of Aamil with his hands in hers, the two of them whispering soft words to each other. Glimpsing the reflection of his son in the window, Aamil motioned for Linh to give the two of them time to speak. Linh tenderly patted Rahim's shoulder as she passed by him. "Can't sleep?" asked Aamil.

"I suppose so," remarked Rahim blankly.

"You're going to do amazing today, you don't need to stress out about this."

Rahim replied simply, "I know."

Aamil chortled, "I'm sure you do. Care to tell your old man what's bothering you then?"

Pursing his lips, Rahim shifted awkwardly, "I'm not sure to be honest, nerves about the unknown maybe? For years I knew this day would come, but it never really seemed real until now. I've known for a long time now what kind of person I want to be, but now that the time has come, I'm worried I'll find out I'm not who I thought I was."

Aamil looked sympathetically at his son's reflection before him, "I know the feeling well. I could reassure you that you are a strong, kind, capable young man...more sure of yourself than I was at your age that's for certain, but I know my words won't get rid of that feeling. Pull me out of this corner and take me downstairs. Maybe there's at least something I can do to distract you and get your mind in the right place."

Gripping the handles on the back of his father's chair, Rahim tentatively turned his father around, rolling him towards the lip of the ramp that led downstairs to the training room. Rahim lowered his father down the ramp with well-practiced hands. His legs in a squat to prevent his feet from slipping forward from the weight and his hands firmly grasping the handles on Aamil's chair.

Descending at a steady clip, they reached the ground level of their home. The hard texture of the ramp gave way to a soft springy mat that spanned the entirety of the bottom level of the home. "Go ahead and hit those lights for me, will ya Rahim?"

Sliding his hand along the wall, Rahim flipped a switch and a bright glare illuminated the room. The light exposed mummy-like training dummies, hitting bags, and a modest weight rack tucked away in the corner. A maroon mat stretched across the floor before him, assorted rips and tears spread across it in a display of age. Strips of tape bound the various sections together, a circle 36 feet in diameter was drawn across the center of the mat.

The faint light of dawn glowed in the darkness outside of the windows that dominated the far wall. Rahim turned to his father who still sat near the mouth of the ramp. Smirking, Aamil instructed his son, "ok start warming up."

A few hours later, Rahim knelt on one knee, his left hand buried in the mat supporting his weight. Struggling to control his breathing, he gasped deeply with a slight quiver in his lungs. Droplets of sweat glistened in his dark curly hair. "It never ceases to amaze me that even though you can't spar with me yourself, you still find a way to be as brutal as ever...maybe even more so."

Aamil rudely stuck his tongue out at his son, "I'll take that as a compliment. Since you're taking this time to complain, I'll assume that the fight isn't on your mind anymore, so you're welcome." He craned his neck upwards to stare out of the window. By now the sun had fully risen to eliminate the harsh contrast the lights had created with the early darkness.

"It shouldn't be long now, grab a mop and clean this place up. Clean yourself while you're at it, then we can head over for check-in."

A short while later, the two of them were traveling at a brisk pace towards the Tower downtown where the municipal fights were being held. The two of them were startled upon seeing the swarms of people streaming in and out of the Tower. Aamil hadn't been in the vicinity of a lower-ranked competition pool in well over a decade.

The sight brought him back as he realized just how many people were stuffed into these centers, all vying against one another for success. Rahim for his part had no frame of reference to judge whether the mass amount of people before them was unusual. Despite that, he was still overwhelmed by the raucous buzz compounded by all of the disparate voices present.

They scanned the crowd several times, spotting Lyall, Tahmejia, and Deandre standing together off to the side of the doors. They walked up, Rahim jumping and waving behind Aamil to get their attention. Lyall noticed them as they drew near and gave a friendly wave.

He was wearing a white tank top and black basketball shorts to match the outfit Rahim was wearing. Tahmejia meanwhile was wearing her trademark jacket, concealing her clothes underneath. Meeting up they touched base, "so have you guys signed in for your fights yet?" asked Rahim.

They shook their heads, "we were waiting for you, do you want to head in now?"

Rahim gave a thumbs up. "Me and Aamil will hang back in the lobby while you guys get that done," Deandre spoke up. Having that sorted out, the three went off on their own to check-in before the start of their fights.

Making their way to the check-in area, they were confronted by an even larger crowd of people. This time packed like sardines in a can, people were lined up behind several Quell Bots, waiting to sign in for their fights. The smell of sweat permeated the air, the proximity causing many of the people to heat up and perspire. "Is it always like this in here?" asked Rahim.

Lyall shrugged, "pretty much. The higher competition pools are significantly less crowded than here, but it's hard to get enough wins in a row to move on to those Towers. Most everyone gets stuck down here, unable to win enough to make it onto the next stage. The injuries you rack up from fighting so many times, and just rotten luck, make it so only the highly trained and the very fortunate move on."

Tahmejia sighed, muttering from under the collar of her coat, "he's right. My biggest win streak is five, I don't know if I'll ever make it out of here."

"Don't talk like that, have some faith in yourself!" Rahim scolded. They were forced to wait for several minutes within the crowd. More people filled in behind them as they moved up in the line. Various groups of people clumped together throughout the crowd.

Many of the groups were wearing one of many shades of blue, each shade sticking together: cornflower, lapis, azure, sky, navy, cobalt, sapphire. Meanwhile, several other clumps were all wearing the same shade of vermillion. The rest of the people present wore ordinary clothing with no visibly identifiable markers to distinguish them. Tensions seemed to be high as elbows dug into one another's ribs, each person jostling for their chance to meet their sign-up time.

The frenzy could only be heard as a dull roar, with the occasional jeer and threat between Reds and Blues being made distinguishable from the cacophony. A pair of women squared off with each other, "get the hell away from me you braindead blue bitch."

"The only red I want to see is when I'm stepping over your bloody ass to get my money! Try me, these colors don't run."

The three shifted in discomfort at the naked displays of aggression going on all around them. "It's best just to keep your head down and ignore it, or else you risk getting caught up in it all," Lyall advised Rahim, Tahmejia nodded in agreement.

Rahim found it hard to listen though, his mind was wholly unprepared for the hatred and divisiveness that permeated the room. Luckily for him, time moved by fairly quickly and they were able to sign in for their fights with the Quell Bots at the front of the room. They wasted no time, scurrying away to meet back up with Aamil and Deandre.

"So, what's the news?" asked Aamil when the three walked over.

"My fight is going to be at two pm, so I'll be fighting first. On floor eleven, room eight, cage two." Tahmejia notified him.

Lyall spoke after, "I'll be on floor nineteen, room fifteen, cage five. Fighting at a quarter to three."

"And I'm up at three-thirty, on floor fifteen. Room four, cage seventeen" Rahim said lastly.

"Well, isn't that convenient timing, we just might be able to watch all of you go." Aamil said, looking up to Deandre who grunted in agreement.

Deandre checked his watch, "we better get a move on then, Tahmejia is up in twenty minutes." The group scrammed to the elevator, managing to get on without too much of a wait. Heading to floor eleven, they walked into a corridor lined with doors all the way down on either side. The hall was significantly more crowded than Aamil was used to, but still less occupied than expected.

Finding room eight midway down the hall, they walked through the door. Rather than the rooms taken up by a single cage, in the matches Aamil was familiar with, this room was filled with several cages. No FilmBots roamed around this room either, as the event was much too low profile to garner any sort of viewership. Several matches were ongoing in the room already, the smell of blood and sweat strong in the air. A smattering of people stood around the room, waiting for their bouts to begin.

Rahim and the others followed Tahmejia to the cage she was set to fight at, a pair of women were already inside beating each other to a pulp. Rahim's gaze became captivated as he locked eyes with a woman leaning off by a wall near the cage.

She wore a platinum outfit with hair to match, swaying across her back in thick locs. The color contrasted her skin, which was a rich brown tone. A scar marred her left cheek, although it was made almost inconspicuous by the penetrating nature of her hazel eyes. So entranced was Rahim, that he almost didn't notice the 'Quell' label written across her compression shorts.

Aamil scowled when he saw her, "she must be Tahmejia's opponent. Why on earth would they send one of their plants this far down the ladder?"

Tahmejia became rather jittery after learning that, "I guess I shouldn't worry since I know how this is going to turn out now," she said dejectedly.

Lyall put his hand on her shoulder, "It doesn't look good, but you've been training your ass off. Nobody deserves this more than you. It's a fight, anything can happen, it only takes one hit." The words didn't seem to offer much comfort to Tahmejia, but she prepared herself anyway. Stripping off her jacket, she dressed down to just her compression shorts and sports bra.

A few moments later, she walked over the smooth grey floor towards the stairs leading into the cage. The hazel-eyed woman followed after her and the two stood on either side of the canvas facing each other. A disembodied voice echoed near the area, announcing the start of the fight. A bell pealed and the two women began their clash against one another. Right off the bat, it was evident that Tahmejia was much more tightly wound than her opponent. Moving very choppily, she pressed forward in her stance towards the other woman.

The woman on the other hand, seemed much looser and more relaxed. Her expression was completely nonchalant, seeming quite unconcerned about the fighter in front of her. Casually moving forward in a Muay Thai stance, she bounced up and down smoothly. Giving almost no indication of her intentions, she launched a vicious body kick that thudded into Tahmejia's ribs.

Tahmejia tried to catch the kick but was much too slow. She attempted to counter with an overhand right, but it was almost as if she was moving in honey compared to the other woman. The punch hit nothing but air, her opponent quickly circled around her.

Rahim and the others shouted advice to Tahmejia from outside the cage, trying to offer some corner side insight to help her chances. Tahmejia tried to take in what they were saying, unsuccessfully. Tahmejia threw a few kicks and a number of punches, to no avail, her opponent easily evaded all of them.

Tahmejia, at last, changed tactics and dropped levels to try and catch the woman's ankle in a single leg. The woman swiftly pulled her foot back though and rained down a multitude of overhand blows on the back of Tahmejia's exposed head. Tahmejia rolled to try and get out of the line of fire but was quickly smothered.

Swarming her, the woman swung with precise aim, landing punches in just the right spots to inflict the maximum amount of pain. It was over before the conclusion of the first round, with Tahmejia curled up helplessly on the canvas. Her body was spattered with blood droplets that had been forced out from the beating she just took.

Rahim and the others had gone quiet at this point, unsure how to handle what they had just seen. Not wanting to cause insult to injury, they chose not to make too many comments and let the matter stand when Tahmejia exited the cage. Tears ran down her face, though from her expression they seemed to be from frustration rather than pain. Even so she was slow to join the group, gripping her sides in discomfort, the blood on her still not cleaned off.

Rahim felt like a bad friend and teammate as he found his eyes not on Tahmejia, but her opponent. The other woman did not give any signs of relishing her victory at all. She walked out of the cage with an emotionless expression. Gathering her things, she walked past them to exit the room, once again locking eyes with Rahim as she left.

It was very slight, but a glint of...something appeared in those eyes as she looked at him. Shaking his head, he forced his attention back to his group and patted Tahmejia on the back consolingly. Not wasting any time, they turned to Lyall to lead the way to where his fight would be taking place.

A few minutes later, they were on floor nineteen, waiting for Lyall's match to begin. Lyall dressed down to a pair of compression shorts that fit slightly too tight for his frame, his sides spilling over the edges. Between the tattoos running up his thighs to his ribs, and his wavy hair pulled back into a ponytail, he made for an imposing figure. Rahim always forgot just how big his friend was, showing the physique of a grizzly bear now that he was dressed down. Upon seeing his time had arrived, Lyall entered the cage, with his opponent soon showing up to follow suit.

If Lyall was a grizzly, this man was a polar bear. Wide Slavic features dominated his visage, a coating of thick blond hair ran all up his body to match the shortly trimmed hair atop his head. The name 'Draco' was printed on his green shorts. Draco stood eye to eye with Lyall. The two of them got into the cage and readied themselves for their match. Rahim looked over to Tahmejia and noticed she was still rather downtrodden from her performance earlier. Hoping to distract her, he asked, "so how do you think he's going to do?"

She glanced over, "I'm sure he'll do fine, what do you think?"

"Oh, it depends. You know what they say about these bigger guys? Whoever lands on top is the one who will win." He said with a wink.

Deandre growled from behind them, "hey I heard that, don't sleep on us big fellas. There's more to it than that!" Tahmejia looked at Rahim and laughed as he was scolded. Soon Rahim and Aamil were chuckling slightly as well.

The group grew silent as the bell rang, beginning the fight. Draco lumbered forward and threw a wide left hook to start the fight. Lyall shuffled to the side and in a move of surprising dexterity for his size, darted low to the ground and scooped Draco's ankle into the air.

A pounding sound resonated from the canvas as the big man jumped on his remaining leg to stay standing. Timing the other man's jumps, Lyall waited till Draco was mid-jump. Yanking the other foot forward, he sent the Slav straight to his back. Lyall pounced atop him when he landed, hooking Draco's leg with his own and assuming half mount. Using that leverage to keep him in place, Lyall started throwing punches at the downed man's head.

After landing two or three big shots, Lyall mysteriously began to rise off Draco. In a feat of strength, the pale giant was forcing Lyall's weight into the air away from him. Their roles were suddenly switched and Lyall was sent to his back, with the bigger man winding his hand to land some overhand blows.

Lyall adeptly maneuvered himself around and past Draco's arms. This stymied his opponent for a considerable amount of time until the bell pealed to end the first round. Deandre rocked Rahim's shoulder, "so whoever lands on top wins, eh?"

Rahim stuck his tongue out and waved him off. Truthfully, Rahim was too worried for his friend to muster any witty retorts, *I hope Lyall can last long enough to find a way to win.* His concern was prompted by the obvious fatigue Lyall showed in his body language. The lengthy scuffle on the ground had thoroughly drained much of his energy.

Rolling over to rise and walk to his corner, Lyall inhaled deeply and contorted his face into a sickly expression. Taking advantage of the water fountain that appeared in his corner, he drank deeply, water spilling all over his chin. Lyall knelt to the ground and took several deep breaths, his back rising and falling as he did so.

A moment or so later, the bell rang, starting the second round. Lyall rose to his feet and met the other man in the middle of the cage. Fortunately for Lyall, Draco seemed a bit more tired than him. His arms were now held quite low, legs shaking slightly under him. Lyall prayed that he didn't get caught by the strength of his opponent, relying on his greater speed to pepper him up on the feet.

Dipping low he slipped in and out of Draco's reach with a series of jabs. Drawing blood after landing three or four shots to the chin. Though he seemed even more unstable than before, Draco bared his teeth and snarled in a show of defiance.

Lurching forward he charged at Lyall to drive him into the fence. Similar to how one would avoid a bull, Lyall jumped to the side and let Draco slam into the chain link. Draco turned to face Lyall, just to be caught by a straight kick to the chest, bouncing him back into the fence. The metal rings in the fence rattled loudly in response.

Seeing his opponent bend over from the kick, Lyall threw a hard uppercut that landed right on Draco's forehead. Another punch from overhead and the fight was over.

Lyall waited to receive his results and headed over to talk with his friends. Collapsing at their feet, he turned onto his back and gasped for air. Sweat was pouring out of every one of his glands, causing a layer of moisture to glisten all over his skin. Rahim bent over and patted him on the belly, "congrats bro, you did great out there!"

"I think I'm gonna die," Lyall moaned.

"You can wait to do that after my fight, we gotta get a move on," Rahim said while looking at the time on his phone.

Lyall flopped his arm on the ground lazily, "I'll catch up. Floor fifteen, right? I'll be there, go on without me." Everyone looked at one another and shrugged, leaving Lyall to catch his breath. They went down the corridor and took the elevator to the floor Rahim would be competing on.

Aamil gave Rahim a once over, observing his son's body language. "How do you feel?"

Rahim's arm was slightly quivering, clenching his fist to still his limb, he looked at Aamil, "nervous, but excited. I'm ready to see if all of this training has paid off." Aamil patted Rahim's back approvingly and turned away silently. They found the room and cage that Rahim would be competing in and waited for his turn to fight. Rahim wrapped his hands and slid them into fingerless padded gloves. Dressing down to his compression shorts, he jogged in place to get his blood pumping.

In that time, Rahim's opponent showed up and approached the cage, whose name Rahim had been informed was Marco. Short and pudgy, his physique was a startling contrast from Rahim's. Rahim stood over a head taller than the man, with limbs that easily outreached his opponents. Marco's stout body was surprisingly energetic however, the man moved in a jittery fashion, quickly shuffling his feet across the floor. Rahim looked to the others and followed Marco into the cage.

Looking across the canvas at his opponent, Rahim visualized all of the actions and possible reactions he planned to make. A shout echoed throughout the room and Rahim turned to see Lyall standing there cheering him on, he had just now caught up with the rest of the group. Then the bell rang and he found himself out of time, it was sink or swim for him now.

Covering ground with a speed that seemed unlikely for his frame, Marco met Rahim on the other side of the cage and tried to corner him. Bouncing side to side, Marco swung big hooks from all angles to keep Rahim contained. After blocking a few of these punches on his arms, Rahim swung his arm down to swim to the outside and shimmy away from Marco. Circling, Rahim reversed their positions and shot an underhand punch into Marco's gut. Marco once again charged towards Rahim, his upper half leaned forward, the bulk of his weight on the balls of his feet as he threw another hook.

It was at this moment, that Rahim chose to roll diagonally, snagging Marco's leg in an Imanari roll. Trapping his opponent in a heel lock, it was a matter of seconds before a hand was tapping out on the canvas.

Getting up, Rahim felt flooded by the thrill of victory. It was a weight off of his mind to have confirmation all of his preparation was paying off. Marco did not seem to be taking the loss well, bitterly punching his fist into the canvas. Rahim leaned over and consoled his opponent, "you have a lot of potential, you just need to iron out your technique is all. Carry this lesson going forward and I'm sure you'll do well in your next fight."

Helping Marco to his feet, he shook his hand and nodded in respect before making his exit. Pausing at the top of the cage, he stopped to get his results from the DistribuBot. "Your victory has been processed and recorded in Quell's database. Fifty credits have been transferred to your personal account and your PQ has been set at twelve."

Rahim was disappointed at how little money he received but had no frame of reference to have an opinion on his PQ score. He went over to celebrate with his father and teammates. Deandre gave him a nod of respect, while Lyall vigorously patted him on the back. Tahmejia stood shyly off to the side and squeaked out, "you did great Rahim, I'm happy for you."

Aamil hummed with pride, rolling over to Rahim he gripped his hand. "I couldn't have done better myself, what a way to handle your debut!"

"So, what did they set your Power Quotient at?" Lyall asked Rahim.

"Power Quotient?" Rahim answered.

"Your PQ score."

"Oh, twelve."

Everyone grumbled in surprise, "twelve?" said Lyall. "That's pretty unbelievable for your first fight, the RefBot must have been impressed with what you showed it to rate you so high after only one fight. I only got a four after my first match."

Aamil intervened, "It is remarkable that he is starting off on such a strong foot, but let's not give any more weight to those scores than we need to. At best focusing on it too much will give you a big head, at worst it can give you crippling self-doubt. Let's just let our work speak for itself, shall we?" Everyone couldn't help but agree, and so the group made their way to leave the Tower.

Nia

Nia stared ahead without emotion, focusing on keeping herself composed. D*on't let them think they're getting to you,* she thought to herself. She stood mostly naked before a crowd of about a dozen or so suits and lab coats. The cold drafty room left gooseflesh all over her skin. She tried not to feel vulnerable, sensing them appraising her with cold calculating eyes like a deluxe cut of meat.

The frigid metallic slap of a pointer rod against her quadriceps threatened to break her concentration. It's wielder a balding man in a white turtleneck with khaki pants. Dr. Galton was his name, stood in the midst of giving a presentation. "As you can see, our subject here, twenty-two years of age, female, has matured into one of the finest specimens that the designer program has produced to date. See the aesthetic facial features, the finely toned nature of her physique. However, appearances are not where her assets end. She also provides peak combat capabilities for her size and weight. With her mind honed to disciplined perfection, the subject is optimal for the task of mitigating resource dispersal from Quell to the general population. I have arranged a demonstration for all of you here today, to give a reminder of the results you can expect this asset to produce."

A curtain opened behind them, revealing a boxing ring on the back of the stage they stood upon. Placing his wrinkled hand upon her shoulder, Dr. Galton leaned in to whisper in her ear, "don't disappoint me, Nia."

Turning, she looked at him with callous eyes, "have I ever?" Shrugging his hand off she strode into the ring.

Clearing his throat, Dr. Galton introduced her opponent. A platform rose underneath the floor from behind the ring. A stoic thirty-something-year-old woman was presented, hands straight as a board at her sides.

"Here we have a subject from the old Spartan program. Unlike the first subject presented, this one has had no gene-editing enhancements. Which era shall win out? The old or the new? We shall see."

The older woman faced off against Nia, shaking her limbs she prepared herself to fight. Nia simply stood there motionless, waiting for the bout to begin. The woman came at Nia aggressively, throwing a combination of punches followed by a roundhouse kick to the body. Nia leaned and shuffled her feet, slipping every single one of the blows attempted by the woman, barely appearing to move at all.

It appeared to Nia like her opponent was moving in slow motion, her movements slow and predictable as if her body was buffering. Switching up her tactics, the woman went low for a blast double takedown. Nia disinterestedly circled to the side, leaving her opponent fumbling for air.

The woman came in again with a straight jab, this time Nia did not evade. Catching her wrist, Nia yanked the woman's arm, straightening it, then jammed her palm into her opponent's elbow, shattering the woman's arm. A horrific scream erupted from the woman's mouth, shattering the calm facade she had been putting on moments before. Shocked gasps rumbled amongst the onlookers, "what do you think you're doing?" Dr. Galton hissed through his teeth.

Nia shrugged, "you said to put on a show, so I put on a show."

Malice gleaming in his eyes, Dr. Galton gave her a good long stare to let her know this wasn't over. Turning around, he spread his hands seeking to soothe the offended onlookers. "Well, it seems our subject has gotten rather carried away with herself. But as you can see, the superiority of the designer program cannot be denied, the results speak for themselves. That should conclude the demonstration, for now. I hope to see you all again when we have completed the newest stage of development that we are working on here."

Upon that obvious dismissal, the group of people began to stream out of the room. Once the last of them bustled out of the room, Dr. Galton snapped his fingers without looking behind him. "Leave the facility and head to your quarters, I will deal with you later." At that, Nia silently exited the room with her nose turned upward.

The building they were in was a cutting-edge research facility, replete with aesthetically pleasing modern design. Big wide-open windows allowed ample light to illuminate the busied work of technicians in lab coats and the hum of various Quell bots conducting the numerous tasks assigned to them.

One of the few places in the world where humans still had real work and responsibilities delegated to them, the utmost care had been devoted to making this a warm and homey atmosphere. An environment adequate in pleasing the people who worked here, enough to make them forget the atrocities their work was helping perpetuate in the broader world.

Nia and her escort were greeted by the sight of lush green vegetation as they walked outside. A grandiose sign with digital print greeted people to the facility they were leaving. 'Welcome to Quell Central, Jewel of Silicon Valley'. Continuing forward, they arrived at the tram that ran alongside a manmade burbling creek. Climbing in, they sat in silence that was broken only by the tumble of the tram's wheels on the trail, and the trickle of the creek running next to it.

* * *

As Nia and everyone else left the room, Dr. Galton stood for several moments with his hands crossed behind his back. He was disturbed from his trance as a voice called out from a dark corner in the room, "Why the long face, Galton? Having trouble controlling one of your lab rats?"

Chills ran down Galton's spine as he recognized the voice that called out to him. A ghastly-looking man emerged from the shadows. Wearing a smokey grey pinstriped suit, the man appeared to be in his seventies or eighties. His demeanor had a timeless feel with the guileful glare he wore over his pale sunken cheekbones. He had a face that inclined one to think he assumed perfect obedience from even death. The pungent smell of sauerkraut confronted Galton as the man approached him.

"What an honor for you to come out to see me, President Rommel. No need to worry sir, she's just a little willful is all. I should have no trouble keeping her firmly on her leash." Dr. Galton said, teeth chattering from the anxiety of being in the presence of the head of Quell.

Saying nothing, President Rommel paced in a circle around Dr. Galton looking him up and down thoroughly. He gave Galton a ghoulish smile, "I should hope so. And how is our...other... program coming along?"

Putting his hands in his pockets to hide their quivering, Dr. Galton nervously replied, "we have made a good amount of progress but AI and tissue synthesis have been a challenge to synchronize. I anticipate that we should have our first specimen ready for examination in about five or six months, sir."

President Rommel appeared to consider this information for a moment before replying, "better make it five rather than six. I hope to see good results...you know I hate to be disappointed."

* * *

It was about a half-hour before Nia arrived at her destination. Before her lay an assortment of cottages situated at the base of a forested foothill near the Santa Cruz mountains. A much larger facility stood far in the background. "Camp Crisp, home sweet home," mumbled Nia.

Stepping out of the Tram, she headed to her cabin. Coming into proximity of her abode, a small log-built structure with a slate roof, Nia narrowed her eyes. A man lay lounging in a patch of sunlight in front of her door. Wearing only white shorts with bare feet and an exposed chest displaying a white fox tattooed across it, Kolby sat there intensely eating an apple. Taking notice of her approach, he looked up and waved, apple juice trickling down his cheeks. "What's up little lady, how was the meet n greet?"

Nia wrinkled her face at him, "Please don't ever call me that again. It went fine, though I think the doc is pissed at me."

Kolby waved his hand in the air, "don't be such a sourpuss, that's probably why the doc is mad at you."

Rolling her eyes, Nia motioned for him to move so she could enter her home. "Whatever, can you please go? I'm tired and don't feel like talking to you."

Standing up, Kolby rudely threw his apple core into the brush near the cabin. "Fine by me. But one more thing, I have a chore for you. I need you to send a message to someone for me, it'll be a bit of a journey."

Always looking for an excuse to get away from the compound, Nia's ears perked up. "Fine, what's the message?"

Kolby tossed an ivory coin in her direction, "just this."

Mitch

Mitch sat at the end of a long extravagant dining table made of African Blackwood. Its polished surface scintillated beneath the sparkling chandelier hanging overhead. His little legs dangled from the chair as his father walked behind him on a phone call. Speaking in adult talk that went over little Mitch's head, fading into a buzz in the background.

ServeBots roamed around the room, half humanoid-like figures made up of a burnished silvery metallic substance. They rotated on spherical balls that propelled them across the floor. Occupied by their various tasks such as cooking and cleaning, they emitted a quiet hum as they executed their work.

Hanging up the phone his father turned to him, "come, Mitch, we are going on a little adventure." Waddling after his father, Mitch hurried to keep up with him as his father's much longer legs threatened to outstrip him. They walked out of their home into a lavish courtyard, resplendent with various exotic trees that gave the area a lively contrast to the ornate marble comprising much of the structure around it.

Walking through an archway, they approached a limousine that was parked waiting for them. Drawing near, the rear door opened automatically to allow them entry. No driver was in the front of the vehicle, yet it took off on its own anyway, pulling off to a preset destination. The interior was plush black leather, stocked with screens and snacks galore to keep the two amused as they traveled.

The clamorous sound of people shouting vociferously awaited them as they exited the gate bordering their estate. A massive crowd joined together protesting and waving signs, stood visible outside of the tinted limo windows. One sign read, 'How can I work to support myself if there is no work?', another read, 'Machines don't need to put food on the table, I do!', a third simply read, 'Capitalist pig!'.

"Daddy why are these people outside of our house?" asked Mitch inquisitively.

His father curled his lip in an expression of distaste, "just losers looking for handouts. They are either too lazy or too stupid to take care of themselves, so now they expect me to provide for them. Minimum skills get you minimum pay, remember that son, maybe if they had a better work ethic they wouldn't be out here making fools of themselves."

Several minutes after the limo pulled away, it made another stop. A man in a black suit with a red tie got into the car, greeting Mitch's father as he got in. "Hello Manfred, it's a pleasure. How's your father doing?"

Manfred indulged the man in the standard pleasantries, "oh, he's doing alright. His health could be better, but I have no doubt the stubborn bastard won't be leaving us anytime soon." Shortly after joining them, the two men became deep in a heated discussion. "It's day and night with these people George, they crowd outside of my property with their protests. I am getting a flood of hate mail both online and in-person, hell I've even gotten death threats. They are making all of these demands of me, but I don't know what they expect, we're just a tech company. It's the government's job to make sure they're taken care of, not mine."

George looked at Manfred for a long moment before responding, "I've worked with you and your father for a long time. I've been more than happy to do your bidding as long as my palms were greased. Mathias has always been the man with the plan, I haven't bothered to look too deeply past what he has asked of me. I can imagine that the high aspirations he has passed on to you can be rather daunting, but just have faith."

Manfred didn't seem content with that answer, "that's all you have to say? What use are you if you can do nothing but blather in a time like this, is there nothing you can do to help?"

George sighed, "look you know I'm the last one who wants to come in and lecture you on how you go about things, but maybe you should consider that this is just reality finally catching up with you. You've spent the last few decades lobbying for tax cuts and deregulation, you've bullied your way into taking on government contracts in almost every sector, what did you think was going to happen? The government no longer has the resources or the authority to effectively intervene."

Manfred grew angry, "big talk from someone who was more than happy to accept my family's money this whole time."

George put his hands up defensively, "like I said I'm not coming to criticize, I'm just explaining the state of reality. I've gotten my hands dirty too, you're right, but getting defensive isn't going to change things. People are upset, people are scared and uncertain about the future. You've monopolized almost every industry, thirty percent of the workforce has been automated away with Quell bots. You didn't want big government getting involved and affecting your bottom line, well now the government doesn't have the power to fix this mess. The chickens have come home to roost, and now the ball is in your court. You hold all the cards here, you hold most of the wealth needed to help these people, it's up to you to figure this out."

Mitch's father crossed his arms over his chest, "and there's nothing you can do?"

The persistence aggravated George, "look I can see if there's any way I can get the rest of congress to approve an emergency relief fund, but that will only buy time. It won't be a permanent fix, and even that isn't a guarantee. Any long-term solution is going to be in your hands now." Manfred huffed in response but let the issue lie, allowing the conversation to turn to more benign chit-chat for the rest of the ride.

Eventually, the limo pulled up to a crowded event, filled with people. They were in a city now, surrounded by towering skyscrapers and shining lights as far as the eye could see. An escort of SecurityBots surrounded the outside of the vehicle as the three of them stepped out. Tall squarish creations that moved about on a belt-like track, long metal arms inert at their sides, while the red eyes embedded in their faces glowed with a hint of danger.

On the building was a massive lit-up digital screen with two men facing off, their fists aimed at one another, the words 'Ultimate Fighting Championship' presented above their outlines. Mitch opened his mouth in awe at the grandiose sight, the hum of the crowd around them filling him with excitable energy, this was a new experience for him.

People shouted and began to take pictures as they spotted Mitch's father walking up to the venue. In response, their SecurityBots tightened formation to shield them from the spotlight. Parting through the throng of people, they made their way inside, where an even larger sea of people milling about greeted them.

A walkway extended in a ring around the building. There vendors sold various kinds of food and drink to satiate the hungry spectators. In the interior of the building, a sea of seats was arranged in a donut shape with the center being taken up by a lone cage.

Trotting down an aisle that ran between the rows of seats, Mitch walked with his father and George to the front row right in front of the cage. A spectacle of colored lights began to flash and strobe across the room as music blared throughout the building. The sound of deep bass and drums rumbled in young Mitch's ears as he looked around in wonder, mystified by the new things he was experiencing.

A tall muscular man entered the cage and strutted around with his chest puffed out. His arms were raised as if he was challenging the world itself to take him on. An older man wearing a polo shirt and black gloves stood quietly near the back of the cage, keeping to himself. Another slightly shorter but still imposing-looking man entered the cage, staring down the first person who entered.

After a few moments of introduction and rigamarole, the man in the polo shirt instructed the two shirtless men to touch gloves, and then the two began fighting. Dancing back and forth, the two exchanged a series of blows. Mitch's father and George clapped passionately as they became engaged in watching the fight.

Mitch's father commented to George, "see these men don't allow themselves to become pitiful by sitting around and whining about the lack of opportunities out there. They buckled down and found a way, putting their bodies on the line and working hard to make a living. The rest of the world needs to take a hint from them."

Turning to Mitch, his father impressed the point upon him, "you see these men Mitch? These men know how to work hard, they don't ask anybody to solve their problems for them, they work hard and get what they earn. Take notes son." Always eager to please his father, Mitch made sure to take his words to heart, nodding in agreement with his father's teachings.

George excused himself midway into the fight and departed, leaving Mitch and his father on their own to watch the event. As Mitch watched the fight, he could only think of the gladiators in the movies his father watched with him sometimes.

Like an action movie, the two men pummeled each other brutally, neither willing to bend his spirit to the other and give in. Late in the fourth round, it was all over. The taller man had delivered a devastating knee to the other's head and knocked him out cold. The both of them emerged bloody and battered from the exchange.

A short while later Mitch and his father were on their way out of the venue. Somebody had let out a tip that they were in there. Another crowd similar to the one they had seen earlier that day, was there waiting for them when they walked out of the building. Once again, the SecurityBots surrounded them, causing the protestors to back away in fear as they walked past them.

"Take the silver spoon out of your ass and feed us!" a concealed voice yelled. "You have more money and resources than anyone could spend in a thousand lifetimes, what gives you the right to hoard this wealth while the rest of us die in the streets!" shouted another. An egg slipped past the SecurityBots defenses and pelted Manfred in the chest, staining the expensive suit he wore. He and Mitch ducked into the limo and pealed off, leaving the protestors behind.

Visibly shaken, Mitch put his hand on his father's leg, "are you ok, daddy?"

Stripping off his blazer, Manfred patted his son's hand, "I'm fine, son." Pausing for a moment he looked off through the window, watching the lights pass by.

Turning, he put his hands on Mitch's shoulders. "Listen to me Mitch, don't ever let anyone tell you that you don't deserve what you have. Our family worked hard to build our wealth, it is our birthright. We earned our position in life by being born into a smart and hardworking family. You are better than the rabble out there that just wants to tear you down for our success. Someday you are going to be a very powerful man, it is your destiny to stand above all others. Just like my father passed the burden of greatness onto me, so must I pass it onto you. We are the chosen few, only we are capable of knowing what is right. If you're going to use your position to its full advantage, you must remember that you deserve to be in the spotlight, you're better than everyone else. We're winners Mitch, the world is ours if we choose to take it." Unsure of how to respond, Mitch stared up at his father with wide eyes and nodded.

Kentrell

Kentrell was disturbed from his slumber, the sound of shouting penetrating the thin walls of his bedroom. He recognized the voices to be his parents, immediately anxiety wracked his mind. His breathing became shallow, his pulse reaching a rate where he could feel his heart beating in his chest. *This always happens because something else is wrong, what could it be?* Kentrell thought to himself.

Lowering his feet to the floor lightly to not cause a sound, Kentrell snuck over to his bedroom door and cracked it open. Standing a few feet away were his parents, red in the face as they spoke to one another in angry tones. "You're a loser Dante, you'll always be a loser! It's because you can't do a damn thing right that we won't be able to make rent this month!" Kentrell's mother screamed with fists shaking at her sides.

"And what about you Talina? What about you?! You're in my face callin me out for not winning fights, but what are you doing? You're out here getting your ass kicked too, not bringing in shit to help take care of our kid!" Dante shot back angrily.

"I shouldn't have to be putting myself out in those cages in the first place! You're a man ain't you? It's your job to be taking care of business and holding me and Kentrell down. What kind of man lets his wife get hurt and his son go hungry? You ain't no man, you're a low down bum!" Talina spat on Dante's shoes as she insulted him.

That sent Dante over the edge, face growing beat red, he aggressively grabbed Talina and shook her. "Who do you think you're talking to? I'm not a man? I'll show you how much of a man I am!" Right as he raised his hand menacingly towards his wife, Kentrell bumped into the door frame out of fright.

Dante heard the noise and looked towards Kentrell's door, noticing that it was cracked open. A look of shame came over his face and he let go of Talina. With one last look at his son's bedroom door, Dante stomped out of the apartment.

It was several days later that Kentrell saw his father again. Dante came back in the middle of the day while Talina was gone. Dante was visibly beaten up, his arm slung in a makeshift sling made from an old t-shirt. A dark expression cast over his face, Dante approached his son who sat on the floor in front of a small television. Turning the volume down on the tv, he knelt to the ground and looked Kentrell in the eyes. "Hey little man, how you been doin?"

Kentrell looked up to Dante, "I'm ok dad, are you hurt?"

"Kind of. I don't think I'll be able to fight for a while. I...I've tried my best." Dante said softly.

"Mom's been sad since you left, are you going to be staying with us again?" Kentrell said hopefully.

The question seemed to cut his father deeply, "I...no, I'm not going to be staying here. Actually, I was hoping you could keep my coming here a secret from your mom. Can you do that?"

Kentrell wrinkled his face in confusion, "but why?"

"I just need you to do this for me, can you promise not to tell her I was here?"

"Ok..."

A tear spilled down Dante's cheek, something Kentrell had never seen before. He didn't know why, but it troubled him deeply to see his dad cry. Dante started speaking again, "I need you to know that I tried my best, ok? I really tried to make this work, I tried to do what I could for your mother and you. I just can't do it...no matter how hard I try, I just fail. You need to know I love you and I'm sorry for everything. You might not see me for a long long time, maybe not ever again. I can't burden you guys anymore, I have to leave Kentrell, ok?"

Kentrell didn't know how to respond, "but where are you going, daddy?"

Dante choked up, "I don't know. There's no way to know what's on the other side...hopefully, something better." Brushing away tears with the back of his hand, Dante leaned to kiss Kentrell on the head and he stood up to go. Pausing at the door before he left, he called over his shoulder, "I love you Kentrell, remember your promise."

Kentrell kept his promise, despite seeing his mother grow more and more despondent as the days went on. He was filled with a sense of impotence as he watched Talina return every day more battered and bruised than the day before, while her mental health seemed to degrade simultaneously. One day, Talina sat Kentrell down and informed him that they were going to have to move because they couldn't afford rent. Kentrell didn't question what she told him and packed his things as she instructed.

Surprise filled him though when he realized that they would be sleeping in a tent for the near future. They pitched camp in a patch of grass under an overpass, the next few nights were cold and restless. Worse than the cold was the hunger, they were struggling to afford food, causing hunger to gnaw at them painfully night after night.

One day, Talina returned to the tent from an outing. Pulling down the zipper of the tent, she looked inside at Kentrell, "come on, we have somewhere we need to go. I think we'll finally be able to get some food tonight." At the mention of food, Kentrell excitedly got up and followed his mother. They turned several times as she led him through the streets to their destination.

Eventually, they arrived at a rather run-down building that stood out like a sore thumb from the well-maintained structures around it. 'Office of Resource Allocation' was written across the face of the building. Entering through the glass doors in front, they stepped into a small line of three people. Kentrell wasn't sure what was going on, but from the other people's malnourished appearances, it seemed they were in a similar situation as Kentrell and Talina.

It was a number of minutes before they got to the front of the line. At the front was a metallic gray box that stood seven feet high. The LabelBot scanned Talina's retina and began to speak to them. "Your application has been processed and granted approval, you qualify to register yourself and your dependent as Dead Weight individuals. Pursuant to this status, you shall receive a monthly stipend, adjusted quarterly by Quell to the amount we deem necessary to provide for your survival needs. Should you enter into this program, you will have the option to opt-out at any time. Do you still wish to accept these conditions as they have been explained to you?"

"Yes," said Talina drearily.

"Your acceptance has been recorded, stand before me and the labeling process will begin shortly." Talina stood before the box and a pair of arms emerged from the side of the machine. Talina twitched as the arms reached out and gripped her head, holding it in place as a laser shone from the machine onto her forehead. A gasp escaped her as the process went underway.

Finishing, she turned to Kentrell, the skin on her forehead red and irritated with an even darker crimson 'DW' printed on her forehead. It was Kentrell's turn, he tried to put on a brave face as the arms grabbed his head. Tears welled in his eyes as the laser burned the skin on his forehead, he clenched his fist to avoid crying out. A few moments later the process ended, Kentrell turned to his mother, with his own 'DW' displayed on his head.

Elliot

"Heavenly Father, glory be to God, in your name we ask for you to shine your light in these troubled times and show us the way. May you thwart the advances of those who would seek to discredit and dishonor your name..." Elliot shifted where he sat, eyes squeezed shut and head bent over to rest on his hands, listening to the pastor deliver his sermon.

Desperately he projected his prayers into the universe, hoping that God was listening and would answer. Thoughts of his sister and his sick mother filled Elliot's mind. He hoped for their wellbeing and prayed that he could find the strength to secure it for them. *Please I need a sign,* he thought to himself.

"...in return we shall have faith in your heavenly wisdom Father, and not question what you deem to be right. For it is in your divine wisdom, that you have created the world that we see before us. We shall not be so arrogant as to question your plan for us. Almighty God we ask that you heal our brothers and sisters harmed in the fires of conflict. So we may once again rise as your soldiers to fight in your name. God, we ask you to bless us with the strength to vanquish those who stand against your will. The non-believers, the unchaste, the sodomites, the lazy, the wicked, and others who would pervert your divine will." The pastor paused for a moment before continuing.

"To close this sermon, I would like to close with a line from the holy book, as I always do. Proverbs thirteen: four, 'The soul of the lazy man desires, and has nothing; but the soul of the diligent shall be made rich.' As we close for today, I would like ya'll to keep this line in mind. Remember to not question why you don't have the life you desire, but what you need to do to get there. The Lord has put the path of prosperity before you, it is on you to realize that path. Amen."

"Amen," repeated Elliot.

"Now if you'll for just a moment, take the time to donate credits to our holy church. Remember to be generous, for the seed you plant here, will be returned to you tenfold by the grace of God."

Elliot eagerly pulled out a tablet and opened the church's website. Going to the donate option on their page, he pressed his thumb to the scanner on his tablet and deposited two hundred credits from his account. *Please God, let this be enough for you to make my mom better, I don't know what else to do.*

Absentmindedly he got off of his couch and turned the TV off, shutting off the image of the pastor still on the screen. "ELLIOT!" his little sister sprinted towards him, tackling and clinging to his leg.

"And how are you miss Victoria?"

She looked up at him with a gap toothed smile, "I'm good, me and mommy have been spending time together in her room!"

"And how is mom?" Elliot asked with a concerned look.

Looking disconcerted, Victoria replied, "she's laying in bed right now, she wasn't feeling very well."

"That's too bad, I'm going to go check on her. You just stay out here and find something to do, ok? Maybe you can find something on the tv to watch." Elliot walked around the furniture and down the hall to the outside of the far doorway.

Rapping his knuckles on the wood frame before entering, he announced his presence. "Hey, it's Elliot, I'm coming in." Pushing the door open he walked into the room, where he saw his mother. She lay in a full-sized bed, resting on a tall frame with a thick white blanket wrapped around her.

Laying on her back, brown hair was splayed across the pillow behind her head. Her breathing came in quick weak inhales. Her eyes cracked open as her son entered the room. Noticing him approach her bedside, a smile cracked her lips. "Hey Elliot, how was your day?" she rasped.

As it always did, the sight of his mother like this made Elliot uncomfortable. He wanted to turn tail and run as far from the image as he could. Instead, he drew closer and grabbed hold of her feeble hand. "My day was pretty good mom. I won my fight earlier this morning, plus I just got done listening to Pastor Campbell's service. I've been working so hard and think I'm close to making it to the next level. I'm going to make you proud mom."

His mother leaned over and placed her other hand on top of Elliot's, enclosing his hand within her grip. "Oh, Elliot. I'm already proud of you, don't you know that?"

"Yeah, I know mom," murmured Elliot unconvincingly. "So how have you been feeling today?"

She turned away and stared up at the ceiling, "you know, as good as the cancer will let me feel. Every day it wears at me just a little more." She looked back at her son, "I don't know how much longer I can keep up this fight Elliot. I need to know you'll be there to look after your sister once I'm not around anymore."

Frustrated tears welled up in Elliot's eyes, "stop talking like that mom. There's a way to help you, they have the cure to your disease. If you can just hang in there a little longer, I'll have the money we need to get you the operation you need to get better. I've been planting my seed and I know God will reward the good faith I've been putting in, he'll make sure you get better."

His mother's face grew deadly serious, "Elliot, you and I both know that there is no guarantee you'll get the money needed to save me in time. I need you to promise me, Elliot."

Turning around to hide his tears from his mother, Elliot conceded. "Yes, I promise. I won't let anything happen to Victoria."

Elliot left their home and went for a walk, losing himself in his thoughts. His next fight wasn't for a few days, and he had been hesitant to return to train with Rahim and the others. For some reason he had just felt repelled whenever the thought came to him.

Elliot just couldn't make himself feel like he belonged there. He felt conflicted because the group had been nothing but kind towards him, but something about the way they lived rubbed against the grain of everything he had been taught. This put him in a bind. For now, all he could do was walk around and feel helpless, pining over his inability to change the world around him.

Distracted, he wasn't paying attention to where his feet were carrying him and bumped into the back of a noticeably larger person. The man turned around and gave him a snarl, baring an ugly snaggle tooth in Elliot's face. "Watch it pipsqueak," he said while shoving Elliot in the chest. Laughter echoed behind the man, coming from the group he was hanging with. Rather than brushing it off, something in Elliot snapped and he decided he was going to take his frustration out on the person before him.

"Or what?" he asked the guy.

Without responding, the man growled and launched a punch at Elliot's head. Elliot ducked and buried his fist in the man's gut, knowing he had knocked the wind out of him by the whoosh of air that followed. The man tried to wrap Elliot up, but Elliot danced away and dashed back in to deliver several more blows to the man's body. The man fell over, and Elliot leaped on top of him, mercilessly punching him over and over and over again.

About a minute later he was dragged off by the group standing nearby. The man Elliot had just beat to a bloody pulp, was on the ground rolling in pain. Elliot prepared himself for the man's friends to attack Elliot out of vengeance, but nothing came.

Surprised, he looked up and saw the three people that had been standing off to the side were howling with laughter. One of them, with a buzzed head and vermillion overalls, reached out a hand to help Elliot up. Elliot cautiously reached out and accepted the hand, allowing himself to be pulled up. "You're not mad?" Elliot said.

The man answered with a country twang in his voice. "Mad? Sheett, ain't nothin to be mad over. You won and he lost that's all there is to it, you're a real man. Tell me, how have I not seen you around the cages before?"

"Must've just been walking around with your eyes closed, I'm not sure either." Elliot laughed.

The man gave Elliot a crooked smile, "Cocky motherfucker ain't you? I'm Hunter, what's your name?"

"Elliot," he replied.

"You from around here, Elliot?" Hunter asked.

"Yeah, I live just around the way."

"Good good, so you must not be a jay. Hell, lookin at that hair of yours, you must be Red all the way down to your britches ain't you?"

"Yessirr," Elliot said proudly.

"I like you, Elliot. Tell you what, you're one of us now and I ain't takin no for an answer."

Elliot thought of Rahim and the others but quickly discarded those thoughts. Hunter and the others were new and exciting, they were like him, the connection Elliot felt was electric. "...ok, so what are all of your names again?"

Hunter gave Elliot another crooked smile, "this here is Jim and Gloria, and that puss on the ground right there is Clyde. What's your PQ Elliot?"

Elliot boastfully pointed his thumbs at his chest, "thirty-four, I'm still in the state competition pool."

The others looked surprised, "well damn, from the beatin you put on Clyde I knew you wasn't no scrub but that's mighty fine. I'm rated at thirty, Jim here is twenty-six, Gloria a twenty-three, and then mister Clyde as I'm sure won't surprise you is a twenty." Hunter paused for a moment before continuing. "Are you a man of God, Elliot?"

"Of course," Elliot said proudly.

"How'd you like to come to listen to a service with us sometime, we're members of Pastor Campbell's congregation."

Elliot grew excited, "no way! So am I! He is so inspirational, I always find comfort in his sermons!"

"That's fantastic, we should meet up and attend a service as a group sometime."

"Hell yeah, I'm down that sounds awesome! I'll be in touch about that, though for now I should probably be on my way!" said Elliot.

"Alright well, we'll see you around, Elliot!"

Elliot moved on and continued his walk, feeling very excited. *Finally people like me, people I can relate to*, he thought to himself.

Rahim

Rahim felt his seat vibrate as the train barreled along the tracks at breakneck speed towards Seattle. He was potentially headed towards his last fight in the regional competition pool before moving into the All-West pool.

The last few years had gone by in a blaze. Rahim miraculously had gone unbeaten, dominating the competition, and advancing at an almost unmatched speed. Almost, because his teammate Elliot, had also enjoyed a tremendous amount of success since he had started fighting. Starting a year after Rahim, Elliot had bulldozed his way into the regional competition pool as well. He was to meet Rahim at the NorthWest regional Tower in Seattle, along with those traveling with Rahim.

Aamil in anticipation of this being a large milestone, had elected to come, along with Dani who was also scheduled to fight today. Aamil was asleep in his chair, which left Dani and Rahim to keep each other company. Departing from her normally colorful attire, she had gone with the simple black and white shorts and shirt that the others wore for their fights. Rahim took notice that she was unusually reserved compared to her normal exuberant self. "This will be the first time I get to see you fight, I'm excited! You're always so fun to watch in the practice room."

Dani looked at him with wide brown eyes, "that's sweet of you thank you, but I'm measuring my expectations for now. We can't all have the rise to success that you've had, I've been stuck in this pool for years now. I'll just be happy if I can string together three wins in a row."

The slight pessimism in her words worried Rahim, "what's the matter if you don't mind me asking? This modesty isn't like you, is there something on your mind? Not that there's anything wrong with it, it just doesn't seem like you."

She sighed, "I guess you've never come along to one of my fights, so you wouldn't know. This is how I usually am on these days. I'm pretty used to the mockery, but it still helps to keep more of a lid on my emotions for these events."

Realization dawned on Rahim, "oh, is it about...that?"

Dani nodded. "To make matters worse, Elliot is going to be seeing me fight for the first time too. He's already enough of an asshole without giving him this kind of ammo to harass me with. Suffice it to say, I'll be practicing my best poker face for the day." The two had always held animosity towards one another, and it was evident in the way she spoke about him.

"I'm aware of what a handful he can be, I'm sure there's an explanation for why he is the way he is, though I know that hardly takes the sting out of some of the things he says." The truth was Rahim did have a faint idea of why Elliot was so ornery. Aamil had simply told him that Elliot had a lot to carry on his shoulders and Rahim should try to be patient with him. "Don't worry about Elliot though, I'll keep a lid on him. If he says anything I'll be the first to deal with him," Rahim said in an attempt to be reassuring.

Dani cast her eyes downward, "I don't need you to do that for me, I can fight my own battles. I appreciate it though, I just want to go in and out without any drama." Their conversation was cut short by the train arriving at its destination. Rahim leaned over and stirred Aamil from his sleep, the three of them then began the walk to the Tower.

A short while later, they arrived and spotted a tangle of individuals in vermillion clothing interacting with each other outside of the structure. A familiar figure disentangled itself from their group. Elliot strode into view puffing out his chest as he walked. "What's up losers, I was starting to think you'd never come."

Rahim rolled his eyes, "we took a couple of wrong turns coming from the station, who are your friends here?"

Elliot casually shrugged, "just some folks that live around my mom's neighborhood, they look out for me, I look out for them. Makes sure the Blue's keep their beaks to themselves."

Rahim stared blankly, "beaks?"

"Blue Jay's dumbass, come on let's be a little quicker here," Elliot scoffed at him.

"What's wrong with...you know what never mind, ready to head inside?" Rahim asked, choosing not to acknowledge Elliot's antics. Upon entering the lobby, the three of them left Aamil to wait while they checked in for their fights.

This Tower was considerably less packed than the ones they previously had competed in, something that did not escape Elliot's notice who was here for the first time. He loudly whistled, "phew what a relief to have most of the rabble gone from here. I could get used to this, nice to be among a higher class of people...present company excluded of course." The subtle shade masked with humor elicited a glare from Dani. They were glad to have a short line to wait behind. Quickly advancing to sign in with the CheckBots at the front of the room.

Elliot signed in first, leaning forward to allow his retina to be scanned. The silver box delivered the relevant information to him, "Edward Stockton, one-hundred-sixty-pound weight class, male. You will be competing on floor thirteen, room seven, at ten AM. Your opponent will be Dawson Parker." Elliot raised his eyebrows at Rahim and Dani, "no cage number? So I'll get the room to myself? Welcome to the big leagues I guess." He seemed very pleased with this fact.

Next up was Rahim, "Rahim Vu, one-hundred-eighty-five-pound weight class, male. You will be competing on floor sixteen, room one, at eleven AM. Your opponent will be Marcello Suha."

"Vu?" Elliot asked.

Rahim realized he had never shared his last name with either of his teammates, "my mom's last name. She and my dad never felt the need to take each other's names or get married at all for that matter." That information didn't seem to sit well with Elliot, his eyes narrowed disapprovingly.

Dani went for her turn to sign in, "Daniel Suarez, one-hundred-twenty-pound weight class, male. You will be competing on floor ten, room four, at ten-thirty AM. Your opponent will be Roman Ester." She closed her eyes as she waited for the comment she knew was coming.

She wasn't left to wait long; if Elliot was critical of Rahim's family situation, learning this information about Dani left him aghast. "Wait, you're a man?"

"Shut up Elliot, leave her be," Rahim growled.

"Her, don't you mean him?" Elliot said incredulously

Rahim walked towards him angrily, looking uncharacteristically aggressive. "I'm warning you, Elliot, say one more word and we'll have a problem."

Dani raised her hand, "what did I say about not needing you to defend me, Rahim?" Rahim looked frustrated but listened to her and quieted himself. "I'm a woman through and through Elliot, I won't argue this with the likes of you, or anyone. I am who I am, if you have a problem with that you don't need to be around me." Elliot sneered, but the daggers shooting from Rahim's eyes cowed him into keeping the peace. He rolled his eyes and followed behind them as they went back to meet with Aamil.

They gave him the information for their fights and he laughed, "well I'm happy the timing works out so none of you are competing at the same time. It must be predestined." The group headed up to the thirteenth floor to watch Elliot's fight. Strolling into the room, there was a lone cage standing in the center of the floor. Loge seating protruded high from the walls, fancily dressed individuals scattered throughout the seats. Screens with still more viewers watching remotely were lined below the seating, a FilmBot hovered over the cage.

"Finally, a proper audience. It's about time my talents were put on display for the world to see." That remark drew a sour look from Aamil, who loathed braggarts. Elliot didn't seem to notice though, strutting forward he dressed down and entered the cage without another word to his companions. The others stood near the edge of the cage as they watched him enter.

A few moments later, his opponent appeared through the doorway. Dawson possessed an unimposing figure, standing an inch or so taller than Elliot with little muscle standing out on his body. Striding over, he entered the cage and took his place across from Elliot. A celebrity in flashy clothes appeared to introduce the two fighters. After they exited the cage, a bell soon sent the match underway.

Elliot in his traditional boxing style came forward with his weight heavy on his front leg. He shot off a flurry of punches at Dawson, playing peek-a-boo behind his fists and twisting to send powerful hooks to the body. It seemed to be no contest for the first few minutes of the fight. Dawson tried to shoot off punches of his own, but kept rolling off of Elliot's shoulders. Elliot pummeled his opponent, leaving angry red welts on the ribs he punched.

Suddenly showing a flash of resistance though, Dawson used an overextended punch of Elliot's to catch the arm and plop down between Elliot's legs. This jump throw sent Elliot rolling to his back. The move was a sharp change from the beginning of the fight and snapped Elliot from the haze of overconfidence he had been lost in. The bell rang before Dawson could take advantage of his position. Elliot went back to his corner with a mystified look on his face.

"What do you think? Was he just trying to lull him into complacency?" Rahim asked Aamil.

"Looks like it to me too." Dani cut in.

Aamil nodded at both of them, "a perceptive observation from both of you. We have to remember that nobody makes it this far for nothing, he must have some skill to be here. It's usually safe to bet some misdirection is taking place if the fight goes this smoothly in the beginning. Hopefully, Elliot keeps a cool head from here on out."

The second round had started and Elliot was indeed approaching Dawson with more caution. Dawson for his part did genuinely seem beat up. He moved backward till his back was near the edge of the cage, Elliot prowled forward after him. Unfortunately, this played right into Dawson's strategy.

Elliot came forward to throw another punch at Dawson but found his arm once again caught. However, this time Dawson pulled Elliot into a clinch where they wrestled for position. From there, Dawson was able to pull Elliot's head into a headlock. Dropping his weight and wrapping his legs around Elliot's body, Dawson pulled him into a tight guillotine.

Scrabbling at his neck, Elliot struggled to break out of the grip, to no avail. The veins in his neck bulged as he refused to submit. A long few seconds passed before his body went limp and he passed out from lack of air. He had earned his first defeat. Elliot was slow to come to after that. When he regained consciousness, he trudged out of the cage with a humiliated expression on his face.

Feeling sympathy for his situation, Dani tried to extend an olive branch and comfort him. "It's ok Elliot, it happens to the best of us. You'll bounce back from this and do better next ti-"

"Shut up tranny. I don't care what you have to say to me, what would a perverted freak like you have to offer me anyways." Elliot spit out viciously. Rahim and Aamil were appalled, Rahim angrily began to chew out Elliot but was silenced by Elliot turning on them next. "Oh put a sock in it. Obviously, I've been wasting my time with all of you anyways. You're a bunch of Blues, I know it. Untrustworthy and unreliable, I'm done with you, you won't have to deal with me anymore." Elliot stomped off and out the door, leaving all of them staring in shock.

"What the hell just happened?" Aamil asked, looking nonplussed. The other two were just as taken aback as he. Turning to Dani he apologized profusely, "I'm so sorry you had to deal with that. I don't know what's going on with him, I'm at a loss for words."

"You don't have to apologize, he is the one in the wrong. There's nothing you can do to control his actions. If he's going to be this way that's on him," Dani assured him.

Rahim chimed in, "I never thought he would take a loss this way. He's always been difficult, but lately, he's been taking it to an entirely new level. I wonder what's going on with him that would make him act like this?" The others were just as stumped as Rahim.

They agreed to table the issue for another time and made their way to where Dani was meant to be fighting. The trip was short and they soon found themselves in a room identical to the one they had just been in. Dani dressed down to a sports bra and compression shorts, donning her gloves she approached the cage.

She tried to embody confidence as she entered the cage, attempting to counteract the feelings of self-consciousness that threatened to overwhelm her. This feeling was compounded by the befuddled stare her opponent was giving her from across the cage.

It was always like this when she fought, the feeling that she didn't belong. Her skin crawled under the scores of judgmental eyes that cast their hate toward her. No matter, she would just have to shine even brighter to remind them and herself of her place in the world. The past and the future don't matter, the dumbfounded stare her opponent was giving her didn't matter. All that matters is now, and at this moment she was determined to dazzle the world.

Aamil sat near the outside of the cage, looking on with the others at his student preparing for her fight, his heart swelling with pride. As he watched Dani settle into her beginning stance, so unusual from the style of most fighters, he began to reminisce on the day he first took her in...

* * *

"Dad! There's somebody at the door, they say they want to train here, with you." Rahim called out to him. Aamil sighed, he had started their school to rake in extra money to tide the family over. However, he just couldn't help but resent the frequency with which his day was interrupted by people arriving to speak with him. There was a constant stream of vulnerable souls wandering in to seek his tutelage. Beyond acquiring enough students to stabilize his family's finances, Aamil was reluctant to take on more students than he had to.

Zoning out, eyes drilled into the floor at his feet, he first became acquainted with her presence by the sound of wet footsteps plopping on the mat. Craning his head upwards he was confronted with the sight of a soaking wet youth in a drenched fur coat, hair tossed over shoulder like a wet towel and makeup profusely running down their face.

"What can I do for you son?" asked Aamil. A flash of annoyance crossed their face, "don't call me that, I'm not your 'son'. That's the dope over there, not me. I'm a lady." She chewed out bitterly. Rahim raised his hands in exasperation, "why do you have to pick on me?"

"Shut up, Rahim," Aamil said with a grin on his face, staring straight ahead at the woman in front of him. "That's my mistake young lady, you have my apologies. What's your name?"

Her aggravated expression morphed into one of satisfaction, she replied, "Dani."

"Well Dani, what can I do for you?"

Pulling a piece of gum out of her pocket she unwrapped it and jammed it into her mouth, chomping aggressively. Remembering her manners, she pulled out another piece and offered it to Aamil. When he softly shook his head, she shrugged and shoved the piece back into her pocket where it likely became smushed into the fabric of her jeans. She then began to speak, "I would've thought that since you're just a torso and head now, that you'd be smart enough to not have to ask. I want you to train me."

Aamil raised an eyebrow at her impertinence, *she's trying to ask for my help and is bold enough to be this rude about it? What a brat.* "You don't seem to have very much respect for me. Why should I do this for you? Surely someone so confident in themselves doesn't need my guidance?"

Dani stood contemplating for a moment as she decided how best to answer Aamil's question. "I'm tired. Tired of a world that thinks the fact that I'm a human being is an insufficient reason to treat me with dignity and respect, but still asks for my respect in return. I'm tired of shrinking myself down, hiding who I am away, just for fear of what others may think. I'm tired of being weak, I'm tired of being so tired. I want you to make me strong, strong enough to carry myself without being afraid of being knocked down. Strong enough to shut up anyone who dares tell me that I'm not good enough. I came to you because you were always strong enough to carry yourself above all the petty contempt of others. With strength left to spare to lend to others even when you had just beaten them. You didn't care about who anyone was or how they differed from you, you showed compassion to those in front of you no matter what. And you of all people should know what it's like to be in a body that is rejected by the world around you. To know that if you didn't have your loved ones to take care of you, that you would just as soon be left out to wither away into nothingness. You were a gladiator in their court and your service means nothing to them. Once you stopped contributing to their bottom line they threw you away like you didn't matter. That's why I came to you."

Even his son had never dared to be so direct with him. Aamil shifted uncomfortably, feeling like the stare of this young woman was piercing right into his very soul. He cleared his throat to try and dislodge the lump that had stuck there. "Very well. It seems we have some time till the rain clears up, we have some spare clothes, go get changed and we can start right away."

Despite her brash entrance, Dani struggled for several days while Aamil tried to train her. Her fearless facade crumbled into frustration as she failed to find her rhythm in their school. Aamil took her struggles personally, interpreting them as a sign of his failure as a teacher. Determined to do right by her, he focused intently on her performance, trying to find some takeaway he could capitalize on.

One day during a training session, he took notice of her exceptional balance and footwork. She continued to lack in other areas, such as grappling and boxing, but her footing was quite sharp. An idea struck him, he knew exactly what kind of style would suit her form.

* * *

"Go get 'em," Aamil whispered tearfully as he watched his student get into her unique stance for her fight.

Dani settled into a lunge with her right foot forward and left foot stretched behind her. She stepped her left foot forward to be parallel with her right for a moment, before sending her right behind her. All while swaying her elbows, she moved rhythmically within her Ginga stance. The rumble of drums filled her mind as she moved gracefully to the beat. Her opponent, Roman, gave her an odd look as she appeared to be dancing before him. Typical for when she fought, her unusual style always gave her opponents pause at first.

Swaying side to side, she sunk deeper into her squat, transitioning her feet in a triangular fashion. Roman grew impatient after a few moments of observing her dance before him and took the initiative. In a direct fashion he came at her with a straight kick to knock her off balance. Nimbly circling to the side, she stepped left. Pivoting leaving her head and leg almost perpendicular to the ground, she slapped the back of Roman's head with her right foot.

Her opponent stumbled for a moment before turning back to face her with a snarl on his lips. Unfortunately, spry as she may be, Dani still lacked a considerable amount of power compared to her competition. Bracing herself for a drawn-out exchange, she breathed deeply and focused on letting her mind dissolve within the rhythm, allowing her reflexes to completely take over.

"I'm amazed every time I see her style, simply beautiful," Rahim said.

"Waxing eloquent, are we?" Remarked Aamil cheekily.

"It's just…you did a great job with her. That's all I can say."

"No, please do say more," smirked Aamil. They watched on as Dani continued her struggle against Roman. Seeking to unbalance her, Roman swept toward her front leg to dismantle her base.

In a shocking display of dexterity, she responded by falling to the side to put her weight on her hand. Spinning, she lithely snapped her legs overhead to land behind him. Continuing the twist, she then turned the tables by kicking his legs out from under him. As he collapsed to the ground, she pounced atop him and began slamming her elbow into his head. Saving him from her fury, the bell rang out, sending them to their corners.

"Fuck yeah Dani, that was freaking sick!" shouted Rahim. Dani waved ardently from her corner in the cage, turning she gulped from the spigot next to her. She turned back, "don't blink," she exclaimed haughtily. As the second round began, Dani resumed her Ginga stance, facing her opponent.

Looking shaken but determined, Roman paced around her much more cautiously than before. Taking care to brace himself to back out of range of her kicks, he tried a new approach. Clumsily he launched himself at her to try and initiate a grappling exchange where his greater strength might triumph. However, it was to no avail as he was not adept at grappling whatsoever.

She swiftly circled around him and took his back, choking him out. In a flash, just like that the fight was over. Peacocking, she strutted around the ring with her arms stretched outward in celebration, "AHHHHHHHHHHH," she cheered non-coherently. Rahim and Aamil whooped and hollered as she left the cage. They celebrated together for a moment before getting their bearings and heading over to where Rahim was set to fight.

Adrenaline rushed through Rahim as he drew closer to his match. *Finally, I might be able to move on. If I go on from here, I'll have made it as far as dad ever did.* They ran into a crowd in the room where Rahim was set to fight. The loge seating overhead was packed with spectators who leaned over their railings excitedly to catch the action as it started. Additionally, people were crowded all over the ground level by the cage, flocking to see Rahim.

Word had spread as to where Rahim was fighting. Fighters from all over the Tower had stepped away from their affairs to crowd the room and watch him compete. Rahim had begun to make a reputation for himself from being undefeated, something that one rarely saw, along with the even more peculiar way he comported himself in and out of the cage.

His opponent had already made his way into the cage ahead of time, dancing around and warming up. As the man spun around, Rahim spotted a pelican with wings extended across Marcello's back. *Nice bird bro,* Rahim thought sarcastically. Marcello was the oldest person Rahim had to fight to date, appearing to be in his early 30's. He was long of limb, looking to stand a few inches taller than Rahim.

Undressing, Rahim walked towards the cage, the crowd dispersing before him like the red sea. Walking into the cage he shook his body to rid itself of any stiffness that remained. Turning around he froze, there nestled amongst the crowd was that girl he had seen months ago. Hazel eyes surrounded by brown skin and a growth of platinum hair. She was a hard person to miss standing amongst the swarm of other people. Making direct eye contact, she gave him a wink before looking away absentmindedly. *Who is she? Why do I keep crossing paths with her?* These thoughts disturbed Rahim's mind as he got ready for the fight to begin.

Aamil arrived being pushed by Dani, "no it can't be," he said as they pulled up.

Dani looked at him quizzically, "what is it?"

Aamil was staring straight ahead into the cage, past his son, captured by the sight of Rahim's opponent. "I've fought that man once before," referencing Marcello. "He was the last person I fought before Kolby did this to me, but what in the blazes is he doing here? He was in this same bracket when we fought."

Dani scratched her head, "I guess he must have continued his bad run of luck and ended up remaining in this competition pool."

Marcello seemed to have caught sight of Aamil, it was evident that he recognized him. A dubious grin stretched across his face from ear to ear. Looking at Aamil and then back to Rahim, Aamil, Rahim, his eyes switched back quickly in disbelief. "Hey, kid?" Marcello called to Rahim.

'Um, yeah?" Rahim called back.

"That wouldn't happen to be your old man in the chair over there, would it?"

Why does he care, what is he asking for? Does he know my dad? Rahim puzzled to himself. "He might be, what's it to you?"

Marcello laughed, "no reason."

Well, that's suspicious. I'm gonna go out on a limb and say there's definitely a reason. Without another word, Rahim started once the bell rang. Bobbing back and forth he stepped around his opponent, waiting to get a read on his style. Marcello did the same, resulting in a standoff with both feinting and circling the other while waiting for the opportune moment.

Rahim was the one to break the calm, going in low with a kick to the calf, which Marcello ate. Having tensed himself for a counter, Rahim was surprised when nothing came. He threw out a straight left which Marcello simply backed away from. Continuing to circle, Rahim wracked his brain for what strategy he should employ next to unsettle his still opponent.

Coming in as if he was throwing a right hook, Rahim then transitioned to power his legs through into a double leg takedown attempt. Marcello then threw a knee that connected straight into Rahim's forehead. Rahim scrambled to keep position by falling to the planted leg of his opponent and gator rolling him to the ground.

Seeing stars, Rahim held on for dear life. This was the first time he had been truly touched, much less hurt, to this extent since he had started fighting. Marcello grunted annoyedly as he was dragged to the ground. Out of his element, he scrambled to try and get out of Rahim's clutch. His eyes still shut in pain from the blow, Rahim wrestled to keep Marcello in his control sheerly through touch. His hands doing what needed to be done through pure muscle memory and body sensitivity.

As they squirmed on the ground, one trying to establish dominance, the other trying to escape to capitalize on his earlier success, the bell rung clear. Tasting blood in his mouth, Rahim staggered to the corner; Marcello wandered to his, fatigued despite the poise he had shown until this moment. Aamil and the others stared off from the side, concern in their eyes at the rare sight of their seemingly invincible comrade hurt.

The second round began, again Marcello restrained himself from going on the offensive. This left Rahim to consider how best to approach his defensively savvy opponent.

Going for a combination, he threw three straight jabs in a row, forcing Marcello to keep his hands up and moving backward away from the strikes. Feinting for a fourth, Rahim instead snapped his elbow down to launch a high head kick, extending his reach. Not getting out of the way in time, Marcello was hit across the cheek with the topside of Rahim's foot.

Marcello hopped backward at that, hands up to maintain defense. "Dude you need to trim your toenails, that totally cut my cheek man," complained Marcello. Rahim shrugged apologetically. Coming in again to throw a combination of punches, Rahim slipped up and opened his side up slightly too much. This allowed Marcello to come in with a sharp blow to the ribs. Steeling himself, Rahim chose not to recoil from the blow, instead using the opportunity to tie up with his opponent. Lunging forward, he snagged an over-hook on the arm that had struck him.

Pushing him up against the cage, Rahim decided to use his superior endurance to tire his opponent, wearing him down enough to weaken his defenses. Pressing forward, he pinned Marcello's arms to his sides and threw a series of foot stomps and up-close knees to the abdomen. They stayed that way for several moments before the bell rung again.

They were sent into the third round, the farthest anybody had ever kept up with Rahim. As this was a championship fight, they had five rounds in total to look forward to should it go the distance. So, Rahim prepared to have to whittle down his opponent in a battle of attrition.

The third round came and went much like the second, with both fighters landing significant blows and Marcello coming out looking considerably more haggard than Rahim.

The fourth round had arrived, Marcello still keeping up a defensive posture, although quivering with the task of keeping his guard up consistently. Rahim's breath was coming a bit shakier than at the beginning of the fight but was otherwise still very energetic. *The moment is coming soon, I can feel it,* thought Rahim to himself. Resigning himself to a brawl, he popped and swayed before Marcello.

Changing up the rhythm and style of his strikes, he came in low snapping from left to right, throwing a barrage of strikes at the body. Feeling the crunch of ribs under his fist as he connected over and over, he hopped away and bobbed back in to land another hit. Marcello lunged forward for a jab. Rahim leaned away for what he thought was enough to avoid being hit, but Marcello had extended his fingers, jamming them into Rahim's eyes at the end of his reach.

An alarm sounded for a timeout as Rahim was permitted to go into his corner to recover from the illegal blow, burning pain seared his eyeballs. Squinting his eyes, Rahim could only see a blur for several moments. The light dazzled him as he tried to wait for his vision to come back.

Marcello absentmindedly stood examining his nails as he waited for the injury timeout to expire. Taking advantage of the break to recover his stamina, Marcello's breath began to come much more evenly.

Across the cage, Rahim was doing much better, though his cheeks were still flooded by the trickle of water squeezing out of his eyes uncontrollably. *Who the hell does that, I swear that was on purpose. Does he think he's a looney toon or something?"* Rahim thought to himself, making a comparison that was now an over a century old reference. A few moments later, he signaled he was ready to go, just seconds before the injury timeout was set to end.

The two began to circle each other again. Marcello now appearing to be much more confident than he had prior to the timeout. Just as they closed the gap to begin a new exchange, the bell rang. Evidently they had been close to the round ending before the timeout.

The fifth and final round was now set to begin. Either one of them would decide the outcome, or it would be decided by the RefBot based on perceived rounds won, according to strikes and takedowns landed.

"I can barely bring myself to watch," Dani said, sounding very concerned. The bell rang at last, squaring off for the final time the two men found themselves standing before one another. Uncharacteristic given his approach the rest of the fight, Marcello was the one to strike first this time. Throwing a left jab, then a right cross, followed by a left shot to the body and finishing with a left hook to the head. Rahim managed to evade the first three blows, but then as he dropped his elbow to block the body shot, he found himself wide open and got rocked by a punch to his jaw.

Gritting his teeth he pressed forward, waiting for the opportune moment. However, the moment he was waiting for did not come. Marcello kept his composure and did not let his technique slip. Rahim was hammered mercilessly by a parade of blows that rained onto him. Feeling his back against the corner, Rahim worried that he might lose for the first time. Blood was running freely from his face, dripping out of the micro-tears in his skin.

Just as he was about to lose hope, a miracle saved Rahim from defeat. Marcello went in for a vicious leg kick, aiming to further destabilize Rahim's base. Responding, Rahim raised his leg and turned his shin to check the kick and CRACK! Marcello's leg bent at a horrifying angle, having been snapped from the impact of his kick.

Howling, he collapsed to the ground, holding his leg. Letting loose a stream of curses, Marcello angrily punched the canvas. He was done, the match was over. Concerned for his opponent's well-being, Rahim knelt to the ground and put his hand on Marcello's back. "Are you ok?" he asked.

"Get the hell away from me!" Marcello snapped. The pain and frustration were too much for him to accept anybody trying to interact with him.

Rahim placed his hands on the canvas and bowed his head to Marcello, "I'm sorry this is the way it had to end. You were the greatest opponent I have fought yet, thank you for giving me the opportunity to become better."

Marcello turned his head towards Rahim after that comment. His eyes burned red, forcing the words through his teeth he snarled at Rahim. "You are just like your old man, do you think I give a shit what kind words you have to say to me? Do you realize what this injury means? I won't be able to compete for months, I'll be demoted way down to one of the lower competition pools. I'll be making dirt money, I might not be able to support myself at all. Do you think anything you have to say is going to make it ok? I have a family to feed, are your words going to fill their bellies? Don't say another god damn word to me."

Rahim recoiled at hearing these words. Their validity cut daggers into his heart and challenged his image of himself. Numbly he accepted what Marcello was saying to him and backed off. Sticking around for the announcer to declare the outcome of the fight, he quickly left the cage to join Aamil and Dani.

They congratulated him, "you did great!" Dani assured him.

Aamil was more interested in his exchange with Marcello though, "what did he say to you?"

"I don't want to talk about it. At least not now, I have a lot to think about," Rahim said, appearing crestfallen. Dani and Aamil nodded, letting him have his space.

The group began to leave when the platinum-haired girl walked across their path. She looked Rahim up and down, appraising him with a smirk on her face. "A little sappy in my opinion, but you're a good fighter. You shouldn't let yourself care too much about your opponents, it weighs you down."

Dani stepped forward, "What exactly is your business with us?"

The woman looked at Dani coldly with her hazel eyes, "us? I certainly don't have any business with you."

Eyeing the 'Quell' label across her clothes, Aamil had a good guess as to why she was here. "Did Rommel send you?"

"That old fart? No, I'm here running an errand for an old acquaintance of yours." Deftly she tossed an ivory coin to Aamil.

Aamil caught the coin and looked it over. A fox was on one side of the coin, a date and coordinates were printed on the other side. "Is this supposed to-" he started to ask, but the woman was already walking away from them.

Rahim called out to her before she could get too far away, "what's your name?"

She turned with a sly smile, "Nia."

Chance

The metallic alloy taste of her pen calmed Chance down as she chewed furiously on the end of it. Having things in her mouth had always been a source of relief for her since she was a child, particularly when stressed out. Although nowadays it seemed she was always under a lot of stress. As a result, her pen had developed indents in it to match the shape of her teeth.

The software engineer corps that Quell employed, one of the few real occupations still available to humans, was a demanding work environment. Her family had been fabulously wealthy before The Great Switch. Rich enough that Chance's parents had never needed to work a day in their lives, and neither did their daughter.

However, they desperately needed a reason to impress their posh friends in the illustrious neighborhood of Hillsborough. So, they had enrolled their daughter in the most extravagant private school they could find, the only schools available anymore. They hired tutor after tutor to drive her to excellence, with the threat of withholding her inheritance should she not apply herself.

So here Chance sat, forced to work long hours day and night on a project, the purpose of which had been ill-explained to her. The transition from Narrow AI troubleshooting to working in the AI Solutions department happened more than a year ago, but the time felt like nothing at all to her. At the moment she was meant to be working on a software program. Although, this particular assignment was proving particularly troublesome for her. This fact did little to please the stern supervisor that she worked with.

"Are you listening to me Chance? Hello? Stop chewing on that damn pen and pay attention when I'm speaking to you!" The berating of her supervisor sprung Chance out of her trance.

"Sorry Joe, what were you saying?" she hastily apologized. Rubbing his fingers on his forehead in a display of impatience, Joe reiterated what he had been saying before. "The boss is wanting this project to be complete ahead of schedule, how far along are you on the code you've been working on?"

"Which boss...?" she asked quizzically.

"THE boss, President Rommel you oaf, should I even have to explain it to you?" Joe exclaimed, his face turning an unpleasant shade of scarlet. "So when do you expect you'll be done."

The mention of his name sent an unpleasant twinge through Chance, she fought to push aside unpleasant memories. Turning her head side to side, Chance mulled the question over for a moment, "what is this project for anyway?"

Joe sighed, "I've told you a million times, I don't know. All I know is we've been given a set of task structures we're meant to complete, and we'll be updated later on. So, can you please answer my question now?"

"Well, it's kind of difficult for me to complete my assignment if I don't know what purpose my algorithm is meant to fulfill, don't you think? As it stands, I'm not sure how long it will take me, maybe a week, maybe two? Who can tell ya know?"

Giving her a good long stare, Joe barked at her unsympathetically, "well I'm telling you, you have one week, that's it. Get it done."

As he turned away from her, Chance stuck her tongue out at him. *Maybe losing my inheritance wouldn't be so bad if I didn't have to put up with this kind of treatment.*

Turning back to bury her face in the screen before her, Chance continued to puzzle over the purpose of her work. The task structure she was being asked to program into this AI was unlike anything she had ever seen before.

What made sense were the ordinary information processing systems that were encoded into AI software. However, this went beyond regular data intake. Somehow, she was meant to program the AI to be able to process complete sensory information as well. Almost as if it was meant to integrate with... "Oh," she said aloud.

Partially swiveling in his chair, Joe looked back, "something the matter?"

"No, nothing!" Chance squeaked. *Could that be what they are having us work on? What could this possibly be for?* She thought to herself. For a moment, she sat there resisting the urge to dig in further. *Just think about everything you could lose Chance. Are you really willing to risk it all just to satisfy some fleeting curiosity within you?* To which the devil on her shoulder responded, *yes.*

Coming up with the first excuse that popped into her head, Chance abruptly stood up, "I need to go to the bathroom." This prompted a resentful side-eye from Joe, ignoring his glare she went to leave the room.

Standing before the transparent automatic glass sliding door, she passed through once the sensors detected her presence and opened the doors. Chance stepped out into a wide hallway with a pewter gray floor and wide-open windows lining the walkway. She traveled for about a hundred meters, enjoying the natural light before she arrived at her destination.

A plaque reading 'Robotics' was displayed above the door in big bold letters. Using her phone as a mirror, Chance quickly fussed over her appearance to make sure nothing was unseemly or out of place. Upon feeling confident that she looked presentable, she then opened the door. Chance walked into the workspace where the robotics and mechanical engineers were consumed with their respective tasks, tinkering on various projects. Catching the attention of a nearby woman hunched over a schematics sheet, Chance politely asked, "excuse me, do you know where Kabir is right now?"

Hardly even taking her eyes off her work, the woman motioned over to a far corner of the room, "he's in his office at the moment."

Thanking her, Chance headed over to where the woman had motioned, 'Kabir Baweja: Head of Design' was printed on a plaque hanging on the door. Knocking on the door, 'come in' was the response that answered her, prompting Chance to oblige.

Entering the room, she saw a man in his late twenties, close to the same age as Chance. A turban wrapped around his head, his face defined by a dark closely trimmed beard. Looking up, Kabir's eyes instantly lit up as he saw Chance enter the room. Seeing that look in his eyes reassured

Chance that her plan had promise. She had always suspected that Kabir had a crush on her and she hoped to use that to her advantage. "Kabir! Do you have a moment? I was hoping to have a word with you?"

"Chance, I'm so happy to see you. For you, anything, just tell me what you need and I'd be glad to help." Clumsily getting up from his desk, he speedily walked around to pull a chair out for her as she went to sit down. "So, what can I do for you?"

Blushing, she fluttered her eyelashes at him coyly, "well I'm embarrassed to say..."

Eyes wide, he leaned closer to her, "don't be, you can tell me anything. I'm all yours, I mean all ears."

"Ok, if you say so. I was wondering if you could tell me whether you guys have received any special projects from the big guy upstairs." Pointing upwards as she said so, "something with restricted information, perhaps you haven't been told what it's for, and maybe even have been barred from speaking about it with anyone...like me, for example."

Appearing on edge, Kabir laced his fingers in his lap and leaned back, looking up at the ceiling. "I may or may not have had something of the sort cross my desk...why do you ask?"

"It may interest you to know, that something of the sort may or may not, have crossed my desk as well over in AI Solutions. As I was, or may not have been, conducting my work on that assignment, a thought occurred to me that my work may, or may not, have a significant amount of relevancy to the work you do over here in Robotics."

The insinuation seemed to unnerve Kabir as he began to shut down from the conversation. Now speaking in a hushed tone, he stared pleadingly at Chance. "I don't think this is something we should be discussing, Chance. You never know if," he pointed upwards, "might be listening. For all we know, the whole building could be bugged. I've already upset my family enough by becoming Patit. If I lose my job here, they might disown me."

Chance leaned over and sympathetically patted Kabir's arm, causing him to jump at the physical contact. "I understand where you're coming from Kabir. You're right, this is a bad place to talk, I should have thought of that before coming in here and putting your livelihood at risk." Leaning further into him, she brought her mouth near his ear. Close enough for the heat of her breath to send tingles down Kabir's spine as she spoke. "What if we spoke over dinner instead?"

Reflexively he began enthusiastically nodding, "th-th-that's something I could agree to."

Chance smiled softly and patted him on the cheek, "ok, I'll see you later then. I'll message you with the details."

* * *

Chance winced self-consciously as the sound of her stilettos clacking against the sidewalk grated her ears. She never was one for playing dress-up and going out on the town. Chance much preferred to be left on her own to fade into the background, but this was a special occasion. Chance was confused on why she felt so nervous, she was only meeting with Kabir after all. Nevertheless, she had still spent a considerable amount of time meticulously fussing over her appearance. She thanked herself for having made a reservation, the parking had been so full she had to direct her AutoBot to park a block away.

She didn't mind though as she enjoyed walking, at least in normal attire she did. Her dress brushed against her leg as she came to a stop; a long black gown, with a collar and deep V-neck, and double slits on either side of her legs. Unused to walking about with this much exposed skin, the cool night air sent a slight tingle down her spine, dancing across her flesh. Looking into the restaurant's wide glass windows that revealed the inside, her mouth watered as she saw all of the people digging into their meals. *Now to wait for my date*, Chance thought.

She cursed her excessively punctual habits, having arrived earlier than the agreed upon time. She wasn't kept waiting long though, soon hearing the approach of her date. Looking up she was astonished at what she saw. Kabir arrived looking significantly more dapper than he did when she saw him around the Quell facility. His hair was braided piled into a bun atop his head. He was dressed up in an elegant black suit with a white undershirt and black tie. "Well, you dress up nicely," she said, looking him up and down.

Kabir blushed, "thank you. You look beautiful yourself, are you ready to head inside?"

"Am I ever, I'm starving," she said excitedly. Linking arms, they strolled inside. A classy atmosphere enveloped them as they walked into the building. The sultry music of a grand piano danced around the interior of the restaurant.

Leaning in for their eye scan to verify their reservations, Chance couldn't help but feel out of place as she always did in these settings. A small ServeBot led them to their table, one of the few still standing empty in the room. Round with a soft white cloth draped over it, their plates and silverware sat awaiting them with daintily folded napkins atop them.

Taking their seats, Chance and Kabir quickly gave the ServeBot their orders, which it processed and sent in for preparation. Finally settled in, Chance and Kabir stared into each other's eyes. Each wondered who would say the first word, the busy hum of the restaurant fading into the background. As usual in their relationship, Chance ended up being the one making the first move, "have you thought about our conversation earlier today?"

"You know, the idea of digging into Quell's affairs still makes me nervous, but if you are committed to this, then I've decided to help you."

Chance smiled, she had known she could count on Kabir. "So, can you confirm the question I asked last time we met?"

"Yes, we were given a special assignment same as you. With rather unusual requests for the specs of the design we were meant to create, and we weren't allowed to hear any context."

"What was unusual about it?"

"As I am sure you know, the designs Quell has commissioned for most of its Bots are each fairly unique and practical. They haven't given much care for the aesthetics of their machines and have mostly demanded functional results. Hence the odd variety of shapes and sizes we see their many products come in. That is, until now. The order we received was rather, should I say...anthropomorphic in design?"

Chance narrowed her eyes, "as in human?"

"Extremely. In almost every aspect, from skeletal structure to implanting artificial blood capsules throughout the frame."

Chance's imagination ran wild considering what Quell could potentially have planned. "An android?" she wondered aloud.

"I must admit, that was the first thought that crossed my mind when I saw the requested design. Although, I can't say for sure as I am unfamiliar with what you've been working on in AI solutions."

"Your description matches what has been asked of us over there. If I am to assume the AI we have been developing is to be downloaded into the structure you've created, the specifics make a lot more sense now. For months I have been puzzling on what purpose Quell would need such a dynamic intelligence system, but if this is the case it makes complete sense. Although, I am still left with one more question."

"What aren't we seeing?"

"Exactly. Correct me if I'm wrong but Quell has never needed to go farther than the process to merge robotics and Narrow AI. However, with this extra information, I presume that they would need to take it to the next step. If we were to dig around, what do you suppose are the chances we could find a unit in Quell developing a silicone flesh replicating polymer? With what we know, it seems like the obvious final step in finishing what we think they're working on."

"I don't know about this Chance, what do you think is going to happen if they catch us digging in their facility?"

"We're already this far Kabir, we may as well see this through to the end right?"

"...I just don't know."

"If you're that worried we could even make a run at it this very night, I'm sure the security is low, and I know a way in."

"You do?"

Chance wiggled her fingers, "I'm a woman of many talents Kabir. You don't even have to follow me inside, you can just be my cover and let me know if anything goes wrong."

"Are you sure this is a good idea?"

"Positive, and you know what's an even better idea?" she said while looking at him seductively. "Finishing up our dinner here and lifting our spirits, before we embark on this mission."

Kabir laughed, flashing his brilliantly white teeth, "now I enjoy that idea quite a bit. Especially if it's with you." The rest of the evening went smoothly from there. Their food arrived in a timely fashion, Chance enjoying an extravagant New York cut steak, and Kabir chewing on a vegan burger.

"Mmm," Chance noised as she chewed on her tender cut of steak, medium well as she always got it.

Kabir looked at her judgingly, "don't people normally take their steak medium-rare?"

Chance rolled her eyes, "Hey dick, I like what I like ok. Besides, aren't you vegan? What would you know about a good slice of meat?"

Kabir shrugged, "that's just what I hear is all." Their conversation went enchantingly for the rest of the evening, with banter aplenty being exchanged between the two. They broke open a bottle of wine and drank the whole thing between the two of them, gaining a pleasant buzz as the night went on.

As they came to the end of their meal, Chance moved them along, "so, shall we?"

Seeming much more amenable and less nervous now, Kabir nodded, "we shall."

The two of them got up and headed out of the restaurant, "we can take my AutoBot," Chance said. The two made the walk down the block to the spot where she was parked, stumbling into each other as they did so.

Passing under the streetlights, Chance put her hand out to stop Kabir, which he walked into. "What?" he asked. Twirling her eyebrows at Kabir, she pushed her hair back and pulled out a joint from behind her ear. "Was that behind your ear the whole time?!" exclaimed Kabir.

"Yup," she said with a grin. "I thought it could be a fun way to unwind before we do the deed."

"Oh, I didn't realize this was an actual date..." said Kabir.

Chance appeared confused, "oh no, I'm talking about breaking into Quell you dolt. Get your mind out of the gutter." She continued, "on second thought though, who knows, maybe if we make a big discovery I'll be so excited you just might get lucky," she said with a wink. Chance pulled a lighter from a hidden fold in her dress and sparked the joint.

"Ok, what do I do, I've never smoked before," fussed Kabir.

"God you're such a nerd," she laughed, "just inhale, but not too deeply unless you want to cough your brains out." The tip of the joint burned cherry red as he took a deep inhale, against her advice, and began a coughing fit doubling over. Chance laughed at him, "what did I tell you? Don't inhale too deeply!"

"I'm sorry," he wheezed, looking up with tears freely flowing down his face. Chance patted him on the back and took the joint back. Expertly she took in a long draw and held it in, finally releasing the smoke to be carried down the street by the night air. They passed the joint back and forth a few times before they put it out and continued their walk to Chances AutoBot in a pleasant daze. They gave the AutoBot directions and it sprang into motion, whisking them away to their destination.

Giggling uncontrollably, Kabir looked at Chance with blood-red eyes, "are you sure this is still a good idea in the state we're in?"

Chance fake cringed, "get those eyes away from me you demon! But yes, I'm still confident we can pull this off. I do have a plan in place after all." She said while wagging her fingers in his face and laughing. The rows of streetlights soon alerted them that they had almost arrived at their destination.

Driving down the illuminated pathway, they pulled into a parking spot near the front entrance. "Alright here's the plan Kabir, I'm going to make my way inside. I want you to stand outside by the car and message me if you see anything suspicious. Ok?"

She was unsure if Kabir had understood her message because he was staring off into space outside the window. Abruptly his head snapped to look at her and he asked, "wait, so how are you getting in again?"

"Like I said, I'm a woman of many talents. If you want to know I'll tell you, but I figured I'd allow you the chance to retain plausible deniability in case anything goes wrong."

"How sweet of you, now that you bring that up, I suppose I can always ask you another time."

Chance smiled, "perfect. I'll see you on the other side then...or I suppose I'll see you back on this side when I return." Leaning in, she gave him a goodbye kiss on the cheek and stepped out of the vehicle. He was left staring at her with a gaping expression on his face. Coming near the entrance to Quell's facility she pulled her phone out of her purse. Fidgeting with the device for a minute or so before tapping a command that opened the doors for her. *Looks like my tenure in Narrow AI is paying off.*

Among her assignments when she worked within the Narrow AI troubleshooting unit, was installing updates into the security intelligence that regulated the interior of Quell's facility. Her rebellious streak had extended back for some time now. She had encoded a backdoor within Quell's system that allowed her access to the command functions of the system. Using this, she opened the doors and deactivated the surveillance systems that monitored the goings-on of the facility.

Confidently strolling in, she beelined to the area she suspected she would find her answers in. A few minutes later she was standing in front of a door labeled 'BioChemistry'. Pulling out her phone again, she sent another command to the security systems, directing the door before her to open. Stepping inside, the motion sensor lights detected her presence and automatically switched on, illuminating the room she was stepping into.

This was one of the few places in the facility that she had never entered before. Workstations with various projects were set up throughout the room. She ignored them and went straight to the supervisor's office, opening the door as she had all of the other ones before. Inside was a simple office with a computer monitor, standing inconspicuously atop a wooden desk. Flexing her fingers outward, Chance cracked her knuckles and got to work.

Within a few minutes, she had hacked into the computer and was sifting through the files stored within. When she came across what she was looking for, she gasped. She found herself looking at plans for a tissue replicating silicon polymer. From the looks of the design, it was obviously intended to match with the humanoid skeletal structure that Kabir was helping to construct in Robotics.

The listed applications were astounding; tactile awareness that allowed for texture and heat sensitivity, with pain sensors that could allow an android to rapidly learn and adapt to its environment. *What on earth are they developing this for,* she was left wondering.

There was another thing as well, something that she had heard whispers of but never had the chance to see face to face. What she saw gave her an inkling of what Quell could possibly be producing androids for.

Not wanting to stick around though, all she had time to do was copy an address. Contemplating where she should go from here, she decided to bring her findings to Kabir.

Heading out of the department, she opened the door allowing the light to spill out into the greater part of the building outside. It was this that caused her to freeze in her tracks, as the light revealed the metallic foot of a Bot standing outside. In fact, as she looked up she could see six SecurityBots waiting for her outside the room, their bright red eyes hovering in the dark. *Oh no* she panicked internally, her thoughts were interrupted by a long slow clap that sliced through the air.

The smell of sauerkraut gave away the source of the noise before she could see the culprit. Revealing himself from behind the Bots was none other than President Rommel. In contrast to the droopy skin hanging over the rest of his face, his eyes were taut and stretched wide, staring intensely at Chance. "Did you find everything alright?

Not again, why did I have to run into him again. What is this creep going to do to me. Awkwardly turning her palms upward she shrugged, "you know, definitely not as big of a selection as I was expecting. The customer service around here sure could use some work."

Rommel's lip twitched, "funny," he said dryly. "Tell me, how did you get in here? We were notified of your presence by the power grid in that room switching on. However, that doesn't explain how you got into the building so easily and without the cameras picking you up."

Fuck I didn't consider they'd notice a few lights turning on. How on edge are these people? Chance thought to herself. "Oh you know, the backdoor happened to be open so I let myself in."

Rommel waved his hand and one of the SecurityBots rolled up to her and grabbed one of her arms, lifting her to hang in the air. Fear coursed through her veins as she was accosted. The metal grip of the Bot bit into her skin uncomfortably and her weight pulled on her shoulder joint, sending waves of pain rippling through her. "You're quite the talented programmer, Miss Ouk, and quite a beautiful one as well I might add. I would hate to lose an asset such as yourself. I've been keeping an eye on you for some time now, watching you scurry about. Tell me, what exactly are you hoping to uncover?"

"I don't know. Something just seemed off with the AI you were having us develop, so I wanted to find out more, that's all." She answered weakly.

"And what exactly did you find out?"

Chance didn't respond. Rommel walked over to where she was suspended and forced her to look at him, pushing his finger under her chin. "Tell me, or your friend outside, Mr. Baweja will join you in punishment."

"Please you can't, he doesn't have anything to do with this. Leave him be," she pleaded.

"Then you will tell me what I want to know, what did you find out?"

Chance looked defeated, "All I found is the silicon skin you've been developing down here. Based on the project I was assigned, I'm assuming you plan to make an android of some kind."

"Clever girl. That is all you found?"

"Yes," she said softly.

Rommel moved his face to less than an inch from hers. His hot and humid breath washed over her face, bringing with it a wave of nausea. Slowly, he dragged his tongue along her cheek, leaving a trail of spittle. "Look at you, helpless before me. I could do anything I pleased and there's not a thing you could do to stop me." He let those words linger in the air, savoring the terror they evoked.

Rommel then snapped his fingers and the Bot dropped Chance to the ground, where she remained slumped holding her shoulder. Turning his back, Rommel walked away from her, his Bots following in tow. "Wait." Chance called out, "so what are you planning? And what are you going to do with me?"

Rommel halted, without turning around he answered her, "I am planning on taking what is owed to me, the world, nothing less will suffice. As for you, you may return to your work. You are too valuable of an asset for me to toss aside. For now, just keep your mouth shut unless you would like me to dispose of Mr. Baweja." With that, he left, leaving Chance to sit and wonder what she should do next.

Kentrell

Kentrell's hands became warm and moist as they were coated by the grease spilling out of the plump cheeseburger he held in his grasp. He sat on a city bench swinging his legs gleefully, stuffing his face with the cholesterol-filled goodness. Taking the burger out of his mouth for a moment, he shoved his hand into the bag of fries beside him, snagging a handful of them to slide down his gullet, followed by a swig of a sweet bubbly soda. It wasn't often that he had such a bountiful meal, so he closed his eyes to savor every bite.

While he ate, a gentle breeze tickled across his cheek, for a moment he was calm and tranquil. *Nothing in the world could take me from this feeling right now.* "Ugh, do you see him? Sitting there and stuffing his greedy little face. We have to go and fight for everything we have, but he gets to sit there doing nothing and eat like a king." These words drifted into Kentrell's ears from afar. Opening his eyes he saw a couple standing across the street shooting daggers from their eyes. *Well, that did it.*

Revile for his own self flooded Kentrell's thoughts as he internalized the words of the couple across the street. *I try everything I can to not cause harm to other people, but the world still hates me. What's wrong with me?* Kentrell dejectedly got up to wander the streets after he finished eating. Since his mother had passed, this was his daily routine, having nothing and no one else to go to.

Shouts and jeers were hurled his way as he wandered. Every now and then, people would even be so bold as to throw old spoiled food at him. The cruel words and harsh gestures had long since stopped having a visible impact on him. He simply turned his heart into stone and kept moving forward, hoping the next day would drag him from his miseries.

His feet eventually brought him near an overpass. Kentrell's eyes fell upon a puddle of rainwater that had collected in a shallow hole. Looking down, he gazed at his reflection in the puddle. His long black hair was in a bird's nest around his head, strands drooping downward, around the crimson DW emblazoned on his forehead. *Deadweight huh? If I really am a burden to everyone then what am I still doing here? Do I even have a future I can look forward to?*

Kentrell sought reprieve from the disparaging thoughts that smothered his mind like a blanket made of knives. He went over to a disturbed patch of earth underneath the overpass. Using his hands as shovels, he dug into the ground. New dirt was forced under his fingernails to join the older material already there.

After about three minutes, he found what he was searching for, a brown glass bottle, half full of whiskey. Inwardly he chuckled at his cleverness upon seeing that his hiding spot had worked. The hole kept any other stray individuals from stumbling across it and taking it for themselves. Walking over to a relatively smooth piece of ground with a view of the sky, he leaned back with his elbow buried into the uncut patch of grass behind him.

Kentrell gluttonously took several swigs from the bottle, unflinching as the bitter rye liquor poured down his throat. Now fully laying down in the grass, Kentrell looked up past the towering city lights, straining his eyes to spot a star in the blurry sky above him. Finding that task unattainable, he resigned himself to staring off at the moon. The numbing effects of the alcohol began to noticeably take effect, settling his limbs and soothing his mind of the troublesome thoughts that so afflicted him. It wasn't long before he drifted into a dreamless sleep, where for a time he could forget.

The pattering of rain upon his face roused Kentrell from his slumber shortly after the sun dawned in the morning sky. Staying still for a moment, reluctant to let the rain stir him from his rest, Kentrell finally gave in to the whims of the elements.

Sitting up with a groan, he winced at the pain shooting through his back from sleeping on the hard uneven ground all night. Wiping the water from his face he pondered for a moment on what he should do with his day. *Food,* was the lone thought that came to him.

As a DW he received a meager monthly stipend, just enough for food to sustain his survival, but not much else. Unfortunately for Kentrell, he had spent the last of this month's credits on his meal yesterday. This left him with another week before he would receive more credits needed to buy food. He now had two options, he could try and beg, or he could go dumpster diving for leftover food that nobody else wanted.

Kentrell knew from experience that most people didn't react kindly to DW's asking for money. Many already thought of him as a freeloader who was living off of handouts, so him asking for help directly left him liable to being berated or even attacked.

Choosing the safer option, he went to go wade through the dumpster behind a nearby Mexican restaurant. Parsing through the assorted ingredients tossed out on their own, Kentrell lucked out in finding a partially eaten burrito still encased in its aluminum foil wrapper.

Too impatient to wait till he had gotten out of the dumpster to dig in, he merrily sunk his teeth into the burrito. He savored the swirl of pinto beans, jalapenos, carnitas, and other wonderful flavors that danced across his palette. Still chewing, he leaned to hop out of the dumpster. Climbing out, he heard vehement cries of outrage echoing down the alley he was in. "What do you think you're doing you thieving DW trash!"

Getting out of the dumpster, Kentrell clutched the burrito to his chest, "I was just trying to find some food."

The person who had yelled at him stomped closer, curly red hair bouncing atop his head. A group of three stood close behind him. The four of them wore matching vermillion sweatshirts. "I don't care, you're stealing! Don't you DW's have enough? You already get handouts for doing nothing, stay off of other people's property!"

Kentrell apprehensively tightened his hands around the burrito, anxious as to how he should proceed with these angry people yelling in his face. Looking down at his feet he stuttered, "I-I'm sorry...I was ju-just hungry and wa-wanted some food. I didn't th-think any-anybody wanted it. You c-can have some, i-if you want?"

One of the lackeys behind the man who originally spoke began mocking Kentrell scornfully. "Can't you even speak right, you Deadweight moron? You c-c-c-can have some," conspiratorially elbowing his friends, he laughed at Kentrell. "No we don't want your garbage food idiot, we want you to know your place and stay off of property that doesn't belong to you." Frozen in place, Kentrell couldn't find the words to say back to the people before him. He wanted desperately to run from the situation, but the only exit was being blocked by the men in front of him.

Staring at the ground by his feet, he avoided the stares darting at him. "Look at us when we're talking to you!" Still burying his eyes by his feet, Kentrell flinched as he heard the sound of footsteps moving threateningly toward him.

A hand shot forward and tangled itself in Kentrell's shirt, yanking him towards one of the men, "god you smell! DW pig!" A fist was then launched into Kentrell's gut, causing him to double over, whimpering in pain and fear. "Pussy won't even fight back, no wonder he's a DW, he wouldn't last one second if he tried to make an honest living in the cages like the rest of us."

"Leave him alone," a voice called from the mouth of the alley. Looking up past the men harassing him, Kentrell glimpsed two brown-skinned men squaring off against the people around him. A third man in a wheelchair sat behind them. The one on the left was broad-shouldered and muscular, with thick tight curls growing from his head. The other was slightly taller but significantly wider, standing on thick powerful legs covered in tattoos. He had wavier hair that was much longer, hanging down his back.

The redhead assaulting Kentrell snarled and spat on the ground, "you?"

Rahim

Rahim lamented the walk home awaiting him, still in serious pain from the fight he had just finished. The idea of pushing Aamil all those blocks sounded like a death sentence with the state he was in. Rahim tried to recruit Dani to help him push Aamil home, but she avoided the chore. Prudently fabricating an excuse on the spot, Dani escaped them. *She won't hear the end of this from me, that's for sure.* Rahim thought bitterly. Aamil for his part, seemed to have no sympathy for Rahim, not indulging any of his complaints.

So, there he was, rolling his father down the sidewalk. Every step seemed to whittle away at Rahim's composure. He tried to shut his mind off until they arrived at home, where he could rest. Fortune seemed to smile on Rahim though, after walking about a block, he ran into Lyall. Lyall appeared to have just finished a trip to the grocery store, brown paper bags hung from both his hands. "How lucky am I, just the man I needed." Rahim exclaimed happily.

Lyall gave a friendly smile, "nice to see you uce, howdy Mr. Jackson. How was the fight? And what do you need?"

"He got his ass kicked," Aamil answered.

Rahim raised his hands defensively, "I mean, I still won. I got rocked though, I can't lie."

Lyall swore, "man, that's just my luck. I miss one fight and that's the time you finally get a run for your money. I wish I was there."

Rahim gave Lyall a devilish look, "ah, it's ok. If you want to make it up to me though, could you push the old man for me?"

Lyall shrugged, "sure, but you gotta carry these bags." Rahim obliged and grabbed the bags from him. "One second though, before we leave let me grab something out of there. Fumbling around in the bag he pulled out a small handful of grapes. Popping one into his mouth he grinned in delight, "mmm, extra soft, just the way I like it."

Rahim curled his lip in disgust, "ew what the hell dude, you like soft grapes? That's just wrong bro."

Giving him a perplexed look, Lyall retorted, "how can you say that man? Nothing beats a tender grape, how can you not like that texture?"

Shaking his head, Rahim argued, "screw soft grapes, it's hard grapes or nothin."

Lyall laughed incredulously, "you're weird as hell uce, I can't even wrap my head around what you just said to me."

Aamil could no longer ignore their conversation, "what is wrong with the two of you? This is such a weird conversation, I feel like my ears are going to bleed." The two laughed at his comment and the three exchanged further banter.

They lost themselves in this absurd conversation for several minutes. It wasn't until they heard arguing, followed by a thumping sound and further yelling, that they were disturbed from their talk. Looking down the alley, they saw four Reds.

They were surrounding a young man curled up on the ground in the fetal position, clutching something to his chest. Rahim was dismayed to see that it was Elliot and the group of people he had been hanging out with before the fight that day. The sight of his student behaving in such an abhorrent manner troubled Aamil. For Rahim's part, he was repulsed by the situation confronting them. Determined to put a stop to it, he handed the bags to Lyall, "take care of my dad." Lyall grabbed the bags and Rahim stepped forward, "leave him alone," he called out.

Elliot looked up from the boy he was beating and narrowed his eyes. "You." he hissed. "Get out of here Rahim, all of you, if you know what's good for you."

Rahim laughed in disbelief, "you think I'm just going to walk away and let you abuse this kid? I've never cared for your attitude much, but I respected you enough to think you were above something like this."

One of the people standing with Elliot interjected, "you didn't see, but this DW here was digging around on private property where he doesn't belong. We're just teaching him a lesson is all."

Elliot raised his hand to silence the person next to him, "you don't need to give him an explanation Hunter. What are they going to do anyway? A cripple, a fat ass, and this chump...against the four of us."

Aamil couldn't keep his silence anymore, "this isn't you Elliot. Think about your mother, is this what she would want for you? You're better than this, this isn't the person you want to be."

Elliot's face reddened to match his hair, growing angry he spat out, "what would you know about it? You don't know me, you don't know who I am. You're a bunch of Godless sinners, your opinion doesn't mean shit to me. Don't you dare talk about my mother either, you're all a bunch of Blues. You don't deserve to even think about her."

Rahim had had enough, "I don't want to hurt you, Elliot. I'm sure you think you have a good reason for what you're doing. After all, nobody thinks of themselves as the villain in their story. As much as I despise what you're doing, I still acknowledge that other forces are responsible for you being led astray, and I don't hold it against you. But nothing gives you the right to go around hurting other people, I won't stand by and let this happen."

These words seemed to give Elliot pause for a moment. Elliot's friend Hunter didn't wait for him to respond though. Cutting in he continued resisting, "And what are a couple of Blues like you going to do about it?"

"Blues? We aren't Blues, we're just human beings who don't care to see you go around abusing defenseless people who aren't even fighting back."

"Not Blues, eh? I guess you aren't wearing those god-awful colors. Well, your skin is too dark for you to be a Red. So either way, you colored folk are gonna have to stop sticking your nose in our business if you know what's good for you. In case you hadn't noticed there's two and a half of you and four of us."

Rahim spat on the ground, "bigoted prick. Are you going to let these clowns speak for you, Elliot?"

Any momentary doubts Elliot had, were tossed away at that moment. Clenching his jaw, he declined to say another word and gave a hostile stare towards them.

Rahim sighed, "fine have it your way, but don't say we didn't give you fair warning." With that, he started advancing towards the young man and his attackers. Snarling, Elliot and his friends abandoned the young man to go meet Rahim halfway.

Lurching forward, the lead of the four threw a wild hook at Rahim's head. Casually leaning backward, Rahim allowed the man to overextend himself. Jutting his foot out, he tripped the man and sent him to the ground. Following after to back up their friend, Elliot and the other two surrounded Rahim.

Lyall, hands full, elected to walk over to the downed man, sitting on him to prevent him from rejoining the fight. "Need any help?" he called to Rahim, the man under him wheezed in protestation.

"I think I'll be fine," Rahim called back. He shot a dangerous smile at the people surrounding him, "three on one? Well, I guess this seems a bit fairer than before, come try your luck." Elliot, Hunter, and the other man all rushed Rahim, seeking to overwhelm him with their numbers. Taking advantage of their disjointed, uncoordinated attack, Rahim ducked under the arm of Hunter. Grabbing the collar of his shirt, he moved the man in front of himself to disorient and trip up the others.

As the third man tried to sneak around his friend, Rahim threw Hunter into him. Elliot then took his chance to swing at Rahim. Rahim sidestepped and pushed his elbow, causing him to unbalance and careen into the wall. Recovering from their previous disorientation, the other two came at Rahim to try and get him with a pincer attack. Again, Rahim used their momentum against them to slip by and force them to crash into one another.

Looking scratched up, pride damaged, the three looked at one another before deciding their time was best spent elsewhere. Motioning to one another they scrammed out of the alley. Noticing this, Lyall took that moment to get off of the guy he had been squishing until now. Seeming to be in considerably worse shape than his friends, despite being the only one to avoid any real fighting, he peeled himself off of the pavement and scrambled to get out of there.

"Are you alright?" Rahim asked the young man, reaching out a hand to help him off of the ground. Taking it, the young man allowed himself to be pulled to his feet.

"I'm fine. Thank you for doing that. You really didn't have to, I'm sure I had that coming to me," the young man said, casting his eyes downward miserably.

Rahim frowned and grabbed the boy by the shoulders, "nobody deserves to be treated like that. You're a human being and deserve to be treated with dignity and respect, no matter the circumstance. What's your name?"

Shell shocked at the kindness he was receiving from this random stranger, the boy quietly murmured, "Kentrell."

"Well Kentrell, it's nice to meet you. I'm Rahim and this is my friend Lyall. Over there is my father Aamil." Lyall waved in a friendly manner upon hearing his name. Aamil gave the boy a tender smile. Looking around with concerned curiosity, Rahim stared deep into Kentrell's light brown eyes. "Are you all alone out here? Is there anybody you can go back to?"

Feeling compelled to answer by Rahim's authoritative presence, Kentrell answered directly, "I'm all alone. I had parents once, but they're gone now."

Rahim had never seen a DW this young before, he hadn't been aware that anyone under the age of eighteen could be registered as one. "How old are you?" he asked.

"Fourteen," responded Kentrell. Indignant outrage at the sight before him swelled within Rahim, felt as a burning hot sensation that set his blood to boiling. "Would you like to come with us?"

Kentrell appeared to be puzzled. He had never had an encounter last this long without it turning into anger, let alone where it ended in the person being kind to him. "What do you mean?" he asked.

"Exactly what I said, I want you to come with us. We'll look after you and we'll teach you how to take care of yourself, would you like that?" replied Rahim.

"But don't you realize I'm a DW? I wouldn't want to be a burden on you."

With a serious look on his face, Rahim grabbed Kentrell by the shoulders, "What did I just say to you a moment ago? You're a human being. You don't have to do anything for me, you don't have to prove anything to me. Even if you did slow us down, I wouldn't care. You deserve my kindness and respect just by virtue of existing, now are you coming or not?"

Still not seeming to quite grasp what Rahim was trying to say to him, Kentrell consented, "I-I guess so."

Rahim smiled kindly at him, "ok then let's get going." He guided Kentrell out of the alley, Lyall turned to follow as they passed him. Patting Kentrell on the back he reassured him, "happy to have you with us boss." Waving his hand across his face, he wrinkled his nose, "we really do need to get you into a bath though." Rahim fought the urge to laugh and punched Lyall in the shoulder, "shut up dude."

Aamil agreed with Rahim's sentiments, giving Lyall an annoyed look. "You're safe with us son, we'll look after you, don't you worry," he reassured Kentrell. Just like that, the three resumed their walk home, with a new friend protectively tucked between them.

Luckily they were only a few blocks away, so they were able to arrive at Rahim's home in a timely fashion. Taking the long way into the living area, up the ramp inside of the house, they strode into the living room.

"Finally, what took you guys so long?" complained Linh as she rounded the corner out of the kitchen. Spotting Kentrell standing between them she gave a surprised, "oh." Her eyes lingered on the DW ingrained into his head before she quickly composed herself, taking on the role of gracious host, "so, who do we have here?"

"Mom, this is Kentrell and he is going to be staying with us," Rahim responded matter-of-factly.

"Oh, yeah um, Rahim can I speak with you for a moment? Aamil you better roll yourself on over here too," Linh said awkwardly.

"Of course." They followed her into the other room where they began to speak in hushed tones. "So, what exactly is going on here?" she asked.

Rahim gave her his best puppy dog look before explaining himself. "We found a bunch of Reds beating on him, he wasn't even defending himself."

Aamil gave Rahim a look as he declined to mention Elliot's involvement in the attack but remained silent. "He's all alone mom, he doesn't have anybody, did you see how young he is? I just...we have enough room for him, and I promise if anything goes wrong, I'll take full responsibility. I just really feel like this is the right thing to do."

Linh chewed her lip, "ok fine, we'll give it a go. I guess what kind of mother would I be if I turned you down when you're trying to do something so noble." They swiftly re-entered the room, whereupon Linh turned all of her efforts to doting upon her newly introduced ward. "I'm Linh, is there anything I can do for you to make you feel more at home?" she said sweetly. Upon finishing her sentence, she caught a whiff of the powerful stench accompanying Kentrell. The smell of years living out in the elements, the only bath in that time being the occasional rain shower.

"It's ok I don't want to be a bother," he said demurely.

Linh forced herself to keep a saintly aura about her despite wanting to gag at the smell. She politely, yet forcefully, urged Kentrell to take advantage of their bathroom. "How about a shower hun? I'm sure it'll feel great to wash all of that crud off and feel nice and clean?" Putting her hands on his shoulders and steering him in that direction as she said so.

"If you say so," he said, allowing her to guide him like a ragdoll. "I'll go grab some of Rahim's old clothes and leave them just inside the door for you," Linh told him. A moment later the sound of the shower could be heard, the faint sight of steam climbing out the top of the shower door. Aamil spoke up happily, "I guess we will be having a new student."

Lyall chose that moment to chime in, "are you sure he can handle that boss? The kid couldn't even find it in him to defend himself when we found him, is this the best plan for him?"

"And that is exactly why we need to train him. We need to give him the tools to stand up for himself, so he doesn't have to keep living that way," interjected Rahim.

Aamil gained a twinkle in his eye. "Exactly," he seconded.

Rahim then took that moment to address the elephant in the room, "about Elliot-" he started to say.

Aamil didn't let him finish, however, "If you don't mind, I'd rather not talk about it for now. I just, I need some time to process everything that's happened with him."

After their conversation had wound down, Kentrell exited the bathroom. He cleaned up nicely, adorned in a plain white t-shirt and baggy brown chinos. The bird's nest that had recently been his hair had turned into a luscious mane rolling midway down his back. His skin a smooth light brown, now rejuvenated, devoid of the dirty smudges that had once coated it. Hugging his arms to his chest he still looked nervous however, "the shower felt amazing, thank you."

Dani

"Your victory has been processed and recorded in Quell's database. Eight hundred credits have been transferred to your personal account and your PQ has been adjusted to thirty-two." Dani stumbled down the stairs of the cage after receiving her results. *Boy am I glad to be going home, I'm getting so worn out.*

Her body hurt all over, over the last few weeks her body had taken an especially gruesome beating in her fights. Competing in the cages had always left her bruised and aching, but lately, the ache had been lingering longer and longer. Perhaps it was due to her getting older. In any case, the prospect of working this way long term was...daunting.

Making her way towards the elevator to leave the Tower, she briefly contemplated stopping by a clinic on her way home to get checked out by a MedBot. Dani quickly discarded that idea though, deciding she would rather suck it up than shell out the exorbitant amount of credits needed to do so.

Perhaps something to distract me from this awful feeling. Dani began planning to indulge herself at her favorite burger shack when the train dropped her off. Thinking about biting into that greasy goodness kept her mind pleasantly occupied while she traveled down the sidewalk to the train.

Paying the toll, she boarded and waited to be transported back to Tacoma. The trip went by in a flash, before she knew it she was walking the city sidewalks. Turning a few corners and walking several blocks, she arrived at her destination.

'Frugals' was displayed above the quaint establishment, though in actuality it was owned by Quell just like most every other business. Walking up to the window, she looked at the ChefBot bustling about in the kitchen.

Placing her order, she stepped away for a moment and lost herself daydreaming while she waited.

A dark-gray cloud formed overhead, capturing her interest for about a minute until she was snapped from her reverie by a hand clamping down on her shoulder. Startled, she jumped, her hand already diving into her pockets for the taser she always carried around.

Dani stopped in her tracks when she saw who had touched her. Dressed in a cornflower blue shirt, matching the outfit Dani wore, was a woman standing an inch or two shorter than Dani. A strand of the woman's hair, the same color as her shirt, fell in front of her face as she raised her hands to placate Dani. "Stacey, what are you doing here?!"

Stacey rolled her eyes, "what do you think I'm doing, looking for you of course."

Dani appeared confused, "I was going to see you at the meeting tonight anyway, why did you need to see me so soon?"

"That's just it, I needed to let you know that plans have changed. The cornflower Blues are being mobilized to meet with the other factions at Wright Park tomorrow night. Zora has summoned the leaders of all the factions to discuss something that she says is of great importance," Stacey explained.

Dani looked incredulous, "Zora is coming here? Why would she come somewhere like this? I would expect somewhere like Seattle or honestly even one of the Cali cities."

A sly look crossed Stacey's face, "well that's where you come in. Zora wants you to connect her to someone, for that she is summoning people to meet here."

"Who could she possibly need me to connect her to?" Dani wondered aloud.

"I'm meant to bring you to her as soon as possible for you to be filled in on her plan, are you free to come along?"

Dani heard a ding behind them indicating her food was ready, "yeah, just let me grab my food. I'll eat while we walk." Not long after, Stacey was leading Dani down a series of streets into an unfamiliar neighborhood. "Where exactly are we going?" she asked.

"Quell has been trying to pinpoint Zora's location due to her efforts to sabotage several of their Bots and facilities. She's become quite the thorn in their side, so she has had to switch locations regularly to avoid capture. She's been relying on the good graces of a network of affiliates and sympathizers; we're headed to the home of one such person right now." Stacey said no more after that, they walked quietly side by side for another half hour.

Eventually, Dani realized they were wandering into a wealthier area, as the apartment complexes gave way to a cluster of small houses. These homes, much like Rahim and Aamil's house, were occupied by fighters who were able to make it to the top-level competition pools and rake in higher incomes.

Stacy stopped in front of a house painted light blue with a white gate in front of its walkway. Although the home was otherwise unassuming compared to the rest of the houses around it. "Give me your phone and go on ahead, I'm going to circle the block and I'll be back for you."

Dani obliged and opened the gate, she went up the stone walkway to the front door and rapped her knuckles on its frame. A beat passed before a bald dark-skinned man cracked the door open. "Can I help you?" he asked.

Dani pulled the strap of her dress to the side, exposing a cornflower tattooed just under her collarbone, "I've been summoned to speak to Zora." The man nodded without a verbal reply and opened the door to let her inside.

"This way," he said, pointing his hand to another door that lay deeper in the home. Dani opened it to see stairs leading down into a basement. She thanked the man and headed down, the door closing behind her.

The rickety wooden stairs creaked under her weight as she descended. The sole source of light in the room was an exposed lightbulb that only faintly illuminated the bottom of the stairs. In the corner, in front of the steps, were multiple crates filled with guns, ammunition, and many other dangerous items. Dani's eyes scanned curiously over the paraphernalia in front of her. Her attention was diverted when she turned the corner and spotted the person she was looking for.

A woman, who Dani recognized as Zora, was hunched over a table along with a bespectacled man wearing a tweed jacket. The two were deep in discussion over plans laid out on the tabletop. Zora looked up as Dani approached them. Dani had only met her once, so she was unsure if she would be remembered. She was delighted to find that she had not been forgotten, however, as Zora looked up with a pleasant expression. "Dani! So glad you could join us on such short notice."

Dani lowered her head respectfully, "of course, I'm always at your disposal. So, what do you need from me?"

Zora's cheeks raised over her high cheekbones as she smiled, "forgive me for the intrusion, but a little birdy told me you know somebody who could be useful to our cause."

Dani pondered who she could mean, "And that person is?"

"Rahim Vu."

That answer gave Dani a sense of clarity, given Rahim's recent spike in popularity, it wasn't hard to guess at Zora's motives. Still, she sought to dig deeper into Zora's intentions, "What do you want from him?"

Zora touched her finger to her chin thoughtfully, "I think that his influence could be the final domino we need to knock down Quell. I'm afraid I will have to keep any further information close to my chest, you understand I'm sure?"

Her words left no room for Dani to question them, "of course."

"Good. Now Stacey should have filled you in on the details for tomorrow night. I would like you to ask Rahim to join me for a private discussion, shortly before we hold the rally."

Dani understood, her blood pumped as she pondered what the outcome of this meeting could be. "Just count on me, he'll be there."

Nia

Nia concealed herself within the throng of spectators, covertly watching Rahim fight. She didn't know what it was, but there was something about him that drew her in like a magnet. *How can he be so strong but so gentle?* Seeing him fight troubled her, it awakened questions about herself and what she had been taught that made her uncomfortable.

Nia was so captivated that the crowd around her, jostling her back and forth, did not faze her. His unprecedented rise to the top and the way with which he conducted himself were quite the novelty. Rahim's persona was so entrancing that lately, a large crowd formed anytime he fought. Nia herself was guilty of being drawn into this buzz. Ever since Kolby had sent her to deliver his message to them, she had returned several times to watch Rahim fight.

Although, she deliberately tried to keep her presence a secret from Rahim. Nia had come to know him quite well from afar, he was extremely predictable once you started to pay attention. Analyzing him compete, Nia had come to notice that he avoided certain openings in the beginnings of his fights. If there was an opportunity for a submission, he would take it every time.

Alternatively, if he had a shot at delivering a knockout blow he would hesitate to pull the trigger. Unless it was a later round and his back was against the wall. It was evident from the mastery in technique he displayed that he wasn't blind to these opportunities. So, Nia could tell that he was purposely pulling his punches.

It infuriated her, especially because he continued to win despite this flaw, it went against everything that she had been taught. Every fight at this point was vital for him, he was only a few wins away from moving on to the national competition pool.

Rahim's opponent was making it difficult for him to find any easy openings. He kept a low stance, preventing any takedown attempts. Circling around him to probe for any shots to take, Rahim shuffled his feet back and forth to throw off the perception of his opponent. Rahim spotted his opportunity and it was over in a flash.

Leading with a jab to distract his opponent, Rahim followed with a low leg kick, turning his foot to scoop his opponents, sending him to his back. In pursuit, Rahim raced to mount him, propping his opponents' leg atop his knee. Swinging his other leg across his opponents' body, Rahim swirled into a leg lock trapping his opponents' knee. Immediately followed by a rapid tapping and Rahim's victory.

Releasing his opponent, Rahim hopped up and reached out a hand to help his opponent up. After lifting him to his feet, Rahim shook his opponents' hand with a slight bow of his head. Nia gritted her teeth at that, memories of her instruction looping through her mind. *Showing kindness to your enemy is weakness.* He always finished his fights this way. It vexed Nia, every time it left her with more and more self-doubt.

Though until now she had managed to contain her emotions and move on, this time something broke and she moved to intercept Rahim after he left the cage. Approaching him, she realized that unlike most of his other fights, this time Rahim had arrived alone. It would just be the two of them...just the two of them.

Something about that idea made her palms terribly clammy. She worked her tongue into knots thinking about what to say to him. Staring at the muscles in his back flex as he bent over to pick up his street clothes, the words jumped out of her mouth, "why do you hold back?"

Turning around, he looked to see who was speaking to him. Recognizing her, he did a double-take, eyes widening. "It's you," were the only words that came out of his mouth.

Having come too far to stop herself, she barked at him, "answer my question."

"What do you mean?" Rahim asked, scratching his head with a stupid expression on his face.

"You could have ended that fight a lot sooner than you did. You held back, why do you do that?"

He appeared pensive for a moment before laughing and shrugging, "you caught me. I guess...I just don't want anybody to get hurt is all."

"They're your enemy, showing kindness to them is just weakness. One of these days somebody is going to exploit that weakness and there's no way you can win then."

Rahim frowned, "what kind of way is that to talk? They are not my enemy, just my opponent. Besides, they didn't choose to fight me, most of these people are only doing this because they have no other feasible option if they want to survive. People are more important than winning. It's not worth it to win if I have to sacrifice my values to do so...if you could even call that winning in the first place."

People are more important than winning? Nia's mind raced as she was reminded of the woman whom she had injured in her demonstration for Dr. Galton. Of the dozens of other people she had hurt in the name of Quell, in the name of winning.

Although now that Rahim was speaking to her; those victories had never made her feel like a winner...whatever that felt like. If anything, she felt like she had lost something with each person she had to step on, a little part of her humanity leaving her. These thoughts awakened a host of painful feelings inside of Nia, feelings she rejected and tried to shut down. Rahim spoke again, interrupting her thoughts, "if you don't mind me asking, why do you work for Quell?"

"I suppose you could say I'm like those people you're so keen on protecting. I don't have a choice in this either."

Letting that be the end of the conversation, she turned around and walked away. "Wait!" he called after her, but she did not turn back. Nia traveled briskly to get as much space between her and Rahim as she could. That conversation had left her feeling weak, something she loathed.

Elliot

A commotion drew Elliot's attention, walking over to the apartment window. Opening the blinds, he saw a stream of people flooding down the street. *Oh shit yeah, that rally is happening, I wonder if Hunter and the others went on ahead without me.* Elliot's friends had mentioned that a large-scale rally was going to be happening in the neighborhood soon. They suggested that he attend with them, but he had forgotten about it until just now. It seemed as though everyone was traveling to the same location, drawn by some attracting force. "Stay here Vic, I'm gonna go check something out."

Making his way outside, Elliot followed the crowd to see where everyone was heading. *They weren't kidding when they said this was gonna be a huge rally.* After a minute or two, he began to hear the faint sound of an animated voice booming over the sea of people in front of him. Pushing his way forward, Elliot squirmed to make it past everyone standing before him, garnering an ample supply of dirty looks as he did so.

Finally, he came within sight of the speaker, widening his eyes, he recognized the person to be a well-known celebrity. *What the hell is Roy East doing here?* The action movie star had dominated the spotlight for many of Elliot's favorite movies growing up. He stood pacing around on a raised stage, giving an impassioned speech to the crowd of people below.

In a rather eccentric fashion, he wore a necklace made of bullet shells. They must have been inordinately expensive, given that guns were hard to come by in this day and age. This accessory was complimented by the rest of his outfit. Complete with pitch-black combat boots, a vermillion flannel, denim blue jeans, and a mullet.

The puissant man boisterously ranted down to the people. Roy's bullet shell necklace bounced on his chest while he yelled into the microphone. Roy's face turning redder and redder. "...are you tired of seeing us hardworking, red-blooded, patriotic Americans having our livelihoods getting sucked out of us by those good for nothing, lazy, drug-addicted DW's? Who just sit around asking for handouts while the rest of us work hard for what we have. Why should they get to sit around on their asses all day, getting a FREE ride, while we work our butts off, put our bodies on the line, to earn ourselves an honest living? Tell me, are you tired of REAL Americans getting dealt the short straw?"

"YEAH!" answered back the crowd, an agitated fervor growing amongst them. "Dead Weight bastards! Stop weighing us down!"

Elliot felt a fervor growing inside him as the clamor of the crowd began to climax. At that moment he looked around at the crowd surrounding him. His eyes saw nothing but red, he was surrounded by people who looked like him. Boldly shouting things that he had only heard whispered in the deepest recesses of his primal self.

"Speaking of people who give us REAL Americans a bad name, let's talk about those damned Blues, huh? Those godless, gutless, brainless blues. Constantly trying to subvert the traditional family with their queer nonsense, and their 'non-traditional marriages'. If they had it their way they'd be teaching our kids that they can marry cats and dogs! Those pussy blues want to taint the PURITY of this country and let just anybody come to live in our community, no matter how dangerous. They're a bunch of ghetto, murderous, thieving, predators who want to destroy our culture and our way of life!"

Walking out behind Roy were some familiar faces, *it's Hunter and the others!* Elliot thought to himself. Roy began to introduce them, "now I've talked an awful lot here today, but I got some friends here from within the community that have something they want to say."

Before they spoke though, Hunter noticed Elliot and grinned. Leaping off stage he shoved his way into the crowd and grabbed Elliot, dragging him on stage. Bringing him to stand with Jim, Gloria, and Clyde, Hunter screamed out, "Blue bastards!"

An angry chant began to take over the crowd, "Blue bastards!" Group consciousness began to form, binding all present to each other and the raving speaker prancing about on stage. Elliot felt himself drawn into that evocative energy.

Feeling light on his feet, lighter than he could remember feeling. Euphoria coursed through his veins as he felt a part of something larger than himself. The call of acceptance and belonging beckoned him, he felt compelled to join the chanting of the crowd, "Blue bastards!" he screamed.

After the heat of the crowd had died away, Roy turned to Hunter "so who's your friend here?" gesturing towards Elliot.

"This is my friend Elliot, he's a real good fighter Roy, you shoulda seen him beat the brakes off of Clyde the other day. Jim and Gloria giggled in the background at the memory while Clyde took on a sullen expression.

Elliot stepped forward with his hand outstretched, "hi Roy, it's a pleasure to meet you. I'm a big fan of your work."

Roy looked him up and down grinning, "Nice to meet you Elliot, any friend of young Hunter here is a friend of mine. Shoot lookin at that hair of yours, it's like you were meant to be workin for me."

"Working for you?" Elliot asked, hoping he wasn't being rude.

"How is it you think, that us Reds are able to mobilize so quickly and efficiently? Good ole top-down leadership, you're lookin at the head honcho of the national chapter. You are a Red ain't you?"

"Of course of course," Elliot quickly assured him. "I had no idea the Reds were so organized, well it's an even bigger honor to be in your presence then. You can count on me, sir. How do you know Hunter and everyone?"

Roy pulled Hunter in by the cuff and rubbed his head, causing Hunter to take on a look of embarrassment. "He hasn't told you? This one is my nephew! My flesh and blood."

Elliot looked at the both of them incredulously, he couldn't see much family resemblance. *What do I know though,* he thought to himself. "I wanted to see if Elliot would come on his own, not because of who I was or who I'm related to," explained Hunter.

"Hunter here says you're one hell of a fighter, how have you done for yourself in the cages?"

"I'm currently fighting in the regional competition pool and hoping to make my way to the All-West pool soon."

Roy's eyes twinkled as he spotted an opportunity, "Big leagues?! That's very impressive Elliot, I would love to come out and watch you do your work sometime. I'm one of the fortunate few who never needed to take part in the cages, due to my acting career, but I have a lot of admiration for those who do choose to take part. Whole lotta blood guts and balls to go in there and dominate your fellow man. Just the thought of it gets me riled up, now that's America for you."

His words brought up memories of Aamil and Rahim. Whom Elliot was certain would have vehemently opposed the words coming out of Roy's mouth right now. *Those sympathetic fools don't know what they're talking about, Roy gets it.* "Well, I fight again in two days, so if you want to come see me I'll be in Seattle fightin for a chance to move on to the next stage!"

* * *

Two days later, Elliot awaited his big regional championship fight. Striding up and down the corridor outside the room he was meant to compete in, he worked up a nervous sweat. *Everything is on the line now, this is where I'll prove my worth.* Unlike most of his fights, he had had the opportunity to do some digging into the person he would be fighting today.

Thinking about it wracked his nerves. Carlton Suggs, a fighter with only five losses on his record. Quite commendable given the sheer volume of fights everyone had to go through to make it this far. He was a bruiser just like Elliot, utilizing a heavy boxing base and packing quite a punch. Elliot found himself mentally visualizing various scenarios that he might end up in and how he would react if he did.

As he did this, he subconsciously swayed and jerked his body around in rhythm with his thoughts, looking like he was fighting a shadow. To enhance his nerves even further, he was under the pressure of wanting to impress his new friend Hunter and Roy, who had come out to watch him fight. Roy had secured the both of them loge seating, where they waited for his time to arrive. Practicing against his invisible opponent off on his own, Elliot worked up a fine coating of sweat until the time arrived for him to go to his bout.

He walked over to the cage and looked up to spot Roy and Hunter seated in their box. Elliot gave them a quick nod and proceeded to dress down. His opponent, Carlton, entered the cage before he did. Short, even shorter than Elliot, the man was quite stocky with a barrel chest and thick compact arms. *I'm going to have to watch out for his power, better keep my distance,* Elliot thought to himself. Following Carlton into the cage, Elliot shuffled around for one last second, awakening his muscles.

The fight soon began and the two were circling each other. Or rather, Elliot was circling, while Carlton stalked after him with an incessant forward pace. Elliot tested the waters with a straight jab, after which he leaned like he was on a tilting cruise ship. Carlton immediately exploded with a huge right hook to try and catch Elliot coming in. Elliot thanked his lucky stars for being able to get out of the way in time. He kept a mental note of Carlton's explosiveness as he formulated a plan of attack.

Switching up his tactics, Elliot threw a teep kick straight at his opponent's quadricep, eliciting a grunt in return. Having successfully landed a blow, Elliot kept that in mind as he continued to probe for weaknesses in Carlton's defense.

Now expecting the counter, Elliot threw the jab again, going straight into the dodge out of anticipation. When his opponent obliged, Elliot ducked under the blow and landed an uppercut underneath Carlton's chin. Carlton's head rocked slightly, but other than that he showed no signs of having taken serious damage.

Elliot went in for another teep kick but fell victim to his opponent's machinations. Swiftly, Carlton was able to catch Elliot's foot and swept him to the ground. He tried to seize the opportunity, leaping atop Elliot to land some blows from above, but Elliot kept him at bay by posting his feet on his opponents hips.

Dragging his opponent's overextended arm to the side, Elliot was able to scooch out of danger and regain his feet. *I suppose I have Rahim to thank for that. If I hadn't spent so much time training against him, my ground defense wouldn't be so sharp.*

Once more circling around Carlton, the two exchanged a series of feints and dodges that resulted in no more serious blows being landed by the end of the round. Going to his corner, Elliot's mind continued racing to answer the puzzle that Carlton presented to him.

Just after his breathing had returned to normal, the second round was upon him. Trying to throw off his opponent, Elliot changed his stance for this round, now electing to lead with his right leg instead of his left. Carlton's bushy eyebrows furrowed at that, but he declined to change his own stance. With his dominant hand in front of him, Elliot was banking on the fact that his more powerful lead jab might be able to make the difference in this fight.

Level changing, he made sure to keep his head constantly moving dynamically. Elliot began throwing a barrage of jabs to the body, to the head, back to the head, to the body again, all to keep Carlton guessing. Most of his strikes didn't land as his opponent was able to block with his gloves or with a turn of his shoulder. Though one of the jabs managed to land and leave Carlton with a bloody nose.

A surge of confidence filled Elliot, feeling that the tide of the fight was going in his favor. Having landed most of the hits in the fight so far, he started to feel untouchable. Swiftly, he switched stances again mid exchange.

Now he began throwing jabs with his left hand to draw away his opponent's defense. When he saw his chance, he struck true with a right hook thrown off his back foot. Carlton stepped back and fell to a knee with that blow, the most apparent sign of pain he had shown yet. Gritting his teeth, he got right back to his feet in a defensible stance. *I gotta give it to him, this fucker is tough,* Elliot bemoaned in his head.

Getting a little more cocky, Elliot became lazy with his technique and allowed his backhand to lower while throwing a punch. This resulted in Carlton catching him off guard and slamming a brutal cross right into Elliot's temple. Elliot fell over...right as the second round ended.

Staring up at the ceiling for a second, Elliot groaned and rubbed his glove over his aching jaw. Rolling over, he forced himself up and stumbled over to his corner. Taking a drink of water he heaved for breath. *Note to self idiot, don't drop your guard.*

He didn't have long to recuperate before the third round started, the bell dinned painfully in his ears. Fortunately for him, his opponent didn't look much better, the both of them had taken a considerable amount of damage at this point. The two wounded warriors both circled each other, this time Carlton had dropped his forward approach.

Breaking from earlier patterns, Carlton struck first with a lunging jab. Elliot level changed, lowering himself to let the jab graze his shoulder. Leaning back to drop his weight on his back leg, Elliot threw a left cross to the head followed by an underhand strike to the gut, then a mid-hook to the side and a hook to the temple. A combination he had practiced for weeks but hadn't broken out in competition yet. Elliot felt relieved to have connected with his shots.

Carlton determinedly tried to stay on his feet, but his legs were buckling and going out from under him. Elliot loaded up for a kick straight to the chest, launching Carlton onto the canvas with a disturbing thud. The victory bell rung and Elliot was the winner. He excitedly jumped in the air as he realized he was moving to the All-West competition pool, *finally in the big leagues.* Stepping out of the cage, he touched in with the DistribuBot and headed to speak to Roy and Hunter.

Roy clapped him on the back furiously, causing Elliot to suppress a wince as he was already in pain. "That was one hell of a fight son! You had us worried there for a second but you pulled through. You're one tough son of a bitch!"

Elliot beamed with the praise that he received from his role model, "thank you so much, sir!"

Hunter rocked Elliot's shoulder, "I guess you beating up Clyde was no fluke Elliot, you're the real deal!"

Roy grabbed Elliot by the shoulders, "you know Elliot, I think you could be valuable to me. What would you say if I offered to bring you into the fold, and take you to see HQ?"

Elliot didn't know how to respond; he had never felt this accepted and sought after before. He had trouble catching his breath he was so excited. "I would be honored, sir, when are we leaving?"

"How about tonight?"

Rahim

"Come on Kentrell, have some faith in yourself, you can do it!" Rahim encouraged. Ever since Kentrell moved into the house, Rahim and Aamil had taken it upon themselves to train Kentrell, to no avail. They had had some success in getting Kentrell to drill his footwork and some combinations against a heavy bag. However, at the moment they were pitting him against Rahim in a light sparring match.

It was here that they were having the most trouble working with him. Rahim continuously tried to build Kentrell's confidence. He took it easy and left him plenty of openings, but Kentrell would freeze up, not budging an inch when the time came to strike.

Seeming to be devoid of all sense of conviction, Kentrell just simply could not bring himself to take the initiative and throw a punch at anybody. "I'm giving you permission to hit me Kentrell, its ok. You have all the tools you need, just do it,"

Kentrell weakly opened and closed his mouth as if he had something he wanted to say but couldn't get the words out. His heart wanted to prove himself, to show what he was capable of. However, his mind refused to allow himself to believe that he was worthy enough to succeed, worthy enough to even try.

After being told for his entire life that he wasn't good enough, that he was lowdown dirty scum, Kentrell had been conditioned to believe those words and internalize them as truth. Even with the kind words he now received, he felt compelled to self-sabotage, to inhibit himself from progressing to prove his ingrained belief that he didn't have what it takes.

Rahim tried to be empathetic and think of ways to break down the mental barriers Kentrell had built against himself. However, his patience was beginning to fray. Rahim was thankful for a reprieve when they were interrupted by the front door opening and closing.

Entering the room was Dani, a stranger walking alongside her. Standing next to Dani was a middle-aged woman in jeans and a cornflower blue shirt. Her hair dyed the same color as her shirt, matching the color clothing that Dani often wore.

Dani hastily got Rahim's attention, "Rahim, there's somebody who would like to meet you. Are you free today?"

The woman next to Dani checked him out, eyes quickly running up and down Rahim, appraising him, "you're Rahim Vu?"

Rahim confirmed, "the one and only. And you are?"

"Stacy," she responded.

Rahim transitioned his gaze from Stacy back to Dani. "Is this who I'm meant to meet?"

Stacy answered before Dani could get the chance, "no, I am merely here to help Dani escort you to a person that believes the two of you may have some common interests."

Rahim raised an eyebrow, "do I have the liberty of knowing who this person is?"

Dani turned her palms upward apologetically, "sorry, Rahim, they would rather remain anonymous for now."

Rolling his eyes, Rahim pressed them further, "how exactly should I decide whether I want to hear out what this stranger wants if I don't even know who it is I'm dealing with? Come on Stacy, not even a hint?"

She laughed, "I'm afraid not. Hopefully, it will suffice that our arrival has piqued your curiosity, there will be a rally at Wright Park tonight. Should you come, all will be made clear then."

Dani tried to coax Rahim, "don't worry, you know me. I wouldn't lead you astray, this is someone you can trust. Just come tonight and everything will be made clear." Stacy turned and left them after that, leaving Dani and Rahim behind. Rahim did his best to pester Dani for more information, with no luck. He was left with nothing to do but wait and see.

Minutes turned into hours as Rahim waited for nightfall, at last Dani alerted him that it was time and began to escort him to their destination. The night air breezed across his skin, leaving him prickly with goosebumps all over. The cold was just mild enough to not be unpleasant though. It would have been a perfect night if he was able to see the stars, something he had rare opportunity to experience throughout his life.

Small clusters of other people moved in the dark throughout the streets. As they walked, Rahim could clearly tell that a great gathering of people was being drawn to one epicenter. They were all traveling in a similar direction as Rahim and Dani. *Well, I suppose Stacy did say it was going to be a rally. But a rally for what?* Rahim wondered to himself. "Dani, what is this event for again?"

She looked over and smiled at him, "all the factions of the Blues are being summoned here tonight. Word is a grand plan is in the works. We've been mobilized to be filled in on our intended part of that plan. As well as opening a space of discussion for any dissenting voices." Rahim nodded despite still being filled with questions.

Seeing glimpses of the other travelers in the streetlights, Rahim noticed that all of them were wearing various shades of blue. He had never thought much about it before, but it occurred to him that he always saw Reds wearing the same shade of red. Though for some reason, the Blues always wore different shades and generally stuck to Blues of the same shade.

Curious, he asked Dani why this was. "It's to help signify our identity markers. Contrary to the Reds, who are quite homogenous in nature, the Blues are heterogeneous and factious. We are composed of many disparate groups who have joined hands to form one coalition. The cornflower Blues, for example, are made up of other trans and LGBTQ individuals like myself. Other factions include atheists, feminists, allied peoples of color, never-Reds, etc. We are all part of the Blue coalition, but we identify with our own tribes." Understanding dawned on Rahim upon receiving this information.

The cement gave way to soft grass as Rahim and Dani entered the park. The clusters of people he had seen on the way had merged into a massive gathering that grew thicker and thicker the deeper he walked into the park. A much smaller arm slipped into his own as he walked, startled, Rahim looked to see who had joined him and was relieved to see that it was

Stacy. She and Dani greeted each other. "How did you find us so quickly?" he asked, wondering if she had some sort of super-vision or something.

"Um, it didn't exactly take much detective work. You do kind of stand out, being the only one here not wearing blue and all." Pointing at his black and white attire as she said so.

Rahim felt stupid for not thinking of that, "oh," he said simply. "So where's this anonymous person?" he asked.

"Shush now, just be patient. I'm bringing you to them, don't you worry your pretty little head," she teased him. They walked quietly for a while, Rahim noticed that they were veering from the path everyone else was taking. Rahim became distracted for a moment by the sight of cherry blossom trees. Their petals glowed faintly in the dim light illuminating the park.

So distracted he was that he didn't notice they were approaching a bridge until the wood planks began clacking under his shoes. Breaking out of his trance, he noticed a lone woman standing in the middle of the bridge leaning against the rail. She wore a dress with pastel straps that darkened in shade into a dark navy blue at the base. A slit ran up the leg exposing her medium-toned skin. Her head turned at their approach, exposing a wide face with comely features.

Rahim put on his best debonair impression and confidently approached the woman, "I never realized I would be lucky enough to have such an admirer. You are the one I'm meant to meet, yes?"

The woman flashed her teeth at Rahim alluringly, "yes." Looking past him, she dismissed Stacy and Dani, "go join the others, you may leave us." Footsteps receding behind Rahim indicated that they were following suit.

"So, who do I have the pleasure of speaking to?" inquired Rahim.

"I am Zora," she stated.

"So Zora, for what reason do I owe the pleasure of your company this evening?" Rahim asked.

"You are a charming one," Zora said with a wink. "You've certainly garnered some wide acclaim over the years, Rahim. An undefeated fighter, seemingly unbeatable, but without the penchant for violence and aggression too common in today's world. A gentleman warrior, a man who not only commands the respect of the people but their adoration, you truly are interesting."

The sound of the beautiful woman singing his praise sent a buzz through Rahim. It almost lifted him off of his feet, but he kept his mind on the task at hand. "You flatter me Zora, but your answer certainly still leaves me with more questions."

Zora laughed, "And also perceptive I see. Tell me, Rahim, what do you think of Quell?"

Staring at her intently, Rahim answered, "I find they and what they stand for to be toxic and vile things, yet, I admire the effectiveness with which they pursue their goals."

"Which is?" she asked questioningly.

"To divide and conquer, the most effective way to rule any empire. In this system they have designed, they've created the ultimate mindset of scarcity. Individuals are forced into a literal fight over resources, convinced that might equals right. Convinced that if you succeed in this world it is because you worked hard and are a better person, and if you fail you're to blame because there must be something wrong with you. They have set everyone up for failure. Setting the stage so that instead of pointing their fingers at Quell, the masses point their fingers at each other and themselves."

Zora's eyes gleamed delightfully at his answer, "rather long-winded," she teased, "but I agree. I'm glad to make the acquaintance of someone who has such a keen eye for the bigger picture." She placed her hand on his chest in an overly familiar fashion. "Can you guess why I wanted to speak with you tonight?"

"Honestly, I'm still stumped on that one, I presume it wasn't for my devilishly handsome looks?"

Zora snorted, "funny, but no." She looked deep into his eyes for a moment, "you really don't know, do you? Think about what I said a little bit ago, you are a man of the people Rahim. As someone who has succeeded so well in this system, you stand in one of the most legitimate positions to criticize it. If you lead, the people will follow. I wish for you to stand by my side and lead the people towards the freedom they deserve."

Her words resonated with Rahim, stirring ideas he had held in his mind but never dared let see the light of day. Curious to hear her response, Rahim asked Zora, "what remedy do you propose to get us out of the quagmire Quell has led us into?"

"Solidarity" she whispered. "We must overcome the suspicion and hatred that has been used to divide people and unite them in a shared struggle. Already I have begun to unite the disparate Blues, bringing all their factions to meet here tonight."

Doubt crept into Rahim's voice as he responded, "what about the Reds?"

Zora took her hand off of his chest and snorted, "you can't be serious? Those bigots and anti-intellectual barbarians? They are part and parcel in perpetuating the system Quell has created. They can't be counted on to overcome the trials ahead, they themselves are obstacles we must surmount."

Thinking of his many negative encounters with Reds, Rahim was forced to internally acknowledge her point. Although he could not concede, doing so would fundamentally undermine his belief in humanity. "You may be right that they will present an obstacle in overthrowing Quell. But I find it difficult to blame them, they are merely pawns who have been conditioned to act against their own best interest. They are still our brothers and sisters, they are still human beings, it may be hard, but we can show them the light."

Turning her back to Rahim, Zora stared out at the water shimmering under the bridge. "I hope you know how exceedingly idealistic you sound. How can you expect us to work with people who are committed to belittling and dehumanizing our existence, who lash out at anyone they see as different from themselves? How do you plan to reconcile this fact with any hope for true solidarity?"

"People are complicated, but they are also simple. If we can convince them that it is in their best interest to join with you, if we are able to bring them into a liminal space where they can understand that Quell is our common enemy, then maybe this can work. Everyone is being harmed at the hands of Quell, everyone is being denied resources so they can dance for the entertainment of the elite. If we can make them see that, then maybe we can turn them to our side."

"You have a kind heart Rahim, perhaps too kind. I want to believe you, I do, but experience tells me it just won't work. People do not surrender their closely held beliefs so easily. Do you think a single convincing argument is enough to make them part from the lives they have led for decades? The Red's have bought into the twisted logic of the system for so long, they have defined themselves through exclusion and spite for so long, do you really think you can turn them over just like that?"

Rahim struggled to respond, grappling with the truth in her words. "I don't know, but I have to try don't I? Otherwise I would just be all talk, and talk is cheap. If I am to believe I can change anybody, to believe I can change this world, don't I have to believe my own gospel to do that? Actions speak far louder than words, if I don't even try to act to sway the Reds, then what good am I to lead anybody?"

Sensing she wasn't going to move his heart, Zora relented, "so you really plan to do it? You really plan to try and unite the Reds and Blues?"

"It was only a distant dream in my mind before, but now that you and I are here speaking, I have decided that yes, yes I am. But I can't do it without your help."

Zora poked him in the chest, "of course you can't".

Not expecting that reaction, Rahim scrambled to figure out what he was missing, "I can't?"

"I happen to know where you can connect to the leadership of the Reds. Information you would be woefully unprepared to find without me." Zora pointed out.

"How exactly did you come across that information?"

"Let's just say that you aren't the first person to try and create a partnership between the Reds and the Blues, although you may not be the last."

Rahim was surprised to hear that, "am I hearing that you have tried to orchestrate an alliance with the Reds?"

A bitter look came across Zora's face, "possibly. Let's just hope that where the touch of a diplomat failed, the respect of a warrior will command them to listen. The person you seek is named Roy East, your best bet to find him will be in Picayune, Mississippi."

"Like the actor?"

"The very same."

"Huh, weird. Thank you though and there's something else I need you to do for me, Zora."

"How the tables have turned, I summoned you here, and now you're the one making requests. Very well, what is it?"

"I will do my best to get the Reds to join us in our fight. But I need you to do your part to smooth things over with the Blues, to make them ready to join hands with the Reds, should I succeed. Even if I get the leadership to go along with it, we will need the masses to be prepared to join together."

Zora smiled wistfully, "I'll do my best. I had already planned on speaking to the gathering here tonight to rally them around the idea of organizing to protest Quell. I suppose I can also try and endear them to the prospect of unlikely allies while I am at it." Rahim thanked her profusely, grateful for her cooperation. He messaged Dani to let her know he was leaving on his own and left to prepare for the journey to come.

Rahim

"Like the actor, Roy East?" Gavin asked, dumbfounded.

"That's what I'm saying! Crazy right?" Rahim said with vigor.

"Where are we going again?"

"Picayune, Mississippi."

"Are you sure that's a good idea?"

"Not at all."

"ah."

Rahim had called Gavin to speak about his conversation with Zora almost immediately upon waking up the next day. Without hesitation, Gavin agreed to accompany Rahim on his mission. Knowing he was originally from the south, Rahim figured Gavin would have enough of a feel for the area that he could steer Rahim away from any potentially unfriendly situations. Additionally, he had an image and persona that allowed him to get along with Reds. "Are you sure you're ok with helping me out here?"

"Of course, I'm sure. You have a good head on your shoulders, Rahim. I may not always follow along with what you're saying but I know your hearts in a good enough place that I'll go along with your little idea. 'Asides, I happen to have family in New Orleans, which isn't too far from where you're headed." Gavin said.

Rahim stared at him gratefully. He had never known any of his grandparents, so Gavin had felt much like an adopted grandfather to him since they met. "Thanks, Gavin, I appreciate it. Ok, so we can buy a ticket for tomorrow to take a Jet to New Orleans and then head from there to Picayune? I guess I'll get a chance to meet your family!"

Gavin shifted uncomfortably, "do you think you'll be able to afford the flight? It'll be around two thousand credits."

"Luckily, I've been able to save a good amount of my earnings from staying with mom and dad, along with staying healthy. Plus, I've been making a pretty handy amount recently from fighting in the higher brackets. I should be good, do you need me to cover you?"

"I can pay my own way, don't you worry about me son. Ok then, well you better make sure you get some rest now, eh?" Gavin said with a soft smile.

* * *

Rahim slept restlessly all night, unable to keep his mind from wondering how he would fare in his journey. *Can I actually change anyone's minds? Do I have what it takes?* Eventually, the sun made its way back into the sky and Rahim prepared for his ordeal to come.

Going through his morning routine, he showered, got dressed, packed a change of clothes, and made himself something to eat. Gavin arrived in an AutoBot, peeking out from the backseat and waving as Rahim approached the vehicle and stored his things inside.

Once he had closed the door behind him, the AutoBot drove itself off, carrying the two of them to the airport. "It's been a while since I've traveled. These jets always stir my insides something fierce when they switch gears, can't wait to get that over with." Gavin grumbled as his way of making small talk.

Rahim had never flown before, so the comment rattled him a fair amount. "Oh yeah? ...is it very dangerous do you know?"

Gavin gave him a side-eye, "I've heard these planes rarely malfunction, haven't you ever flown before?"

Swallowing his embarrassment, "to be honest, no," Rahim confessed.

Gavin looked incredulous, "I mean I know it's quite costly and all, but your father was a very successful fighter in his day and you're a stud yourself. You've never had reason to fly?"

Rahim looking unusually anxious replied, "dad never really wanted me to watch him fight, he hates what Quell has done to martial arts. As for me, well, I've made due just taking the bullet train to LA for the few out-of-state fights I've had so far. Also, I'm kind of...scared of heights."

Gavin burst out in laughter at Rahim's expense, "so, the kid does have a weakness. I would have thought you'd have bigger balls than that. I'd have never guessed, just wait till I tell Elliot," he said mischievously. That comment gave Rahim pause, Gavin hadn't been told yet what was going on with Elliot. Not having the heart to tell him now, Rahim declined to continue the conversation.

Rahim sat in tense anticipation the rest of the drive until they arrived at the airport. The humongous facility stood looming outside of the car window. A huge expanse of tarmac housed large sleek passenger jets that waited to take their occupants to their destinations.

Rahim and Gavin checked in via retinal scan upon entering the terminal and walked over to wait for their flight. The enticing smell of the cafeteria followed them as they approached their gate. They were onboarded in a timely fashion, finally settling into soft seats and reaching to strap themselves in.

The experience was new for Rahim, he struggled to find the appropriate matching pieces for his buckles to secure himself. He was envious of Gavin, resting with extra legroom in the aisle seat, while Rahim had his legs crammed in by the window. Rahim fought waves of vertigo that washed over him as he looked down and saw how high he was sitting above the tarmac. Imagining looking out while the plane was taking off made the feeling even worse.

The sound of AttendBots distracted him for a moment. Rolling back and forth along the aisles, on tracks, making sure all passengers were taken care of before the jet took off. Before long the Jet's wheels were moving and it was positioning itself on the runway.

Rahim rigidly gripped the armrests next to him as he felt this happen. He tried to force himself to stare forward to spare the fear of seeing them elevate to dangerous levels above the earth. Succumbing to horrified curiosity within moments, he compulsively stared out the window.

Skating along the runway, the plane began to rise through the air, without any physical indication it was leaving the ground. Rahim's fear turned into stupefied wonder as all the structures beneath them grew smaller and smaller. The world began to take on an entirely new perspective.

The glory of blue sky with brown and green earth, the manmade symmetrical squares cut into the metropolis below. All of it left Rahim speechless. Gavin leaned over and nudged him in the ribs, "not so bad after all, huh kid?"

"I guess you're right. It's...so much more beautiful than I ever imagined. It makes me feel so small. Makes you consider how petty and indifferent our struggles are in the grand scheme of things. We fight, we die, but this landscape...it will remain long after we're gone."

Growing quiet, Rahim remained transfixed by the rugged canvas of the earth creeping by below them. Once they broke the cloud line, Rahim wondered how high they would go. A purplish tint infused the sky as they rose, the craft then began to level out and tip forward. A sickening thought entered Rahim's mind, he was right.

The craft lurched forward into lightning-fast acceleration, aided by the gravitational pull of the earth. Rahim's stomach slammed into his rear at the sudden change in speed. However, after a few minutes became accustomed to the new pace and his body settled down.

Gavin was quite amused by Rahim's struggles, "what did I tell ya about the gear switch? That second boost will put some hair on your chest, eh?" Rahim was ghost-faced and weakly nodded. All in all, they arrived in New Orleans about an hour after taking off. Rahim had mostly overcome his anxiety but still found that his legs were slightly shaking as he got up to leave his seat. Dread already hovered over him as he thought about the inevitable flight back.

The memory of his ordeal soon fleeted from his mind though, as he realized they were going to stop to visit Gavin's family. "What are your folks like?"

Gavin awkwardly looked off to the side, "I never know how to talk about them, best you just see for yourself. We won't be staying too long, so don't expect to get too acquainted."

Rahim sensed something was off but shrugged. He was sure Gavin had his reasons for responding the way he did. Logging onto his phone and paying five hundred credits, Rahim ordered an AutoBot to come for them, which arrived in a few minutes. Climbing in, the vehicle took off towards the preset directions Gavin had given it.

The skyline of New Orleans entranced Rahim. It was a significantly larger city than Tacoma, but also quite a bit smaller than Seattle. He looked out the window of the car excitedly as the tall buildings moved by. They made their way into the French quarter of New Orleans.

This was one of the few areas left that one could still get a feel for the old world. Vivid colors and vibrant scenery decorated the structures that made up this district. An unseen artist filled the air with the soothing vibrations of a saxophone, serenading them as they drove along.

An inkling of the meaning in Gavin's words, occurred to Rahim, as they pulled into a cemetery. Exiting the car, they silently walked side by side until they reached a grouping of graves. Gavin stoically knelt down, pressing his gloved hand to his lips and then touching each of the headstones.

There were four of them; displaying the names Susan Potter, Rolland Potter, Mary Potter, and Rose Potter. Standing, he remained still for some time, looking downward at the resting place of his family. "Did you ever know your grandparents?" Gavin asked quietly.

"Unfortunately, no, they passed before I was born."

Gavin put his hand on Rahim's shoulder, "figures. Old age is something people rarely get to see these days. This life of ours has a way of breaking people down far before their time." Gavin paused for a second, "I never knew mine either, but my father knew his. From what he told me, once upon a time it wasn't terribly unusual for people to hit a hundred years old."

Rahim grew concerned as he noticed Gavin was quivering, a sign of vulnerability he had never seen from the older man. "I'm older now than my father ever was, there he is right there, Rolland. Next to my mother Susan, my wife Mary, and my sister Rose. I've outlived all of them. All of them suffered tragic, completely avoidable deaths, but stories like that are all too common these days. So, I can't exactly wallow in self-pity. But do you know what breaks me down, Rahim?"

"What?" asked Rahim breathlessly.

"It's the crushing isolation. Having all of these memories, all of these painful and yet wonderful memories, but nobody to reminisce over them with. Nobody who truly understands what it's like to travel along the hard trail of life for so long. Arriving at the end of the path, turning around and realizing you're the only one who made it."

They remained still without speaking for a few more moments. Rahim was touched and honored that Gavin was comfortable enough to share these emotions with him but overwhelmed by a feeling of ire at the sheer injustice of it all. *What was it all for? We have the resources and ability to make sure that almost nobody must live a life of squalor and hardship, only to die prematurely. So, what was it all for?* "Can you promise me something, Rahim?" Gavin asked.

"Anything."

"Whatever you intend to do here, whatever you're planning, just make sure it's for a world where most of us don't have to die before our time. Where the rest of us don't have to grow old and alone."

Rahim patted Gavin on the back, "I'll do everything in my power to make that happen." He then turned and walked back to the AutoBot that was idling in the parking lot, awaiting their return.

* * *

The countryside was unlike any environment Rahim had ever witnessed as they made the drive to Picayune. Marshlands sprinted in and out of view as they drove along. Bigleaf magnolias sprouted out near the roadside, white-flowered swamp titis looming nearby. AgriBots could be seen in the distance, tilling, and maintaining the fields. The lush greenery kept him entertained for the duration of the drive, which lasted about a half-hour.

Transitioning into less populated areas, approaching Picayune, the change in scenery was dramatic. The area was a harsh change of pace from what Rahim was used to. The large cities that he was used to were meticulously well kept and maintained by Quell, however, this much smaller area was dilapidated and run down.

Potholes were littered across the streets, making it difficult for even the AutoBot's acute sensors to avoid crashing into all of them. Trash littered the sidewalks, representative of the decrepitude that lack of investment had allowed to seep into the area.

It occurred to Rahim that he didn't have an actual address to search for to find Roy East, Zora had simply given him the town. Hoping to find another perspective, he mentioned this to Gavin. "It's a small town, I'm sure we'll be able to find him lickity split. It's just a matter of getting the locals to divulge the information is all," assured Gavin.

"If you say so," replied Rahim, resigned to let him lead the way. A familiar flash of vermillion hit the corner of Rahim's eye. Catching notice, he turned and spotted a group of Reds mingling outside of a brick-built bar sporting a sign displaying the name 'The Weary'. Consulting Gavin, the old man agreed, "good eye, that'll be a good place to start."

Directing the AutoBot to pull over, they stepped out and approached the people hanging outside The Weary. A group of four stood there. There were two women who appeared to be friends by the look of their matching outfits; flannels tied into a knot that drooped over black jeans. They were in the midst of politely entertaining the advances of two men, who were aggressively leaning into the women's personal space as they spoke. "Howdy, would ya'll mind pointing us in the direction of a friend of ours?" Gavin said, taking the lead.

Catching notice of Rahim standing off to the side of Gavin, they narrowed their eyes and stared him down instead of answering. One of the men, medium-length light brown wispy hair with a birthmark on his upper lip, spoke up in an accent as thick as motor oil. "A friend of yours?" he spat on the ground. "You don't look like you're from around here, at least your pal over there doesn't. I doubt you know anyone from Picayune." The two women leaned close together, whispering behind him. They got the man's attention, "wut was that?" he said.

The taller of the two women talked to Rahim, "you're that fighter ain't you? The one out West everyone been 'talm bout? The undefeated kid?"

"One and the same, ma'am," Rahim confirmed.

The small group began a new round of hushed whispers at that. The man with the birthmark spoke again, "so how's it that a hotshot like you knows someone out here, and who you looking for exactly?"

"I suppose you could call them more of a mutual acquaintance than a friend, we're looking for Roy East," answered Gavin.

"Wudda yu want with Roy?" the shorter of the two women chimed in. The others had surprised looks on their faces, puzzling to themselves what these strangers could possibly have to do with Roy.

"We have a mutually beneficial proposition that we'd like to pitch to him, we'd prefer to keep it to ourselves until we meet with Roy."

The man who had yet to speak flicked the brim of his hat and looked up at Gavin and Rahim. "Well, yah came to the right place. I'll take yah to him, but first, are yah armed?"

"No, sir," they both said. Signaling to his compatriots, the others got up and patted down Rahim and Gavin to verify they were telling the truth. Indicating that Rahim and Gavin should follow, the man in the hat lead them inside the bar, leaving the others to stay as they were.

A modest interior greeted them on the inside, beat up brown stools strewn here and there. A BarBot roamed around aimlessly as it waited for a new customer to approach and give it something to do. The man in the hat led them to a side door in the bar.

Pressing his thumb on the handle, a covertly hidden fingerprint scanner read his presence and granted them entry. The door swung open, revealing a set of stone-hewn stairs that descended into darkness. "Wow," exclaimed Rahim, "well I guess we got lucky finding the right place on the first try."

"It wasn't luck," responded the man, "there are entrances to the tunnels in locations all over the town. Had you gone to any other gathering area, you would have had a good chance of finding a route to Roy."

"A network of tunnels going through the city. He sure must be an interesting character to know," commented Gavin.

"The tunnels have existed under the town for quite some time, Roy merely appropriated them for his own use. He's a...cautious man."

Rahim and Gavin exchanged glances, "sounds like a real fun guy," remarked Rahim dryly. So accustomed to the sleek and modern visuals that Quell had built into most areas, Rahim was amazed at the stone structure of the tunnel that he walked within. He had found himself experiencing that feeling of novelty a lot on this trip.

They traveled for some time, the only light being the occasional lamp that was posted every several dozen meters or so. At last, they reached a rusted steel door with two guards posted in front of it, armed with assault rifles. Never having seen a gun in person but knowing of their deadly nature, Rahim eyed the weapons uncomfortably. The man in the hat leaned forward and spoke to the guards. Nodding, they allowed them to enter.

The room they walked into was an unnerving sight. Mounted animal heads adorned most of the stone walls, exotic skins were laid across the floor. Doors leading into other tunnels such as the one they had just exited, were stationed at regular intervals around the edges of the room. Reds walked about, going in and out of the doors, going about their business.

"This way," said the man in the hat. He led them into an antechamber that veered off the side of the main room. In this room was an even more elaborate collection of taxidermized animals: a lion, several geese, a fox, and most peculiarly a Komodo dragon. On the floor sprawled the skin of a polar bear being used as a rug. Its teeth bared near the booted feet of the man they sought, Roy East.

Reclining in a throne, his bullet shell necklace sagged off to the side of his hairy exposed chest. *What the absolute fuck did I just walk into,* thought Rahim. Roy's eyes grew interested as he saw them enter the room, "Rahim Vu, isn't it? What a surprise to be making your acquaintance."

Hoping to use flattery to set the conversation in the right direction, Rahim responded, "Roy East? I almost didn't believe it was you, you look taller in person than you do in your films."

Adjusting his posture to seem even taller, Roy gave a big grin at that, "thank you thank you, you know the screen never did do me justice. Although I could say the opposite to you, to be honest...you're a bit shorter than I would have expected. It seems you've traveled some distance to reach me, what can I do you for?"

Unsure of where to begin, Rahim sought to test the waters, "what do you think of Quell?"

Roy appeared confused, "you came all the way here to just ask me that question? I mean you're one of their star fighters aren't you? You should know better than me what they're about."

"Just humor me."

Scratching his chin, he thought for a second. "I suppose they've certainly done well for themselves, haven't they. Owning half of the world and then some, that fucker Rommel is definitely living the American dream," he laughed after the last remark. "I suppose that leads us to the question, what do YOU think of Quell, Rahim?"

Rahim chose his words carefully before responding, "I think they're dishonest. They preach competitive excellence but have gobbled up almost every industry for themselves and have deterred any future competitors from rising to challenge them. The-"

Roy interrupted, "hold on now, they've worked hard and made brilliant inventions to get where they are, how is that not honest? They've given everyone a fighting chance to succeed, pardon my pun, how's that not honest? Sounds like sore loser talk to me."

Concealing his annoyance, Rahim continued, "I can't argue against the fact that they have made many incredible inventions that have changed the world and solved many of its problems. How did they stay in power though? And how did they grow their power so expansively? The answer is they lobbied heavily to remove any regulations inhibiting them from market domination. They mercilessly stomped out any rival businesses that sprang up, and they have exploited the vast majority of people in this nation. This isn't sore loser talk, this is concern that this stopped being a competition period and is just a facade for Quell to win no matter what."

Roy had nothing to say to that. Rahim continued, "They're also disloyal. Despite all of the technological advancement they have given us, can you really say that things are better for Americans since Quell took over the nation? You can look all over the country and see that people are living shorter lives, constantly set at each other's throats. People are constantly unsure of whether an unforeseen injury is going to ruin their economic security, unsure of where their next meal is going to come from, unsure of if they are going to see their loved ones tomorrow." Rahim glanced at Gavin as he said so. "Quell doesn't care about the lives of Americans, it just cares about soaking them up for as much profit as they can until they're bone dry."

Roy responded, growing flustered, "now now, you may have a few good points there about Quell. But the real issue is those DW's soaking up all of our resources. They just sit on their asses accepting handouts while the rest of us work hard for what we have. If they weren't constantly taking, there would be enough for us, us hard workers, to make enough to live comfortably. You want to talk about setting Americans at each other's throats? You need not look any further than those dastardly Blues! They're the ones dividing us! Constantly trying to despoil our American culture; forcing their 'racial tolerance on us', trying to take God out of our lives, teaching our children that it's ok for two men to kiss, or that a man can suddenly become a lady if he wants to. That's what's dividing us and keeping our country weak!"

Rahim felt his hackles raise at the foul ideas that Roy was shooting off but fought to control the fire burning in his chest. *Remember why you're here Rahim, keep a level head and try to speak a language that he might understand.* Gavin chose that moment to intercede, trying his own level of tact to win over Roy. "Listen I know where you're coming from Roy I do. At the end of the day, we just want to create strong people who can stand on their own and contribute right?"

"...right," echoed Roy.

"As it stands, we're all, except for actors and such like yourself, made to fight in Quells system, right? Blues and Reds alike. They control the resources; they control how people have to live their lives. So, do you think that they would allow DW's to soak up so many resources that they couldn't make hand over fist in profits? I don't know if you're familiar at all with the process of becoming a DW, but it's incredibly strenuous. You are burdened with a significant level of proof to qualify to be one. It's not easy. So do you really think that those people are the problem? When we live in a world where people are literally made to fight one another and view each other as obstacles to success, do you think Quell is more to blame or the Blues? Who stands to benefit the most from that?"

Roy scratched his chin, "so, let's say I go along with this idea that you're pitching me, Quell is terrible for society. Then what? What are you trying to get out of me here?"

Rahim cleared his throat, "You have a considerable amount of influence over Reds all over the country, right?"

"I suppose you could call me a figurehead of Reds nationwide, yes."

"I am asking for you to lend your influence to my cause?"

"Which is?"

"To force Quell to dismantle the system of oppression that they have constructed, and properly distribute resources so that everyone can be assured of their health and safety. Isn't that the godly thing to do? The just thing to do. Think of all the people if this happens, when they hear the name Roy East, they won't think of an actor, they'll think of a messiah, somebody who helped deliver them from pain and suffering."

Roy stroked his hands through his beard, "I do like the sound of that...so how do you propose we carry out this plan?"

Of course you like the sound of it, you egotistical prick, Rahim thought to himself. "Here is the part you may not like. We would like to coordinate between you and Zora an alliance between the Red's and the Blues. If only we could arrange a coalition that included both groups, there is nothing that we can't-"

Roy growled, "that bitch put you up to this? Everything is beginning to become clear." He stuck his fingers between his lips and emitted a loud whistle, summoning a group of armed guards who encircled the two visitors quickly and efficiently.

Entering the room with the guards was a familiar head of red hair. "Rahim? Gavin?" said Elliot in disbelief. "What the hell are you doing here?"

"Elliot?" they both exclaimed simultaneously.

"Elliot, you know these two here?" Roy asked, looking between Elliot and the pair.

Elliot glared at them, "unfortunately."

Roy laughed, "what a small world. You'll have to fill me in on the details when I finish my business here. For now, just stand in the corner and watch. I don't want any interruptions." Pulling an antique looking revolver out of his waistband, Roy rubbed the barrel against his temple in a maniacal fashion, appearing to be contemplating something. "You've come in here with a lot of fancy talk and flattering words, but if you're working with that cunt there's no way I can trust you. Tell me why you're really here."

Alarmed at the sudden aggression manifesting before them, old-timer Gavin frantically wondered how they should proceed. Gavin took the first step, "sir, I think there's been a misunderstandin here-" Not waiting for him to finish his sentence, Roy swiftly raised the barrel of his gun and pulled the trigger, sending a round into Gavin's shin. "AHHHHH" Gavin screamed, collapsing, and holding his leg. Splatters of scarlet blood decorated the floor around him and seeped out of his leg, soaking the left side of his pants.

Elliot jumped and turned pale at the suddenness of what just happened, "Jesus." he yelped.

Roy pointed his gun at Elliot, "What did I say about interrupting boy? You're lucky I don't whoop you for using the Lord's name in vain in here. Now stay quiet." He pointed the gun back at Gavin. "Did you think you could just come in here and smooth me over with that southern drawl of yours like I'm some gullible child? If one more word comes out of your mouth, I'll put you out of your misery old-timer. I want to hear the boy talk."

Rahim gritted his teeth, a swell of emotions filling him: concern over Gavin's wellbeing, despair that their plan was failing, anger over the treatment they were receiving. Aware of how thin of a line he was dancing on, Rahim breathed deeply and fought to regain his composure. "I don't know what boy you're referring to, as there are none before you."

"You've certainly got balls speaking to me like that with a gun in your face." Roy laughed, not in a friendly way, but in a calculated way meant to intimidate. He lowered his gun to rest in his lap, "speak then. And hope I like what you have to say."

Squeezing his fists at his sides to alleviate tension, Rahim answered, "it is as I have told you, we have no hidden intentions in coming here. I just want what's best for our people, Blues and Reds, and that is the dismantling of Quell's power hold. Quell doesn't care what groups we align ourselves with. They would just as easily toss any of us aside like trash if it would widen their profit margins. By protecting others, we protect ourselves, Zora understands this and this is why she has expressed willingness to work with you. Time and time again, I hear Blues referring to Reds as uneducated, bigoted, heartless tools. Wouldn't the perfect way to throw that in their face, to make them look like judgmental cynics, be to subvert their expectations and join us in this fight? Whether any of us cares to admit it, we need you and your support."

Roy ran his fingers through his beard absentmindedly. "I've seen you fight, Rahim. You seem to be a strong and capable man who can stand on his own feet. Your presence here is certainly a sign that you've got no shortage of commitment and guts. But I'm afraid I'll just have to agree to disagree, there's no way I could stand up in front of my people and tell them to work with Blues. Our values and way of life are just too different, we are seeking a more...traditional life for people to pursue."

The meaning of his words did not escape Rahim, who was losing more and more faith in being able to secure a positive outcome from this conversation. "If you don't mind, I'd like to be alone now. My men will escort you back where you came from."

Rahim turned to Elliot, "and you? Are you just going to stand there? Do you have anything to say?" Elliot didn't respond, having a semblance of shame on his face for the first time since Rahim had known him.

Roy wagged his finger, "you don't need to talk to my Elliot, be lucky I'm letting you leave here alive. Move on now, before I change my mind."

Rahim gave one last resentful stare at Elliot before leaning over to help his friend. Gavin groaned as Rahim helped him off of the ground. Moving him so he could cling to Rahim's back and be carried to avoid putting any weight on his leg. Rahim could tell that Gavin had already lost a considerable amount of blood, so he rushed his pace to get Gavin to help in time.

The walk up the tunnel was much slower than the walk down had been. Along with the additional weight, stress seemed to make time stand still for Rahim.

Kolby

Kolby was wracked with a deep ache, penetrating him through and through. He suffered from a battered body, a tired mind, and a wounded soul. Yearningly he sought comfort in the memory of Veronica's arms, whom he knew was waiting for him at home.

This was no time to distract himself with pleasant reminiscing, however. He was here to do something he had been anxiously contemplating for some time now. Kolby waited on a bench along a pier staring out at the Puget Sound.

The deep blue water rolled out into the distance, making his worldly concerns seem petty in comparison. The view and the chill sea air washed over him, almost freeing him of the apprehension that gripped him, almost. The bumping sound of wheels traveling on pavement alerted Kolby to the arrival of the person he was meant to be meeting with. "Hello Kolby," he heard. Turning his head, he saw Aamil sitting next to him with a burly man keeping ahold of Aamil's chair.

"I see you got my message, who is your large companion?" Kolby asked.

"This is Deandre, he's a long-time friend of mine."

"Hello Deandre," a grunt was all he received in return.

Aamil flipped the white coin to Kolby, which Kolby deftly caught. Aamil folded his hands over the blanket in his lap, "so why have you summoned me to speak with you? And why now?"

Kolby had thought long and hard for a while now about all the things that he wanted to say to Aamil. Now that the moment was here, however, he found himself freezing up. "I suppose you could say I've had a change of heart over the years, about a lot of things. There's so much that I'd like to ask you. As for the now...well, I guess I just happened to hit my breaking point is all, had to happen sooner or later."

Kolby got off the bench and bent over to one knee, looking straight at Aamil, "I'm so sorry, from the bottom of my heart. Not just for what I did to you, but for all of the wrong I have done in my life."

Aamil looked past Kolby out at the water, "Is that all you wanted to say to me? Sorry?"

"Look Aamil, I can't give you your legs back, I can't take any of it back. I was just following orders, doing my job. I don't know if there's anything I can say."

Aamil laughed harshly, "how about accepting some fucking agency over your life? 'You were just doing your job.' So much harm has been done Kolby, from people just putting their heads in the sand and refusing to question their role to play in all of this...shit."

Turning his head to the ground, Kolby slammed his fist into the wood planks of the pier, drawing blood. "You're right Aamil, you're right. I've been resigned to just be a pawn in other people's games..."

The chastising tone Aamil took with him reminded Kolby of Veronica. "I've hurt people, so many people, with these hands. Until now, I've let myself be convinced that I'm not worthy enough to challenge the status quo. That I should just look out for myself and keep my head down, but now that I have something to lose..."

Aamil looked at him with knowing eyes, "so who's the woman? Or man, sorry to assume."

Kolby laughed, "You have keen eyes. Her name is Veronica."

Aamil took on a wistful expression, "I can see where you're coming from. I'm a believer in self-reliance, but there is something to be said for having that special someone come into your life and kick you in the pants to make you want to be a better person. Someone to give you something to give a damn about."

Aamil paused, without looking he grasped Kolby's shoulder comfortingly. "I'm not sure what you're wanting from me, but I can't take you where you want to go, I can only show you the way. If you want to make amends for the life you've led, actions will speak much louder than words. People matter Kolby, not just the ones that can do something for you or who don't bother you, all people. Human life is inherently valuable, LIFE is inherently valuable. Anybody who disrespects or disregards that fact is undeserving of power. Regardless of if you explicitly hold malice towards others, if you aid in their demise even through omission, you are complicit. If you want to make amends, you must work in service of others. You must do what you can to break this cycle of hatred and violence that is breaking our world apart."

Kolby sat in silence for several moments absorbing Aamil's words. "You've given me a lot to think about. I'll...try to take what you've said to heart. Does this mean you no longer hold a grudge against me?"

Aamil looked at Kolby sagely, "grudges are for children. However, that doesn't mean I've forgotten the things you've done. If you want that to happen, you'll just have to give me something else to remember you by."

Bowing his head at Aamil's feet, Kolby thanked him profusely. They spoke for some time after that, basking in the open ocean air.

* * *

Kolby found Veronica fast asleep in their bed when he returned to Camp Crisp the next day. Looking down at her before him, she lay in the fetal position, wrapped tightly around a pillow, her face scrunched in a disconcerted expression.

I wonder what she's dreaming of. Smiling softly, Kolby kneeled and brushed his finger across her cheek lightly so as not to wake her. Reacting to his touch Veronica's face took on a more peaceful look.

A sense of resolve washed over Kolby. Nodding, he turned around and began bustling about their small cottage intently. Grabbing the bags he had left near the front door, Kolby plopped them into the center of the floor.

Slowly, the bags began to fill as he stuffed them with clothes, toiletries, and other valuables in the home. About an hour later, Kolby had nearly filled all the bags. Tapping his foot thoughtfully, he contemplated what important items he might be forgetting. Feeling the hairs on the back of his neck stand up, he spun to see Veronica watching him from the bed.

"You're awake."

"I am," she responded. "What are you doing?"

Kolby strode over to Veronica's side and clasped her hand. "Taking us far away from here. We can't stay any longer. I've secured an AutoBot for us and rigged it so they won't be able to connect us to the vehicle."

"Where are we going?" she asked him with piercing eyes.

"I-I don't know, I just know this is no place for us. I can't stand by and take part in this madness for one more second," Kolby's voice cracked as he said so.

Veronica reached out and tenderly pulled Kolby's head into her chest. Running her fingers through his hair, she asked, "what happened while you were gone?"

Nuzzled against her, Kolby filled Veronica in on the conversation that transpired between him and Aamil. Listening carefully, she waited until he came to the end of his story. "I see," was all she said when he finished.

Kolby seemed relieved, "so you understand? You'll come with me?"

Veronica pushed him away and kissed his forehead, "I would follow you to the ends of the earth, my love. Let me ask you one thing though."

"Anything."

"It seems you are shouldering a lot of guilt over your history working for Quell. From what you have said, you want to take action and atone for this by leaving. I want to know, who do you think this will help?"

"I won't have to hurt anyone anymore, nobody will have to suffer at my hands ever again. More importantly, I know how much you hate being used by Quell. You won't be trapped here a moment longer, this will help us." Kolby said, seeming frustrated.

"Do you hear yourself? This isn't about anyone but you. This is about you assuaging your own sense of shame. You feel bad about being used by Quell, so you're running away from them. But don't you see, they will just replace you without a thought. Those same people you don't want to harm will end up hurt anyway by somebody else's hands. You know that. It's just like Aamil told you, even omission is enough to make you complicit in these people's suffering. I love you and will stand by you no matter what, but I can't stand to see you lie to yourself like this."

A lone tear raced down Kolby's face, "you're right but...I don't know what else to do."

Veronica gestured broadly, "you stand here amidst one of Quell's most closely held secrets. You have long held Rommel's favor and serve here as one of his most trusted agents. You can't think of anything you can do?"

Kolby laughed at his short-sightedness, "you are far too good for a bone-headed lout like me. I swear I don't know how I managed without you all those years." Kissing her hand, Kolby looked intently into Veronica's eyes. "You have convinced me to stay. Even so, I need you to leave. The world be damned, I couldn't live with myself if I let something happen to you."

Now, Veronica, was the one crying. "If you think that's what's best, then I accept that. Do you have a plan?"

* * *

Standing in a patch of wilderness just off the road, about a mile from Camp Crisp, Kolby and Veronica tenderly said their goodbyes. Pressing their foreheads together, Kolby sensually ran his fingers through her hair. He took a long moment to soak in her presence with all of his senses. At last Kolby opened the door of the AutoBot he had brought for Veronica.

"I'll come for you when I think it's safe"

Veronica stared at him for several heartbeats, "you better," she said, smiling gently. Getting into the vehicle, she closed the door and drove off into the distance.

Waiting till she disappeared, Kolby slowly clenched and unclenched his fists. A torrent of emotions swirled inside, threatening to overwhelm him. *You don't have the luxury to break down right now pal, there's work to do,* he thought to himself.

Kolby then began the walk back to camp, focusing on his breath to reign in his thoughts. As he walked, he reached behind him and pulled out a revolver. Kolby had pulled it from the luggage moments before sending Veronica away. Rolling it between his hands, he eyed the piece somberly before tucking it in his waist band. Minutes passed by until the buildings came into view. As he approached the encampment, he stopped in his tracks.

An AutoBot was parked just outside of Camp Crisp. Initially, Kolby wondered if Veronica had had a change of heart and come back. That notion was soon dispelled, however, once an unfamiliar woman stepped out of the vehicle. Short of stature, hair black as midnight, brown skin, well-groomed, and wearing a Quell uniform.

Clearly a woman of means, she must be one of the techies. I haven't seen her before though, it's unlikely that Quell gave clearance for any new staff to be brought into the facility. Increasing the peculiarity, Kolby noticed Nia approaching the woman. Appearing surprised, the woman exchanged words with Nia, after which Nia hastily ushered the stranger into her cottage.

That's it, something fishy is definitely going on here. His suspicions validated, Kolby began to approach Nia's dwelling. As he drew near, another flicker caught his eye. Craning his head, he observed a blonde figure dashing towards the main facility. *That doesn't bode well,* he thought soberly.

More immediate matters commanding his attention, he put the observation on the back burner for now. Softly pressing his ear against the grainy wood of Nia's door, his eyes widened as he heard the conversation ensuing inside.

Chance

Several months had passed since Chance returned from her reconnaissance into Quell. Kabir had been very confused when she returned with no information to share. Not wanting to worry him with the details of her experience, she chose to keep the fraught encounter to herself.

Though keeping this secret caused a well of guilt to arise in her whenever she encountered Kabir after that day, Chance promised herself she would tell him after she had completed her work for Quell. That way she could feel confident they would be preoccupied in their designs and no longer sniffing after her trail.

Once Chance neared completion of the project assigned to her, she was plagued by doubts. *Do I trust Quell to do the right thing with this technology? What harm could I be causing by helping them create this?* These concerns left her conflicted as she worked. For most of her life, she had kept her head down, trying to stay out of trouble, but this situation felt like it demanded her to act. Putting those thoughts aside, she worked with new vigor to finish her project. At last, she was done.

Chance bided her time, then, one day, she felt a window of opportunity. Rushing to exit the building after work, she raced to get into her AutoBot. Plugging in the address she had memorized when she broke into Quell, she was whisked off to her destination. Chance was pleasantly surprised to find out her destination was not far, merely a short drive to near the Santa Cruz mountains.

The route followed the creek running near Quell's facility, giving her a scenic view as she traveled. Soon she arrived, stopping the car. She was a bit perplexed as she saw the collection of dwellings interspersed amid the trees. *Well, this certainly isn't what I expected.*

Maintaining confidence that her Quell uniform would shield her from too much scrutiny if she was caught, Chance began snooping around. At the entrance was a large arch with a sign above it reading 'Camp Crisp'. *Subtle,* she thought to herself humorously. She observed several small housing units, with a big facility near the back of the development. Several other lab coats like herself wandered in and out of the structure. As Chance looked around, a twig crunched behind her, followed by a voice.

"Who are you?"

Turning around, Chance spotted a woman with long platinum locs going down her back, a scar ran across one of her cheeks. The woman held an intense intimidating look on her face, "I'm a research associate here, just decided to stretch my legs."

"No, you're not. I would know if you worked here, now tell me the truth."

Chance felt a sense of panic take over her, her brain short-circuited. Nothing came out of her mouth but, "um, uh, um." Finally, she just decided to take a chance on telling the truth. "Ok, I'll fess up here...but can you promise not to rat me out."

The woman smirked, "ok I promise."

Oh, I didn't think that would work, Chance thought to herself. "So...I actually do work for Quell, in their main facility. I've been investigating some shady activity in Quell and I happened to come upon this camp, so I thought this might be a place I could go for answers. My name is Chance by the way, who are you?"

"Nia," the woman responded.

"You seem reasonable Nia. I'm not sure why you're being so nice to me, but could we go somewhere where I can ask some questions?"

"Let's just say you're not the only one who has issues with Quell," she muttered under her breath. "We can talk in my house, it's just over here. That's where I was headed when I approached you."

She beckoned for Chance to follow her into her house. Walking in, Chance was surprised by how little there was. A twin-sized loft bed stood tucked away in the corner with a desk and chair underneath it. A small bathroom branched off in the corner, a stove, cupboard, and fridge occupied another corner of the room. Other than that the room stood bare.

Nia pointed to the chair under her bed, "sorry I don't have much seating room in here. I don't ever have company; you can take the chair though." Chance made herself comfortable and sat down. Although, she immediately regretted it as she was now awkwardly staring up at Nia, who remained standing and staring down at her.

Chance slowly found the words, "so, what's going on here?"

"This is where Quell trains and houses its genetically enhanced fighters. The successor to their original Spartan program which merely housed and trained unaltered children from birth to be fighters."

"Wait, so Quell is sending you into its Towers, why? I thought they already had fighters voluntarily contracted to them, why take this extra step?"

"Why do you think? Money. Consider us an insurance policy, in case more transparent means don't follow through. They don't want to pay out more resources than they need to. So, they send us to rig the matches in their favor, or at least greatly increase the odds they win. If they maintain the illusion that everyone can succeed if they just work hard enough, they can manipulate people into blaming themselves and not rebelling against the system."

Chance's head was reeling. Due to her family's inherited wealth she had never needed to take part in the Towers, but what she was hearing sounded diabolical. *So that must be why*...an epiphany struck her and everything became clear. "I think you may have just given me the answer that I've been looking for."

Nia turned her head, "what do you mean?"

"What I do for Quell, Nia, is I am one of the main contributors on developing AI software. Recently I have been doing some digging, as I told you, and uncovered designs for an android. They are seeking to make Robots that can pass as human beings. I have been wracking my brain since discovering this, asking myself why Quell would be developing this. Until now."

Nia's mouth opened, "you don't think?"

"Exactly. I believe Quell is planning on slipping these androids into the cages. With them, they will have absolute confidence in their ability to control the flow of resources trickling down to the main population. That's just the tip of the iceberg. Who knows what they could pull off if they can convince everyone those androids are real people."

"I couldn't agree more," an unfamiliar voice spoke. Chance and Nia swirled to see a tall man leaning in the now open doorway.

"What are you doing here, Kolby?" Nia snarled.

Chance reeled, *is this THE Kolby Balgair? The White Fox?*

Kolby shrugged, "I apologize for eavesdropping. I saw you pull this strange woman into your home, and I became curious. So, I decided to drop in."

Chance looked back and forth between the two, uncertain if she should speak up or let them battle it out. "What are you going to do then? Are you going to go running to Quell like the lapdog that you are?" asked Nia.

"More like lapfox am I right?" quipped Chance.

"Shut up," shot Nia.

"Didn't you hear me when I walked in?" said Kolby innocently. "I'm with you, I think something needs to be done about Quell. They are a parasite that will just keep sucking more and more lifeforce out of this country unless somebody stands up to stop them."

"So what, you've been doing Quells bidding for all of these years and you suddenly decide that you can take it all back? You've just decided that being cold-hearted doesn't suit you anymore, and now want to turn over a new leaf and expect everyone to just forgive you?"

"I'm not asking for your forgiveness, Nia. I can't expect anyone to just let go of the things I've done, but that doesn't mean I can't still try and stop things from getting worse. For all of these years, I've thought that kindness and compassion for others were signs of weakness, but in them, I have found my salvation. I've been so wrong for so long, that for what time I am able to, I'd like to be right for a change."

Nia turned her back to him and stood with her arms crossed, her body ever so slightly trembling. Chance took that moment to place her hand on Nia's shoulder, "we only just met Nia, but I can tell you're a good person with a big heart-,"

Nia shrugged off Chance's hand, "what do you know Chance?"

"Look, every person in this room is complicit in working for Quell. Quite frankly, me most of all. The both of you were born into their grasp, I ultimately chose to work for them. I can't even put into words how it makes me feel, knowing that not only have I been living a lie for most of my life, but that the work I have done has actively made the world a worse place. I can barely process it, part of me wants to deny it and run from that feeling, but that won't help anybody. Which, ultimately, is all we can do to atone, right? Make sure to do as much as we can to not let anybody else get hurt by this system."

Nia stood there for a moment without answering, after a long pause she nodded. Turning around she looked at Kolby, "ok what would you have us do?"

Looking Grave, Kolby answered, "I have a friend that I think you should bring this information to. But first, we need to get out of here, I'm not the only one who saw Chance come in here."

It was at that moment that a loud banging rattle the front door. "Open up the door Nia, I know you have an outsider in there," barked a harsh voice.

Nia looked at Kolby with Panic in her eyes, "Han," she whispered.

Chance was unsure how to react to the situation, "should I be worried? Is he going to hurt us?"

Nia gave her a look that suggested the worst. Meanwhile Kolby peeked through a window that lay near the door. Looking at Chance, he asked, "can you start your AutoBot and get it ready to leave?"

Nia interjected, "what's the situation outside?"

Kolby glanced at her, "Han has brought ten fighters with him, plus two SecurityBots"

Nia appeared incredulous, "oh, is that all?! Going out there would be suicide, we can't escape from that!"

Ignoring Nia, Kolby looked back at Chance, repeating his question. "Well, can you?" Nia looked about to speak up again, but Kolby calmly placed his hand on her shoulder, "don't worry, I got this."

"Y-y-yes, yes, I can do that," Chance stammered, already fumbling in her pocket for her phone to do as he asked. More banging shook the door, startling Chance and causing her to fumble even more as she did so.

"I'm going to open the door now; follow my lead. When I tell you to run, the both of you need to get to the AutoBot as fast you can. Get the hell out of here. Find Aamil Jackson and tell him what you have learned. Chance, you should be able to find where he lives on Quell's database, don't waste a second getting there."

"But what about-" Nia began to say.

Kolby harshly interrupted her, "don't worry about me, just do as I tell you." Not wasting another moment, he flung the door open to reveal them to the small crowd waiting for them outside.

Han stood in front of the group, his expression twisted into a cruel smirk. Though this smug look transformed into a look of annoyance as Kolby walked out of the cottage with Chance and Nia. This only lasted a moment, however, as he quickly began to emit a dark chuckle.

"Well, well, well, look who we have here. Now this right here is some serious deja vu, huh Kolby? It seems like anytime I'm about to deal with this girl, there you are to stand between us."

Kolby shrugged sheepishly, "what can I say; I guess I've always been a killjoy. Sorry to spoil the fun."

Han waved his hands in the air, "I guess it must be fate; who am I to question these things. No matter, it only adds to the fun. I've wanted to deal with you for a while now." Coughing, Han motioned behind to the group of fighters and the SecurityBots positioned on either side of the group. "Though I am certain of the answer, I suppose for courtesies sake I should ask anyways. Stranger, who are you and what are you doing here? And Nia, what does she have to do with you?"

Chance began to respond, but Kolby shook his head. "I don't think these girls will be answering any of your questions today."

Snarling, Han spat at him, "if you want to make this difficult, so be it. No sweat off my back, we can do this the hard way if you want. You know how persuasive I can be." Raising his hand, the SecurityBots began to roll forward, before stopping almost immediately when Han shouted, "wait!"

Gleaming metallically in Kolby's hand, pointed directly at Han's face, was a revolver. Keeping his eyes on Han, he turned his head ever so softly to speak to Chance and Nia behind him. "Now."

Blustering, Han barked at them, "don't you even think of trying to leave." Glowering, he looked back to Kolby, "I don't know where you got that contraband, but you know damn well that gun won't put a dent in these Bots."

Kolby smiled coldly, "sure you got me there. But it can kill you easy enough, can't it now?" Han blanched at that. "Go now, don't worry, I got you covered."

Slowly backing away, Chance and Nia retreated from the area. Just as they had gotten several dozen feet away, they gasped as they noticed a blur moving towards Kolby's blind spot. One of the fighters at the back of the group had slipped away without Kolby noticing, sneaking to the side of his peripheral. In a mad dash, the figure tackled Kolby to the ground, the gun flying out of his hand into the dirt.

Nia gasped, "no!" she screamed.

"Just go!" Kolby screamed back desperately. As he said so the fighters were already dashing towards Chance and Nia.

Fortunately for them, they had already drawn near to the AutoBot. Scrambling, they got to the car and flung themselves inside. Frantically, Chance directed the vehicle to leave and they pealed away. The last thing they saw were the SecurityBots suspending Kolby by his arms and Han burying his fist in Kolby's gut. Moments later, the scene left their vision and they were headed far away.

Rahim

Rahim had been consumed by a terrible feeling of remorse when he
escorted Gavin from the hospital. The old man refused to inform Rahim
on how much the visit had cost him. Rahim just hoped that Gavin would be
able to adequately support himself after their ordeal. He tried not to let
these thoughts weigh him down, choosing to focus on the task at hand. It
had been a couple of days since his harrowing experience. Rahim had
contacted Dani the previous day and arranged for her to connect him and
Zora once more.

Rahim sheepishly approached Zora. He prepared himself to notify
her that his plan to align the Reds with them had failed. Foul thoughts
brewed in his mind, dreading the massive 'I told you so', he was about to
receive. Dressed much less lavishly than the last time they had spoken, this
time she wore plain street clothes. High-waisted blue jeans over a white t-
shirt tucked in at the waist. Standing in front of her, he cleared his throat,
"Hey, just got back from my trip."

"And?" she asked without looking towards him.

"It uh, it...didn't end up working out. He just wouldn't see eye to eye
with me and I couldn't bring them on board to join us."

"I told you so."

"I knew you were gonna say that! I hate you!"

Zora laughed, "well I don't know what you expect, I DID tell you so
after all. I am sorry that it didn't work though, just know that I more than
anyone wanted to see you succeed, the fact that you didn't is a loss for
everyone. So are you ready to prepare for the real hard work ahead of us?"

"What have you been able to come up with?"

"I have been in contact with all of the other factional leaders amongst
the Blues, all of them are ready to participate and direct their followers into

action. I am thinking of coordinating protests at all, or at least most, of the Towers around the country. We won't have the numbers to make any sort of effective stance, however, so it is going to be on you to motivate people to turn out."

"Thank you for all of the work that you have put in to make this happen, this wouldn't be possible without you."

Zora waved him off, "I still think a concentrated strike towards Quell would be our best bet, but for the sake of idealism, I am willing to try your idea of a peaceful protest out. Let's just hope that Quell doesn't take advantage of your idealism and use this moment to silence all of its detractors at once."

"I think that destroying the system is a worthy goal, but what will replace it? If we truly want lasting change, we need to capture the hearts and minds of the people and motivate them to want better for their country. After being divided and set against each other for so long, we need to find a way to bind people together."

"I don't disagree that that is a worthy ideal to pursue, but how pragmatic is it? Certainly noble, but what are ideas worth if they can't be put into action?"

That last statement conjured a funny expression from Rahim. "You know that makes you sound a lot like my father."

Zora grimaced, "why would you think that's a comparison I'd like to hear?"

Rahim chuckled, "I'm not sure, it's just all that I could think of in the moment."

Winking, Zora waved her hand at him, "I'm only teasing you. I hope you do understand what I am saying though." She grew more serious, "I will allow you the opportunity to do this your way, but aggressive action will be our only option if this falls through."

Rahim nodded, *I don't like it, but if I can't pull this off I can no longer deny her.* "I fight for the championship in six days, I will make my move then. You will know it when you see it, once you receive the signal, begin making plans to mobilize immediately." Having agreed on this, Rahim departed for home to prepare himself for the trial to come.

* * *

Six days later, Rahim sat in the window of a jet preparing to fly to Los Angeles, a mere twenty-minute flight away. Unlike his first trip with Gavin, he only felt slightly nauseous about the idea of flying through the sky. He mused to himself how much his life had changed in the last few years. Leaning his head back, Rahim became lost in contemplation for the further changes that were to come in the next few days. *Everything is riding on this, I cannot afford to fail.*

He didn't have long to dwell on his thoughts though, for the flight was over before he knew it. It was an odd feeling for him, traveling alone. It gave him considerable unease as he got off the plane. He boarded the AutoBot he had ordered to transport him to the Tower. His eyes widened as he neared the Tower, a massive crowd was gathered around the building.

Unlike the local Towers that were crowded with fighters trying to scrape by, this was a national Tower that was reserved for only the elite of the elite to compete. It was odd that so many people were assembled here. *I'm confident that these aren't spectators, as the tickets for these events are quite pricey. So what are all of these people doing here?*

He soon was given his answer, spotting dozens of signs within the crowd bearing his name and messages of encouragement. Getting out of the car, several people began to get the other's attention, screaming maniacally, "it's him!" they yelled.

The feeling of celebrity was a new one for Rahim and one that he did not feel entirely comfortable with. The fans swarmed him, many simply just wanting to touch him, others shouting questions in his face. "You're my hero Rahim, a true man of the people!" "Hey, champ, ready to continue that undefeated streak?"

He politely smiled and waved, doing his best to seem appreciative of the turnout. Squeezing his way through the crowd, Rahim finally made his way into the building. Significantly more opulent than the Towers that he had fought in before, the national Tower was a sight to behold. White marble floors sheened under his feet, a big domed ceiling loomed above the foyer.

He turned his sights to the elevator that waited on the other side of the room. On his way, he stopped to check in with the CheckBot. The experience felt rather odd because there was barely anybody else there to check-in. A big change from the check-in stations in other fighting venues he had taken part in.

At last, he walked into the elevator, jumping at the sound of the contraption speaking to him once he was inside. 'What floor do you wish to arrive at?' spoke a hollow-sounding voice. Rahim marveled at the smooth blank interior of the box he stood within. Devoid of any buttons, he assumed his only option was to verbally direct the machine. He answered, "18th floor."

Although he did not feel the space he stood within move at all, it was only 3 seconds before the doors opened, spilling him onto the floor he needed. Rahim's footsteps echoed around him as he trod along an arched hallway, replete with more marble and gold. *This seems a bit over the top.*

At long last, he entered a large domed room that housed a single cage in the center of it. People in fine clothing stood around mingling with one another. A ServeBot rolled around, delivering glasses of champagne to the guests.

Many of the guests took notice of Rahim's presence when he walked in, they excitedly lined up to try and shake his hand. Opposed to the admiration and excitement that awaited him outside of the building, this encounter felt more like he was an object on display. The wealthy elitists looked upon him with bemused expressions, as if they were visiting a zoo and he was the main exhibit.

Not wishing to engage with them any more than he had to, Rahim smiled politely and continued moving, wishing to get on with this as quickly as possible. Dressing down, he entered the cage and awaited the arrival of his opponent. Shuffling could be heard as the guests outside the cage began to take their seats, awaiting the fight to come. A rather more subdued sound of excitement could be heard as Rahim's opponent arrived.

He was a fighter with little to no renown, one of Quell's inserts. A pale man with a buzzed head and an impressive physique entered the cage. Staring forward while entering, he seemed to look through Rahim, his eyes dead and soulless. A light lit up from above, providing better illumination for the cameras to view the cage.

Descending from the ceiling, a microphone entered the center of the cage, followed by a man in a sparkling black tuxedo entering the cage. In an excitable tone, he introduced Rahim and the other fighter to the audience. He spoke boastingly of their laurels and accolades that landed them in this arena.

After he finished his shpeal he offered the mic to the fighters. Giving them the chance to make a statement before their fight began. The other fighter spoke first in a flat voice, "I want to thank Quell for giving me this amazing opportunity to prove myself and show what I am worth. It is because of them that a guy like me can make it to the top just by working hard and pulling myself up by the bootstraps, they have really changed this country for the better."

Rahim rolled his eyes at the obvious propaganda coming out of the other fighters' mouth. Stepping up to the mic, suddenly all of his previous worries and fears vanished. Readying himself to unleash the words he had been preparing for weeks, he was overtaken by a sense of calm.

 Clearing his throat before delivering his message to the world, Rahim's eyes found the camera, "since I was born I have been raised to be a true martial artist. The values of hard work, discipline, and perseverance have been dear to me my entire life. However, there are other values that I find to be just as important, values that define who I am as a martial artist. I believe in the idea that as iron sharpens iron, so does one person better another. In this spirit, I believe in maintaining respect for my opponent and the work they have done to get to where they are. I believe in caring about their well-being, making sure everyone has a fair chance to succeed so we can bring the absolute best out of each other. It is because of these beliefs, that I do not support Quell. They deny the necessities of survival to most, and the ones they do provide for, they stigmatize to set the rest of us against them. They do not care about the spirit of fair competition, merely in the strength of the privileged over the weakness of the deprived. They would leave the majority of people to suffer without healthcare they could easily provide, to starve without food they could easily give, and to languish with broken spirits. It is because of this that I reject Quell, I reject their legitimacy to lord their wealth and power over the rest of us. I reject the system they have created that has set us against one another. It is because of this, that I cannot, in good conscience, participate in this system anymore. So I will be forfeiting this fight and shall boycott the system Quell has created. Fifteen days from now protests will be held at Towers all over the US, I'll be there, I hope the rest of you will join me."

Elliot

First, he has to turn up sticking his nose where it doesn't belong. Then, he has to go acting all high and mighty like he's better than me. What exactly does Rahim think he's going to accomplish; I can't wait for that loser to get cut down to size. Elliot's thoughts dwelled uncontrollably on Rahim. It had started with the scene in Picayune with Roy, the incident with Gavin causing Elliot to doubt himself. Rahim's stunt on national tv only further fueled the flame of Elliot's obsession.

Back and forth, his internal monologue flipped from reassuring self-affirmations to crippling self-doubt. His mind was so twisted that he had started to dissociate, his sense of self fraying at the edges. It was in this mindset that Elliot ran through his usual routine, preparing for the biggest fight of his life. He was moments away from competing in his first fight within the All-West competition pool. It was finally time, Elliot was the first to enter the cage.

Dancing around he got a feel for the layout of the space he'd be competing in. His opponent, Connor, entered soon after, causing a level of dismay for Elliot, quite unlike any he had experienced before. Although Connor certainly had an imposing figure, it was his eyes that crawled under Elliot's skin. Framed within a gaunt bony face, were a pair of dead soulless eyes. His gaze appeared to pass over Elliot, barely registering his existence.

Feeling considerably perturbed, Elliot fought to not let himself be distracted from the task before him. The fight soon started and the two fighters circled each other. Elliot's opponent was unusually passive, resting in a basic stance with very little in the way of motion.

Elliot circled him to pick his first shot, Connor responded by turning with him, albeit in a very slight and choppy motion. Elliot took his chance and shot in for a low kick to the calf. Elliot's cheeks turned red and he had trouble breathing as overwhelming pain followed. He felt like his shin had just struck iron.

Pulling his foot back, he had trouble with every step afterward. An unpleasant sensation shot out from his leg every time he tried to put weight on it. Connor, meanwhile, seemed to be unfazed by Elliot's kick, not even budging a centimeter when hit.

That's unlike anything I've hit before, what the hell is this guy made of. Elliot approached more cautiously this time, testing the waters, he threw a low jab to the midsection. Even with the gloves to cushion his fist, his knuckles sent screams of protest up and through his arm. Again, Connor seemed to be barely fazed by the hit, although his pace did pick up, his movements becoming more fluid.

Elliot's mind short-circuited thinking of a way to take this guy apart, *is he even human,* he wondered. *I'm not much of a grappler, but it seems so far like that might be my only route.* Feinting as if he was going for a punch to the head, Elliot level changed, blasting through his opponent with a double leg. Successfully, he took him right to the ground, although his chest became bruised from slamming into Connor's knees. He immediately regretted his choice though, for Connor's hands then dug into Elliot like a vice grip.

Without the grappling proficiency to wriggle from the grasp, Elliot found himself being controlled. No visible strain on his face, Connor pushed Elliot off of him and switched their positions, pinning Elliot to the ground. Reaching his arm back, he slammed home his first punch. He hit Elliot in the face, resounding in a sickening crunch.

Elliot felt his nose pulverize, his face awash with blood after the first hit pounded into him. *There's no way he could be human.* Seeing his opponent raise his arm to deliver another blow, Elliot knew there was no way he could possibly withstand this punch. Closing his eyes, he waited for the sweet release of death. The punch never came though, for the bell rang, saving Elliot.

Flailing about with minimal body control like he was in a drunken stupor, Elliot dragged himself to his corner. Frantically he considered how he was going to get out of this situation. *There's no way I can throw in the towel, in front of all of these people? I'd be a laughing stock for the whole world. Think Elliot, think.*

Try as he might, he saw no outcome that ended positively for him. While his mind raced, he looked across the octagon at Connor. Those cold lifeless eyes looked right through him. *That impossible toughness, that crushing strength, those dead eyes. Something is up here, consequences be damned, I'll reveal this to the whole damn world if I have to.*

The beginnings of a plan formulated in Elliot's mind, really more of a last-ditch effort than a plan, but it was all he could think to do. The bell rang and the time of reckoning was upon him. Now would be the moment that Elliot would prove his constitution.

Connor's movements were even more fluid than the previous round as if he was learning and progressing on the spot. Effortlessly, his feet glided across the canvas and he began throwing a series of combinations at Elliot. Scrambling on his heels, Elliot barely managed to avoid the bulk of them. The only exception being a low punch that barely grazed his ribs, still sending tingles rippling through Elliot's body.

Still doubting what he intended to do, Elliot pattered around, waiting for the perfect opportunity, one that he knew was unlikely to come.

At last, Connor took the choice away from him by landing a roundhouse kick to the side. Elliot wheezed and a trickle of blood came out of his mouth, but he managed to hold on to the leg. Leaning forward with the last of his strength, the edge of his fingers jammed into Connor's dead eyes, ripping downward. A horrific tearing sound ensued, as Elliot ripped the skin off of his opponent's face.

Thick blood-like goop seeped out, a cold metal interior revealed. Previously sewn-in skin now hung loosely off of the thing's face, the gray metal underneath spotted with bloodstains. A commotion could be heard outside, as the mortified onlookers witnessed the grotesque thing that now stood in the cage. "No fucking way," said Elliot.

Even with his earlier suspicions, he had never imagined something so insane would be happening to him. Seeming unfazed by its face hanging from its head, the machine continued crushing Elliot. This time Elliot knew there was nothing he could do.

His face barely had time to register the panic he felt before Connor cocked its hand back to slam into Elliot's skull. Dangling limply before the might of the machine, Elliot's neck snapped back with a crack. The Bot crushed his skull, goop spattering all over its gloves and arm as it did so.

Elliot's corpse slumped over to the canvas, blood pooling around him. As this scene unfolded, it was as if the world outside the cage seemed to set on fire. The physical viewers were terrified and flooding out of their seats, the virtual viewers stunned.

Rahim

Rahim, Kentrell, Aamil, and Linh sat huddled around the TV, awaiting Elliot's debut fighting in the All-West competition pool. Aamil had done some digging and discovered Elliot was fighting today. The others were conflicted over watching, but he had insisted that they still support him from afar. Rahim didn't have the heart to sway Aamil, so he relented.

A sudden slamming on the door broke their concentration. "Go check that out," Aamil told Rahim. Walking to the door, Rahim was shocked to see Nia standing in front of him alongside an unfamiliar face. Next to her stood a woman with jet black hair tossed over her shoulder. She wore expensive clothing and a pair of spectacles that sat a little too low on her face.

With little explanation, Nia barged the two of them past Rahim into the room. "Sorry, this is very important. You were the only people we could think to turn to."

Scratching his nose, Rahim was flabbergasted, a sentiment the rest of his family shared. They puzzled over the identities of the two women now standing in their home. "...uh, who are your friends, Rahim?" asked Linh.

Before he had time to answer, Nia looked at his father, "Aamil, I presume?"

"Yeah, uh, you guessed right. Is there something I can do for you?"

Nia hesitated, exchanging a look with the woman beside her before replying, "Kolby sent us here, he said you could help us."

Aamil looked annoyed, "Kolby? What the hell, just because I forgave him doesn't mean he can send whoever to my home. What does he think I can help you with?"

At that remark, Nia appeared to almost wilt, becoming uncharacteristically diminutive. The stranger placed her hand on Nia's shoulder comfortingly. Seeming to draw strength from the gesture, Nia responded slowly, "...we...don't really know. Everything just happened so fast and...all he could tell us was that we should come see you." Nia's voice cracked as she finished speaking.

Sensing the anguish threatening to overwhelm the composure only barely maintained by Nia, Linh rushed forward to embrace her. "There there," she cooed while gently rubbing her hand across Nia's back in a circle. "You're safe now, just take your time." A look of confusion briefly formed on Nia's face, but dissipated shortly as she melted into Linh's embrace. Linh turned her head slightly to speak to Aamil, "I think something terrible must have happened."

Aamil sighed, looking dreadfully weary, "I suspect you are right." Wheeling forward, he tenderly placed his hand on the small of Linh's back as a signal for her to move for him. Once she stepped aside, Aamil looked closely at Nia's face. "Do you feel ready to tell me what happened?"

Nia nodded and began relaying what she and Chance had witnessed at Camp Crisp. Aamil waited patiently while she spoke. When she finally told him what happened to Kolby, he nodded knowingly. Leaning forward, Aamil spoke with a tone of deep sincerity, "you did everything you could. All of you. Let us hope that Kolby is within our ability to help and his act of redemption is not his final act."

Rahim stepped forward, "there's one thing that still needs explaining though. I understand why Nia and Kolby were at that camp," Rahim paused and looked at the stranger. "But who are you and why were you there?"

Having been in the background of the conversation till now, the stranger appeared surprised to suddenly be addressed. "Oh hi, yeah my name is Chance!"

Nia piped up, "she works for Quell like me, except not as a fighter."

"Worked," corrected Chance, "although I suppose I haven't technically tendered my resignation yet." Fidgeting nervously with her hands, Chance continued, "I've spent the last couple years working in AI Solutions for Quell" That comment seemed to put everyone visibly on edge. Throwing up her hands defensively, Chance placated them, "I promise I am no longer working for Quell, I'm on your guys's side. Just listen to what I've discovered."

Chance spent the next several minutes going over her research and what she had uncovered going on at Quell. The group's faces got more and more horrified as they learned of the plot that Quell had been cooking up to further their oppression of the population. "Androids?!" exclaimed Rahim. As he was about to ask more questions, a scream emitted from Linh, "Elliot!" she sobbed. That prompted everyone in the room to look at the tv. With horrified expressions they saw what had happened to Elliot.

Numbness gripped Rahim as he witnessed the Bot standing over Elliot's mangled body. Blood dripped down the knuckles of the Bot, its face dangling off its metallic skull. "I guess the cat is out of the bag for the whole world now," Nia said. Everyone gave her a dirty look for the insensitive way with which she framed the comment. The group mourned for several minutes, lamenting what had befallen Elliot. The terrible reality of what Quell was doing settled in the air.

Rahim thought back to the fight that he had forfeited, to his opponent's dead soulless eyes. *Is that what they were planning on doing to me?* Relief at still being safe and sound washed over him. A feeling immediately followed by guilt for considering his well-being while Elliot now lay dead on the ground. Rahim looked at Chance and Nia, "there is somebody we need to speak to, they will be able to help us stop Quell."

Hours later, after back-and-forth communication, they were on their way to meet with Zora. Rahim was unable to keep his thoughts in order, constantly fidgeting to eliminate the nervous energy consuming him. Nia and Chance traveled silently alongside him, giving him his space to grieve and dwell on his feelings.

Eventually, they arrived at a quaint house deep in the interior of the city. A Blue lacky of Zora's opened the door for them, directing them to the basement. There Zora stood, leaning over a table kneading her fingers into her temples. Without looking up she greeted them, "so, you've arrived, welcome. I guess we have much more to consider than we previously did our last meeting."

"Just so," said Rahim.

Nia looked at Zora and back at Rahim, a spark of jealousy smoldering in her eyes. "Are you going to introduce us or what?" she snapped at Rahim. "Zora, this is Nia and Chance, guys this is Zora. Chance would you care to fill in Zora as you did me?" Waiting for Chance and Zora to finish speaking, Rahim took Nia to the side to talk to her. "So, why the change of heart?"

Nia blushed and shifted uncomfortably before answering, "I guess I just had a lot to think about after the last time we spoke. I was confused and didn't know what I should do. Then, I ran into Chance and found out what Quell has been doing. I can't deny that self-interest played a part. I assumed that I would soon be replaced if this trend continued, but I also just couldn't live with the weight anymore of aiding in these heinous acts. Especially after what happened to Kolby..."

Rahim looked deep into her hazel eyes and saw only truth in the words she spoke, "I'm happy to hear that you were able to come around."

Having finished conversing about the recent events that had come to light, Zora and Chance looked over at the two of them. "Would you two like a room or are you going to join the rest of us in planning how to deal with this catastrophe?" Zora commented dryly. Sheepishly, Rahim and Nia ended their conversation and walked over. The four of them delved into the logistics of how and when they would mobilize people for the protests against Quell. Coming to an agreement the three then left Zora to her own devices.

May 3ʳᵈ, 2170

Rahim

The day finally came when it was time for the rubber to meet the road. Rahim found himself looking over a massive crowd of people with Zora by his side. They were near the Tower in Tacoma as he had requested, they staged the main site of protest there.

Most attendees were dressed in their respective shades of blue. Surprisingly though, there were also a significant number of plain-clothed individuals who did not identify with any of the Blue factions. Additionally, a large amount of DW's had turned out, visible by the red letters emblazoned on their foreheads.

A rumble of conversation emerged from the crowd, the separate discussions merging into one loud buzz. Rahim and Zora scanned the crowd, observing for the moment when they felt all had arrived. Everyone became absorbed in their own bubbles, waiting for the leaders of the event to speak.

Similar gatherings were being staged near Towers all over the country. Large screens were assembled so that everyone could simultaneously participate in viewing the main speakers heading the protests.

"Now that I'm seeing everyone here at once, it's kind of overwhelming. Are you sure it's a good idea to let me speak? What if I mess everything up?"

Zora kindly patted Rahim's shoulder, "you'll do just fine, there's no need to worry. Well, maybe there's a little reason to worry, but still, I have faith in you. Just remember that these people are here to seek guidance from you. They are likely feeling even more lost and helpless than you are, so just speak from the heart and trust that they will understand."

"Thank you, Zora, that actually helps a lot. How much longer do you think we'll be waiting before we go up?"

She scanned the crowd, "oh, I think we will likely be able to start this up in about ten more minutes. I'll get them warmed up for you." She finished with a wink. The time went by a flash and soon she left Rahim's side to go address the crowd. Her speech was impassioned, sending a fervor throughout the crowd. However, she was interrupted by an unexpected sight.

Approaching the protest were thousands of Reds marching in a loose formation, riding a horse at their head was Roy East. *What is this guy's deal, a horse? Really?* Rahim thought to himself. Then he asked himself the larger question of why these people had shown up here today. Steeling themselves for what appeared to be an imminent conflict, they waited to discover the group's intentions.

Brandishing a megaphone Roy revealed their reason for coming, "we have no love for you Blue sons of bitches. You folks are people that we despise almost more than any other. Quell has crossed the line though, they have hurt both of us the same. It was our boy out there killed by their Bot, we cannot tolerate that sort of treachery. While we would not stoop so low as to befriend you, we believe that at this moment we have a common interest to fight against Quell. So, we are willing to put aside our differences for the time being and stand beside you."

From her stage, Zora looked down on them. Slowly, she nodded in acceptance of the proposal that Roy put forth. Just like that, the Reds lined up alongside the rest of the crowd, the two colors split along a clear divide. Roy walked up to join them on stage, Rahim had a bad feeling gnawing at his gut as the man drew closer. The feeling intensified once Roy came within a few feet of Rahim.

A shiver seized Rahim's spine when he looked into the lifeless eyes of Roy. The deranged glare previously present in those eyes had disturbed Rahim, but now he found himself perturbed at its absence.

Thousands of eyeballs glued to his every move, Rahim second-guessed his gut and decided against making a scene. *I'll bring it up to the others after we're done. Hopefully, it's just the jitters getting to me. Zora* continued her speech, welcoming Rahim onto the stage for his turn to inspire the crowd.

Rahim walked up nervously to present himself before the masses, *there's no turning back now, just say what you have to say.* "Let me first say, I am happy to see all of you gathered here today. You have all decided to show up and take action, the most vital ingredient to securing freedom. There are many wise individuals, who, throughout the ages, have expounded on the nature of existence and morality. Though their ideas profound and influential, it is not their originators who lit the annals of history with the fire of progress. That honor belongs to those who declined to resign themselves to mere pontificating and choose to put those ideas to good use, to ACT. It is this fact that has inspired me to question how I ought to live my own life, how I ought to ACT to live up to my ideals. These are the thoughts my ponderings have led me to. I have a moral obligation to do something if I think somebody is being harmed. I think it is not only possible but necessary to care about the welfare of other people as well as ourselves. Some might say that they have a responsibility to take care of themselves, but I think that line of thought is damaging. I am not a religious man, but I find a lot of wisdom in old proverbs. "He who is without sin may cast the first stone." I think sin is a harsh word, but the point is that all people are fundamentally flawed. "To be human is to err." We all make mistakes. The point is, nobody is perfect. "Many hands make light work." We all need help sometimes if we are being honest, we all have found ourselves burdened by a load too heavy to carry alone. When we deny others' cries for help, we often are denying our own imperfection and our own humanity. We are placing a bar for ourselves that we can never achieve; causing internal unhappiness, and external neglect to our moral obligations to each other. We all make mistakes, but with a helping hand, we can make our way. If everyone helped each other, if everyone was willing to make a small sacrifice of our time and energy, we would all have the assurance that we won't be allowed to fall. If you cared about others, and they, you, in return, you could have security in knowing you will be ok. To get there, somebody has to take the first step, somebody has to ACT, and it has to be you. This is what the essence of democracy is all about; all men are created equal, of the people by the people for the people, the

UNITED States. We are the most united when we are caring for and looking after each other. As I said, to be human is to err, so in turn, we should have empathy for those who have trouble hearing this message. After all, we have spent so much time in this world with everything telling us that it is a sign of weakness to struggle. Telling us that to get to the top you have to be ruthless and step over others. If you fail then it's because it was your fault, you have to pick yourself up by your own bootstraps. These messages are subtly sent to us every day of our lives, of course, some people are going to be buried in their twisted philosophy. If we are truly to embrace our moral obligation of caring for one another, we must be gracious and do everything we can to bring them to the light. After all, they are only human too. We must preserve and cherish that which makes us human. This is why we cannot continue to let this system that sets us against one another stand. Like most of you here, I have lived my entire life under the thumb of Quell. We have all had our human dignity denied to us for no other reason than to increase the wealth of a small group of people who could never possibly spend what they already had to begin with."

Rahim paused in his speech for a moment, noticing a flicker of movement within the ranks of the Blues, as well as the Reds opposite them. Helplessly, he witnessed several individuals within each group unveil guns that they had been concealing until now.

Bangs resounded, people opening fire, indiscriminately mowing down protestors. A red mist filled the air as blood and screams took over. Pandemonium quickly ensued and people scrambled to escape. People hysterically knocked each other down as they ran to save themselves.

Rahim stood motionless, his brain trying to process what was happening. It seemed that Reds and Blues alike had been caught off guard, the mass crowd of people were thrown into chaos.

Fingers possessing strength they should not have had, dug painfully into Rahim's arm. Too shell-shocked to care about the physical pain, he numbly looked to see the hands owner. Cackling, Roy hooted at the mayhem. Despite his animated body language, his eyes still held no life in them.

"That was a pretty speech boy, all that talk about humanity and such. Too bad for you I ain't human." Grinning wickedly, it grabbed Rahim's face with its other hand. Rahim hung limp in its grasp, catatonic. Roy growled and dropped Rahim, Roy turned its head to look behind it and Rahim saw Zora standing there, a determined expression on her face.

As Roy turned around fully, Rahim saw a knife sticking from its back. Zora screamed past Roy to Rahim, "get off your ass, Rahim! We need to get out of here or we're both screwed!"

Roy snorted, "what makes you think I would let you two get away? You're dead bitch." It started pacing towards her. Seeing Zora in trouble stirred Rahim into action. Adrenaline pumping through him, he got off the ground and approached Roy.

Heaving, Rahim planted his foot between Roy's shoulder blades and kicked it off the stage. Rahim tried not to notice the sickening thump as Roy landed atop the already large pile of corpses that had accumulated in front of the stage.

Having saved Zora, his mind threatened to retreat back into itself until Zora madly shook his shoulder, "we need to get out of here right now Rahim! If we stick around here we both might be dead!" Without responding, he allowed himself to be dragged off by her, following her away from the scene.

How could this have happened, he thought, numbly trying to process the awful reality that had just unfolded. He was broken from his shock by the thought of his parents, Nia, Lyall, Chance, Kentrell, and all of the others who had been in the crowd. Pulling at Zora's arm he screamed, "NO, NO! WE HAVE TO GO BACK! WE CAN'T LEAVE THEM! I HAVE TO PROTECT THEM!"

Zora refused to let him go, grabbing his face in between her hands, "you have to keep moving Rahim! You have no way of knowing where they are, all you will be doing is putting yourself in danger. You have to escape and hope that they got out ok. We will look for them later, but for now, we have to get out of here!"

He knew she was right, but still, it tore his heart in two to think about what might have happened to his dear family and friends. Tears gushed out of his eyes as he deliberated over what choice he should make. Knowing in his mind that Zora was right, he went away with her, running to leave the chaos behind them.

Eventually, they got far enough away that they could stop and breathe. Rahim quietly sobbed, "it's all my fault, it's all my fault. All of those people...all of those people are dead, it's all my fault."

Zora gave him a perplexed look, "what are you talking about Rahim? Cut that out, you didn't do anything. It was the Reds, they showed up and then everything went to hell, you saw it didn't you?"

Rahim snapped at her, "no it wasn't the damn Reds Zora, can you set aside your vendetta for one god damn second. Just think about Roy, you stabbed him in the back and he didn't even flinch. Did you see what happened, there were Reds and Blues both opening fire out there. Just ask yourself what you think all of this means."

Zora seemed shocked, "Blues...are you positive you saw that? I don't...I don't know what to make of that. Unless, no...Rahim, you think Quell sent androids into the crowd to cause this madness?"

Rahim nodded, "That seems to be the most obvious explanation to me right now, given what we know. But...I'm still the one who gathered all of those people there, I'm the one who provoked Quell, this wouldn't have happened if I hadn't-"

A stinging slap interrupted his train of thought, Zora stood before him fuming. "Don't you dare take all of the blame onto yourself! You don't think I'm feeling awful about what happened here too? Or do you just want to throw a pity party so you can say woe is me? Now, we can sit here and feel bad for ourselves if we want, or we can go get the sons of bitches who did this. This has only increased the urgency to deal with Quell, now we know just how far they are willing to go to get what they want. The time for diplomacy is over, they have taken that option away from us. Any hope for cooperation between the Reds and Blues is gone for a very long time now. Hell, mobilizing any new people won't work. People are going to be far too confused and scared to try and stand against Quell now. We have to organize the dedicated forces we already have. This is the time for us to take action."

Mitch

Mitch gazed out the window of his office, looking over the city jutting from the landscape. The crinkling of papers could be heard behind him; his advisors prepared to brief him on the tumultuous situation brewing in the world outside of his company.

A polite cough alerted Mitch to the fact that they were ready for him. Rolling his neck around to bring his attention to bear, he turned to speak with them. Pacing around the room he came to the head of an oval table where seven suited men obediently awaited his signal to start the meeting.

Taking his seat, he waved at them in a dreary manner, indicating that they may begin speaking. "Sir, the situation has grown increasingly dire. We have been experiencing dramatic costs associated with the mass protests underway throughout the country. Organized efforts have led groups to sabotage company Bots, destroying hundreds of units and counting beyond repair. The production costs to recoup these units have resulted in significant losses. More broadly, unemployment in the nation has hit sixty percent and rising. The protests have been growing exponentially in size, along with the militant uprisings that come along with that."

Mitch sorely rubbed his temples, this news agitating him as if a swarm of bees was flying around picking at his brain. "Of course, these people have too much time on their hands. How else would they respond rather than using that time to tear down their betters? How have our preparations been coming along?"

A ruddy man in a bowtie answered, "We have neared completion on the construction of the main sites across the country, those projects should be finished in about two weeks. Also, the people that you requested we summon arrived at HQ this morning."

Mitch seemed satisfied, "I'm happy to hear it, it is imperative that we have this done in a timely fashion before I make my announcement. This house of cards is quite precarious right now, nothing but perfect timing will suffice. We must give the people something to hold onto so anarchy does not ensue." Their meeting proceeded in a standard fashion from then on, going over various logistical outlooks and discussing the particulars of their plan going forward.

A few hours later, Mitch felt giddy as he walked into his penthouse apartment, located on the top floor of his company HQ. Twenty individuals, ten men, and ten women were seated in the center of the room awaiting his arrival. Several SecurityBots were stationed at the corners of the room and on either side of the doors leading into it.

These individuals were all highly acclaimed MMA fighters. Standing in their presence left Mitch overjoyed. His father had instilled in him at an early age, a love for the sport and admiration for the work ethic of fighters.

Coming to the front of the room, he rubbed his hands together and addressed the people sitting before him. "You all are probably wondering why I have gathered you here today. Before I answer that, I just want to lay out exactly what it is I am offering you, before I tell you what I will require in return." So far he still had everyone's attention, so he continued. "As I'm sure you know, things in the outside world are not ideal. Poverty is running rampant, the streets are becoming more and more dangerous every day, it is a stressful situation to say the least. I am prepared to offer all of you extravagant homes in an area of your choice, plus a handsome sum that will give all of you a level of wealth you never dreamed possible."

"What's the catch?" one of the people chirped.

"There is a tumultuous transition ahead of this nation, one my organization will be leading the charge on. I cannot disclose all of the details to you now. That information shall be classified until I address the nation collectively. However, what I can tell you is I will be requiring you to employ the skills you have refined throughout your lives in the service of this company. More importantly, I have a bigger sacrifice I require, to satisfy the terms of the agreement I lay before you now. You shall commit to partnering with another person here and having a child. You will, of course, receive fertility assistance should there be any complications in this regard. The children that you have, will be bestowed into my organization's custody, along with any legal rights and claims to them."

An uncomfortable silence followed after that statement. Looks of confusion were aplenty amongst the small group that Mitch spoke to, "um, what the hell for?" asked one woman in the group.

"To the same effect that you would be serving in my employment, albeit with a more concentrated approach. The children will be given the best training and resources to allow them to reach their fullest potential as fighters."

"Would the children have any choice about whether to participate in your little program?" queried one of the men.

"As much choice as they would have presented to them. They would not be competing until they turned eighteen, at which point they would be contracted to work for Quell. They would not know any life to turn to besides this one."

The casual manner with which he spoke of these things, along with the words themselves, didn't seem to sit well with the group. "That uh, that kind of sounds like slavery, if I'm being completely honest." The earlier woman said.

Mitch seemed unfazed by this suggestion, "I promise they would be adequately compensated for the services that they provide me."

"Ok, but that still sounds like slavery."

At that, Mitch shrugged, "if that's how you would like to view it. I have told you what's in this deal for you, these are my terms. The decision is yours to make." When it was all said and done, fifteen people stayed, with the woman voicing the objections being one of the five to leave.

Mitch snapped his fingers as the five left the room. Two SecurityBots coasted over the floor, following them. Muffled screams and audible thuds could be heard outside of the room. Those present visibly turned pale, flinching at the implications of what they just heard. A smug expression rested on Mitch's face, "I'm so glad you decided to cooperate with my venture."

* * *

A week later, Mitch prepared himself to speak in front of the whole nation. He sat in a leather armchair while a FashionBot meticulously applied his

209

makeup and adjusted his outfit. Mitch repeated the news he would break to the world over and over in his head. Soon it was time for the crucial moment. With a snap of his fingers, the set he sat within was cleaned up. A desk was placed in front of him, and cameras rolled out to face him.

A moment later, a red light flicked on the camera, and the recording began. "Hello America, I'm Mitch Rommel. I'm speaking to you today to address some serious problems that have plagued our nation for some years now. Although we do not bear the authority and responsibility invested within the governments of these United States, nonetheless we find ourselves obligated to extend a helping hand to you, our loyal consumers. I am proud to say that my company, Quell, has a long cherished history of efficiency and problem-solving. It is this competitive excellence that is required to solve the afflictions facing this country and the world. Our leadership and technology paved the way to solving one of the gravest crises facing the human race, climate change. When our planet was wracked by volatile natural disasters: blistering droughts and wildfires, floods and rising sea levels, devastating hurricanes, land erosion and dust storms, Quell stepped up to the plate to lead us into salvation. The company my grandfather built, god bless his soul, through hard work and innovation, developed the world's first stable nuclear fusion technology. This solved our energy needs and paved the way for several revolutionary creations; carbon and methane capture technology to clean our atmosphere, effective and efficient agricultural automation, previously unthinkable medical miracles, just to name a few. Luckily for all of us, the work of Quell has been able to touch almost every sector of the economy, giving us the chance to meaningfully touch your lives in a myriad of ways. Unfortunately though, as is often the case, where one problem is solved, another arises. Our innovations have rendered human involvement in most areas of the economy, obsolete. The government has failed to adequately transition people into new areas of work. Perhaps it is because they lack the competitive pressure to create solutions like we in the private sector are so used to doing. Whatever the reason, we at Quell have decided that it is our duty to help the fine people of this nation. Help them have a fair chance at the American dream, a chance to seize opportunities for themselves. After watching unemployment rise uncontrollably, millions out of work, poverty rising uncontrollably, we said to ourselves that this isn't the America all of us were promised. You deserve better, and we're going to give you the chance to take better for yourself. I am proud to tell you, that Quell once again will be making a world-changing innovation that will put the power in YOUR hands to fight for a better life for yourself. Beginning a week from today, Quell will unveil several centers around the country. There, anyone who has the desire to better their life, can go and seize the opportunity of a lifetime. You will have the choice to sign up with our program and take control of your destiny. This program pits ordinary everyday people against each other in organized fighting matches. You will receive compensation just for participating, with higher rates for winning and higher rates as you maintain high performance over time. I know, this may not sound appealing to many, and that's ok, you have the freedom to take other routes in life to earn prosperity if you wish. This is a chance though, for anybody who wants to stop the guessing game and start being in control. For people to be their own boss and set their own hours. If you work hard enough, you could even be as wealthy as me one day! I am offering you the opportunity to stand on your own two feet, to be self-reliant! You won't have to worry about taking from the generosity of others to support yourself. If you are willing to work hard, you can pick yourself up by the bootstraps and seize the life that you've always wanted. The choice is in YOUR hands! I look forward to seeing all of the intelligent entrepreneurs who decide to seize this opportunity. To all my fellow patriots, good luck and good night."

Rahim

The hours until Rahim and Zora discovered whether the others had emerged from the fray alright, were some of the most stressful of Rahim's life. The worst possible scenarios ran rampant through his mind, his heart clenched with worry.

When the others finally started trickling in to meet at his house, the relief was palpable. Nia and Chance walked in first, his parents, Kentrell, Gavin, Tahmejia, Dani, Lyall, and Deandre arriving a few moments after. He tried to stay strong for the others who undoubtedly had been through worse than him.

Rushing over, he gave each a strong hug, even Chance whom he barely knew. "I'm so happy all of you are ok." It was a while before they were able to collect themselves enough to have a lucid conversation about what had just transpired. Zora took a second to pitch their theory to everyone, the encounter with Roy and how they suspected Quell had sent in androids to send the crowd into a panic. "That is the most plausible scenario. I mean your interaction with Roy alone is pretty incriminating," echoed Chance. Rahim who had yet to speak, asked the million-dollar question, "so what now?"

"Isn't it obvious?" said Nia, "we make the bastards pay."

"How do you propose we do that?" asked Linh. "They have an army of bulletproof SecurityBots to get in our way if we tried anything, on top of androids that can surprise us when we least suspect it. A direct strike at them will only result in more needless death."

"So we should just roll over and let Quell continue their reign of tyranny?" questioned Zora. Dani nodded, agreeing with her sentiments.

"I think there might be a way we can do this with minimal bloodshed," voiced Chance. "I have someone on the inside who may be able to get us in without too much hassle. If we get that far, I feel confident I can turn the tides in our favor."

Aamil looked at her quizzically, "how exactly would you do that?"

A mischievous look flashed in Chance's eyes, "as some of you already know, I have extensive experience working as a software engineer for Quell. First within their Narrow AI troubleshooting department, then in AI Solutions. Throughout my time there, I have become intimately familiar with their operating systems and procedures. From time to time in my work, we would experience unit infidelity. In these cases, we would be required to remotely deactivate the unit for troubleshooting or decommission. Now, this next part is where it gets tricky. I don't have any direct experience with this but have heard rumors measures have been taken to make this possible. Somewhere in Quell HQ is a kill switch designed to boost the signal we use to override individual units. This would broadcast that frequency to power down all Bots in Quells system at once."

Zora spoke up, "I'm a big fan of the idea of hamstringing Quell like this, it would be the perfect fell swoop to take them out...but I see one hole. Our society is almost entirely dependent on the work that these Bots perform, aren't we risking a nationwide collapse if we turn off all of those machines?"

"We will certainly experience some adverse effects from this plan, I am confident that there will be a significant amount of panic nationwide. However, we needn't worry about the long-term effects. We can always reboot the Bots and bring them back online after we have deposed the heads of Quell. With the Bots under our control, we can direct them as we wish."

"Which begs the question of what we plan to do with the Bots if we pull this off," Dani pondered aloud.

Rahim waved his hand, "we'll cross that bridge when we come to it, we have bigger things to worry about first." Everyone nodded in agreement, with their plan of attack settled, they began discussing logistics for how they would execute this plan. "So, when should we schedule our flights to San Francisco?" asked Nia.

"NO!" shouted Chance, "that is a terrible idea. Quell undoubtedly has identified almost all of you as resistors and will be tracking your movements. Taking one of their jets will give them way too much time to prepare for you. AutoBots will be much more ideal, although I will have to tinker with them to disengage their tracking mechanisms. Fortunately, I have already taken the liberty of doing so to mine. Now we only need one of you to offer your vehicles and we will be able to drive down to Quell HQ."

A long silence greeted her, "um," said Dani, "none of us have AutoBots, those are far too expensive for any of us. We've always just used Quell's ferrying service."

Zora stepped forward, "actually I have an AutoBot. I've been fortunate to be able to raise an ample amount of funds from the Blues, it comes in handy for mobilization efforts. Do whatever you need to it, I'm happy to donate it to the cause, then we can be on our way." Just like that their plans were in motion.

* * *

A few days later they were on their way to San Francisco. Rahim, Nia, Chance, and Zora in one car. Lyall, Dani, and Kentrell in the other. It was a hard decision, choosing who to leave behind. Aamil's condition and Gavin's age limited them from coming along for the mission.

The others had been harder to sway, Rahim managed to convince Deandre he needed to stay to watch over his father and Gavin. Wanting to protect Linh and Tahmejia from danger, Rahim had simply given the hard truth that he wanted them to stay behind. Rahim still dwelled on the hurt they had shown in their eyes, but he convinced himself he did the right thing.

Rahim now sat in tense silence next to Nia, he wanted to lighten the mood, but due to his inability to make small talk, he was stumped. The only reprieve from the quietude was the brief chatter of Chance, who had no such limitations. Casually, she made observations of what she saw out the window as they drove along. Zora, sitting up front with Chance, occasionally indulged her by engaging in light conversation.

At last, they neared their destination, the iconic visage of the golden gate bridge standing brilliantly before their view. Driving by towering skyscrapers contrasted by narrowly built rustic neighborhoods, the group pulled into the Silicon Valley area. The reflective glass donut that was Quell Park greeted them.

They stopped some distance away to get their bearings and touch base with the other group. Stopping in a shaded parking lot, the two vehicles emptied their passengers, who proceeded to review the situation with one another. "How was your drive?" Rahim asked Lyall and the others.

"It was long but very pleasant," Dani answered first. "Kentrell here is quite the interesting fellow, it was nice finally getting to know him!"

Kentrell blushed and looked at his toes, "thanks Dani, I like you guys a lot too."

Lyall stretched and gave an ugly face, "my ass is killing me though, jeez that was a long few hours."

"You're telling me," muttered Zora in an uncharacteristic fashion.

"Does anybody have an idea of the situation we are stumbling into yet? Anybody see anything fishy when you drove up?" questioned Dani.

"I did see a few more SecurityBots than normal roaming around the entrance to Quell Park," answered Chance. "It seems they are prepared for some sort of retaliation, even if they may not have specific details. I wouldn't be too worried though, if they knew we were coming, I assume the security detail would be larger."

"Do you think we should gather more information before we make our move?" Rahim asked, "we were planning on striking at night and there's still daylight left, so if we want to do recon, now's the time."

"I have been in contact with Kabir, he is giving me updates on the status of the interior of the building. They are keeping a close monitor on who is entering and leaving. He can't go examine the exterior without arousing suspicion. According to Kabir, several fighters have been brought into the building to provide extra security, they are scattered throughout the structure."

"I'll go check out the outside," volunteered Nia. Rahim began to object but was silenced, "aside from Rahim I'm the fastest one here, and I'm also the least conspicuous. I can get around the area without being noticed. I have a lot of practice going through covert operations."

They consented to her plan, Nia went off on her own to scour the area for potential dangers to their mission. An hour later, the last hours of daylight leaving the sky, she returned with her findings. "There are SecurityBots stationed throughout the park, three standing guard over the main entrance, two over the side entrance. It doesn't appear we have an option to enter the premises without a struggle, at least none that have presented themselves to me anyway."

Rahim scratched his chin, thinking for a second. Sighing, he agreed, "well I guess the old-fashioned way it is. It's a good thing we brought equipment for just such a scenario."

Zora walked over to the trunks of the AutoBots, "yep, it's all in here." Opening the trunks, they revealed several poles that appeared similar to scythes. Though much shorter, with straight triangular-shaped blades on the sides instead of curved ones. They appeared much more suited to close-range combat with the piercing power to stab a hole in whatever they were slammed into. Alongside them were several rifles with a large box of ammunition.

Lyall balked after seeing those, "what exactly are we supposed to do with these? Everybody knows that SecurityBots are too dangerous to take in a fight. Are you expecting us to engage them? They're bulletproof for one, and what exactly are those stick things going to do?"

Zora smiled, "don't worry your pretty little head about it. My people have been combating Quells Bots for some time now and we are well suited to the task. You are right that SecurityBots have advantages that would make it normally unwise to confront them. However, we have planned around their weaknesses. They are very strong and durable yes, but not undefeatable. These sticks here are pikes that were designed to blow past the SecurityBots defenses. The SecurityBots exterior is composed of aluminum melted around a metal composite foam, the blades on these pikes are made of carbon steel. The design of the pikes is such that they allow you to deliver an exceptionally powerful punch. When delivered to places with thin protection, such as the heads of the SecurityBots, it allows us to penetrate and destroy the system functions of the Bot. You are also right that SecurityBots are normally bulletproof. However, these are not ordinary rounds, these are armor-piercing. We don't have many though, so make sure you are using your shots wisely. I am going to send in a squadron of Blues to cause a diversion. They'll draw in as many SecurityBots as they can, so we can sneak in mostly unmolested. Hopefully, we won't have to actually use these."

"What about the human fighters they brought in, how should we handle the situation if we encounter them?" Dani asked.

This had been a moment of tense debate between Zora and Rahim, but they had managed to reach a place of compromise. Rahim answered Dani, "first and foremost try to evade them as much as you can, but if conflict becomes unavoidable, aim to wound as much as you can and not kill. I would say preferably try and stick to hand-to-hand combat, but that is a privileged thing for me to say and not my place to make you risk your lives in that way. For all we know, the human fighters are armed as well and that kind of engagement won't be possible. I can't tell you to try and enter a battle you don't think you can win. Use your best judgment and just make sure your first priority is your own safety." Everybody nodded solemnly, grim looks of resignation on their faces for the harsh reality yet to come.

Having figured out their plan of attack, Zora sent her followers to assemble at the main entrance of Quell Park. The rest of them gathered near a side entrance, awaiting their chance to rush into the campus. A thunderclap rippled through the air, an explosion boomed near the main entrance.

Tall pillars of flame and smoke plumed in the sky, heat warmed their skin even though they were hundreds of meters away from the explosion. Rahim grew worried, he gave an irate look towards Zora, "you could have warned us you were planning that, that better not have hurt anybody"

She was unapologetic in her response, "what do you want from me? I'm doing my best here." Security all around the area stirred a commotion, swarmed to the site of the blast. Shots could be heard as Zora's people began to pick off the Bots under the cover of smoke.

Once they felt the coast was clear, the group rushed onto the grounds and began to beeline towards the facility. They were relieved to see that the doors of the facility were clear as they approached. Ducking near some shrubbery, they waited for Chance to notify them that Kabir had opened the doors to the building. She gave them a thumbs up and they walked in through the doors.

From there the real search began, "Kabir should have deactivated the camera systems, so we ought to be able to move around without them knowing our movements. They still have security on the inside though, so keep a low profile and try not to make too much noise. Let's disperse, if anybody needs help, notify the others. We'll be looking for a room labeled 'Command Center' so let me know if you find it. There are multiple levels to this building, so I say, Lyall, Dani, Kentrell, and Zora should go down to investigate the lower levels. Rahim, Nia, and I will proceed upward and investigate those levels as we go. Sounds good?" Everyone agreed to the plan and they parted ways.

Rahim walked off with Chance and Nia, investigating the upper levels. They tentatively peeked around every corner, making their way to the stairs. Strangely most of the base floor was clear of any dangers, no souls present to get in their way. A few moments later they arrived at the stairs which went upward several levels. Tiptoeing up the first flight, they peeked around the corner and did not see anyone in the immediate vicinity of where they were.

Seeing that the coast was clear, they slid onto the first floor, passing by several department doors that Chance assured them were pointless in investigating. Their first hiccup was when they reached the end of the hallway and approached a socializing area, set near the next flight of stairs. Vigilantly posted around the various sofas and armchairs set around the room, were two SecurityBots and what appeared to be one of Quell's fighters. The fighter was a blonde man of middling height, "somebody you know?" Rahim asked Nia.

"Yeah, his name is Brandon, you shouldn't have much trouble with him." She hesitated, "try not to hurt him though, he's not a bad guy."

"Surprise surprise, the ice queen has a soft spot," Rahim teased.

"He's the least of our problems anyway, those Bots are very sensitive to movement. So, unless we play this perfectly, we are going to get in a scuffle earlier than we'd like. We'd probably end up alerting everyone else in the building," Chance said in a hushed whisper.

Rahim thought for a moment, "if we could just draw them into one spot then maybe we could take them all out without too much of a sound. They have three-hundred-and-sixty-degree vision, so our odds of sneaking up on them are low. Unless they happen to be preoccupied, even then, any strike will have to be sudden. You guys have your pikes?"

They both pulled theirs out from where it was slung on their backs, "right here," Chance said.

"Ok," said Rahim. "I'm going to stay low and out of sight, I'm gonna try and take out Brandon in one move. The Bots are going to come over to take me out when I do. I want you to come in low once they move towards me and spring on them from behind to strike their soft spots."

The girls seemed nervous about the idea but ultimately agreed. Rahim got low to the ground and carefully crawled behind one of the sofas in the room. He took the utmost care to place his hands and feet as softly as he could, one after the other. He could not make himself completely silent, to his dismay, even the slightest sounds he made caused his heart to feel like it would beat out of his chest.

Fortunately for him, the guards seemed too preoccupied looking out of the window at the commotion outside and didn't seem to notice his bumbling. He was close enough now to Brandon that he could smell the slight perspiration wafting from him.

Concentrating, Rahim visualized his approach intently, there would be no room for mistakes here. Tensing his muscles, he coiled himself up and sprung himself to wrap around his opponent like a boa constrictor. Rahim's arm quickly snapped around Brandon's neck and latched onto his other bicep. His legs wrapped around his opponent, locking Rahim into place.

In one motion, he and Brandon went crashing to the ground. Brandon scrabbled at his neck to free himself, all the while his face turned redder and redder as the air was squeezed from his body. The SecurityBots almost immediately turned to apprehend Rahim. They approached him with a menacing glare in their mechanic eyes.

Praying this plan would work, Rahim held on and hoped that Nia and Chance could pull through. Just as the claw-like hands of the SecurityBots began to clamp around Rahim, their metal exterior chilling him as they made contact, a WHAM! erupted from behind them and they crumpled atop Rahim and Brandon.

Rahim winced with pain and struggled to keep his grip after the impact. He managed to hold on until Brandon slumped in his grasp, all resistance fading away. Nia and Chance pulled Rahim out and helped him to his feet. Looking over he saw the pikes buried in the heads of the Bots, their circuits chopped up and exposed around the blades of the weapons. "Thanks, guys, that had me worried for a second, glad to have you on my side."

Nia punched him in the shoulder, "come on have a bit more faith in us, it's not like there was any chance we would let ourselves fail this early in the game."

They retrieved their weapons from the heads of the Bots and zip-tied Brandon's hands behind his back. Nia gave him one last sympathetic look as they did so. "Shall we move on?" Chance asked, indicating with her hands for them to take the lead up the stairs. Moving upward, they made it to the third floor, "this is the floor I work on," Chance informed them. "I'm certain it's not here, so we can just move forward. There are only two floors above us, so it'll either be there or it will be in the lower levels that the rest of the gang are digging into."

They traveled down a corridor and up another flight of stairs. Peeking around the corner to scout the fourth floor, they spotted the ankles of three fighters and a lab coat standing a distance away from them. Ducking back down the stairs they moved away till they felt they were out of earshot.

"I'm not sure if we can scout them out without giving ourselves away, what do we do?" Nia asked. Rahim was stumped on this one, he had no answers. The only thing he could think of would be to bullrush and hope that the people weren't armed.

"I have an idea, but there's still a chance they might see us," said Chance. "I have a small makeup mirror in my pocket, it's possible we can peek it around the corner to get a glimpse of the situation. There's a small chance they spot the mirror. Do you think we should risk it?" Nia and Rahim looked at each other, they didn't have a better option at the moment so they agreed to Chance's plan. Chance went ahead of Nia and Rahim to look into what they were up against. She was sweating bullets as she neared the top of the stairs again.

Carefully she extended the mirror out and angled it so she could see what was around the corner. Chance's hands shook anxiously, fortunately, she got a good view without being found out. She spotted two of them holding guns, while the other two appeared to be unarmed. It appeared that their initial count was correct and there were no more people on this level.

Chance rushed back to Rahim and Nia with her information. They were dismayed to hear the situation awaiting them. Rahim seemed conflicted, he was hesitant to resort to armed force but his eyes kept resting on the rifles they brought with them. "I hoped it wouldn't have to come to this," he said.

Nia seemed much more adamant about their course of action than he, "we don't have much other option. It's either we give up now and let Quell win, or we do what must be done and get our hands dirty. There's no other way. Not only are they armed, but we're outnumbered, brawling isn't going to get us out of this."

Chance thought about it for a second and proposed her own idea, "look I don't like the idea of such violent tactics either Rahim, but I also agree with Nia that we don't have a ton of options. What if we tried a stalemate, if we got the drop on them we could threaten them into giving up their weapons and get them out of the way peacefully."

Nia didn't seem convinced, "But what if they call our bluff and start shooting? I know these people, and they will do anything to win, anything. I wouldn't put it past them to just shoot anyways without regard for their own safety."

Chance shook her head, "look you're right, but I just can't think of a better way. Unless we think of something else, the only choice is to get blood on our hands, and I'm not sure if I'm ready to do that."

Nia glared at her, "and how much blood will be on your hands if we let these people continue to get away with exploiting and using everyone?"

Rahim began to interject but his attention was caught by something on the ceiling of the corridor, "Chance is that what I think it is?"

Chance look puzzled, "it's just a fire alarm why do you ask? Ohh..."

Rahim smiled, "so you're following what I'm thinking?"

"I think so, but how exactly are we going to play this? We still won't know how they'll react if we set the alarms off."

"We'll just have to hope things go our way on this one, hopefully, they will be disoriented enough that we can rush them and if worst comes to worst then we can go with the nuclear option." They then discussed and put themselves in position. Rahim accepted a lighter from Chance and went on his tiptoes to hold the flame near the smoke detector. Almost immediately, sirens began going off and sprinklers rained water from the ceiling.

The group quickly became drenched, their gambit paid off though as they could hear the people above scrambling around in confusion. Darting down the stairs, the fighters ran past where Nia and Chance were hiding without noticing them. Just as the last of the people passed, they jumped out and tangled the ankles of the last two, knocking them down and sending their weapons flying from their hands. The front two, a fighter and a lab coat turned around and began to raise their weapons to point at Nia and Chance.

Nia was astonished to recognize the lab coat standing in front of her, none other than Dr. Galton. Glancing at the people she had downed, she recognized one of them to be Han. Nia snarled, "great, a get-together with all of my least favorite people. I'm so sad to have been invited."

Dr. Galton sneered, leveling his gun at Nia, "sorry to disappoint. Luckily, you won't have to worry about any future reunions."

He was disrupted by Rahim coming from behind, kicking Galton to the ground, and throwing a vicious hook to the fighter's temple. Dropping down, he rained another punch onto the one he just hit, finishing them. He turned to deal with the one he kicked, who was now rising.

Meanwhile, Chance and Nia had desperately pounced atop the ones they had tripped up, hitting them. Chance was quickly becoming overwhelmed by the superior strength and ability of the one she was on. Nia held her own against Han but could sense the tide turning against her as the person next to her dealt with Chance. Flinging Chance off of him, the man sent her flying painfully into the hard stone stairs, where she cried out. Turning he went to help Han, who Nia was rapidly punching and elbowing in the head.

Noticing she was now outnumbered, Nia somersaulted off of her former teacher and spun to face them both. Back against the wall, her heart began to race as she worried she would be overtaken. Han seemed flustered by Nia getting the drop on him. Wiping blood from his face with the back of his hand, he spat at her. "You always were a terrible student, I think it's time for your final lesson."

Flashbacks ran through Nia's mind as she remembered all of the merciless beatings she had received at the hands of the man in front of her. Gritting her teeth, she growled at him, letting him know she was no longer afraid of him. She knew she was outnumbered though and was concerned she might not be able to handle the both of them.

Her concerns were alleviated though when the man next to Han was dropped by Rahim. This just left Han facing both Rahim and Nia, trying to goad Nia, he shouted at her, "so this is how it is? You're too afraid to take me on your own? Just as pathetic as when you were a child. You're just as weak as Kolby, and you'll end up dead like him too."

Rahim put his hand on Nia's shoulder, "don't let him provoke you, let's just take him out."

She pushed his hand away, "I don't care, let me have this." Nia paced forward to meet Han, his widows peak dipped in concentration. He shot out like a cork out of a bottle, swinging savagely. Though he was larger and stronger, he possessed a key weakness that she did not.

Nimbly she dodged his opening punch, cocking her leg back, she slammed it right between his legs. Face turning scarlet, he doubled over in pain, the wind knocked out of him. Malevolently she grabbed fistfuls of his hair and yanked his head to meet her knee. He fell to the ground moaning in pain. A fiendish expression on her face, Nia grabbed her pike from where it lay.

Rahim moved to stop her, "Nia, he's done. You don't need to do this."

She snapped at him, a dark look in her eye, "get away from me if you know what's good for you, Rahim. He's going to get what's coming to him and you won't stop me." Turning the spike away, she ruthlessly beat the blunt end of the metal pole into Han's ribs. "TELL ME WHAT HAPPENED TO KOLBY!"

Whimpering, too dazed to answer, Han held his hands up, "please show mercy." He wheezed weakly.

Nia cackled, "don't you remember Han? Kindness is weakness." She turned the sharp end of the pike to face him and raised it, but it was stuck in place when she tried to bring it down.

Rahim stood behind her, holding the pike, "You've had your fill of revenge on him. Any further and you'll go down a path you might not be able to return from. I don't know what this man has done to you but debasing yourself for petty revenge only lets him win. Let's do what we came here to do." Nia's expression softened, she sagged into Rahim and let him take the weapon from her.

"How poetic."

Rahim and Nia turned to see who had spoken and were horrified to see Dr. Galton had come to. He was standing over Chance, who still lay prone on the ground, pointing a gun at her head. "Get away from her," Nia hissed.

Dr. Galton wagged his finger, "now now, you wouldn't want to make me angry, would you? I could get so worked up that my finger just might slip." Rahim and Nia were frozen, like a deer in front of the headlights, they saw only their ends before them.

Just as despair consumed them, a thump resounded, and Dr. Galton made a peculiar expression. He fell forward comically onto his face, standing behind him was a man wearing a turban, holding a fire extinguisher. Kneeling, he tenderly put his hands on Chance's shoulders, concern was written all over his face. She slowly came to and looked up, putting a hand on his cheek, she whispered, "Kabir, when did you get here."

"Just in the nick of time it seems, are you alright?" he asked.

She nodded and looked to Rahim and Nia, "are you guys ok?" They indicated that they were.

Rahim then received a call, it was Zora. Answering the phone, she spoke without waiting for him to greet her, "we found the room, it's on the bottom floor." Rahim was ecstatic to have all of the guessing taken away, "we'll be right there," he responded. He then relayed the information to Nia, Chance, and Kabir.

The group bound Galton and the fighters and hightailed it downstairs. "I'm happy we found the place, but couldn't it have happened before we went to all of that trouble? That was such a waste of time," Chance moaned.

"Look at it this way, we were going to have to deal with them at some point, so better we got it out of the way now, right?" Rahim reassured her. They went as fast they could without stumbling and hurting themselves down the stairs. They ended up having to travel down three floors after reaching the base level, just to get to the bottom. Once they got there, they found a trail of four destroyed SecurityBots and a zip-tied fighter on the ground.

Going forward, they eventually reached the other group, "so it seems you guys didn't have too much trouble handling yourselves. Is anyone hurt?" Rahim asked. They all confirmed that they were fine, their group stood before a door labeled 'Command Center'.

Opening the door they were surprised to see an empty room, well, almost empty. A platform stood in the center of the room, and a door was set in the far wall. Entering, the platform lit up with a hologram of none other than Rommel. "Somebody loves their theatrics," Lyall muttered behind Rahim.

"So kind of you to join me, your entrance was most spectacular. The explosion was a nice touch, you dealt with my security in short fashion. If I was actually here I would be in big trouble. Chance, darling, it's so wonderful to see you again, I was wondering if I ever would after you stopped showing up here. And Nia? Now that is a surprise, you were always so faithful in your assignments, I never expected you would turncoat. Since you are here, I suppose all of you are searching for the kill switch? Quite the clever plan, astute of you to know that you could never defeat me without it. However, unfortunately for you, it was a fruitless endeavor, as that control is safe and sound with me in a place you will never reach. I am not without my manners though, so I have taken it upon myself to leave some company to entertain you in my absence."

As the last word fell off of his lips, the image of the hologram was disturbed by a pair of figures walking through it. The door on the other side of the room was now open, standing before the group was a man and a woman. The both of them had perfectly proportional features, matching one another right down to the dead eyes that peered out from their faces. The only difference between the two being that the man had a taller and slightly wider build. Rahim had an ugly feeling about what they were up against, he remembered his encounter with a similar individual when he forfeited his last match. "I don't like this at all," he voiced to the others, "anybody have any ideas?"

The pair didn't give anybody time to answer, speaking in unison, their voices echoed eerily towards Rahim and the others. "Hello, won't you join us? You have shown admirable fortitude in making it this far, it would be a shame to waste the talents you possess. Forget your endeavor and stay with us for a while...so that we need not hurt you."

"Yeah, fuck this noise, what should we do?" Lyall bemoaned.

Chance spoke up, "I think I might know where Rommel is, but I don't know if we can bring everybody without being slowed down. Not to mention, I have a funny feeling our new friends here might be in hot pursuit if we try to leave."

Zora stepped up, "go on ahead, you and Rahim go after him. We will stay here and do what we can to give you time, just do what needs to be done."

Rahim nodded and began to leave with Chance, but felt his arm grabbed. "I'm going with you guys," said Nia.

"Of course you are," Rahim agreed.

"I'm coming with you too!" announced Kabir. Chance tried to argue but he wasn't having any of it, "I'm not going to let you go into danger without me, I'm staying by your side." She relented and the four of them went to leave. That left the rest of the group to face off against the androids that stood before them.

* * *

Rahim, Chance, Kabir, and Nia raced up the stairs and outside to get off of the premises. A battle zone awaited them when they got out of the building. Zora's followers and the Bots had been in the thick of it while they were in Quell's facility. Broken down Bots were strewn all over the grounds. A few Blues could be seen beaten down and dead near the main entrance. Pained by the site of the carnage, they kept moving to get back to where Chance's

AutoBot was waiting for them. "So where do you think Rommel is?" Rahim asked Chance.

A dark look came over her face, "the only other place where I know he spends his time, his home. He lives near where I grew up so I'm very familiar with the location of his estate, although I've never been inside personally. Once we get inside it will be a complete mystery to me. Knowing Rommel, I'm sure there will be more than a few nasty surprises in store for us."

The others grimly nodded, soon thereafter they reached Chance's vehicle and they were being whisked away to Hillsborough. The atmosphere among the four was tense, anxiously waiting to arrive at Rommel's residence.

Although the drive was short in actuality, time seemed to come to a standstill, every worst possible scenario playing through their minds. Finally, they pulled up to their destination. The giant wall encircling the neighborhood, stood tall consuming their view. A suspicion came over Chance as they drew near, "I think we should go the rest of the way on foot."

"Why?" asked Nia.

"Something tells me that I won't be able to get access to the gate, if Rommel is suspecting us then he likely barred me from the system."

Kabir chimed in, "what other way in is there though, Chance? The wall is too seamless and too tall to scale. At least to my knowledge, this is the only way in."

"I mean, what harm is there in trying? Worst case scenario we can't get in and then we have to try another way right?" suggested Rahim.

"I guess..."

"Ok then, let's do this."

They drove up to the receptacle where Chance leaned out of the vehicle to have her retina scanned. To her surprise, it went through and the gate opened. As it opened though, they could spot about a dozen SecurityBots waiting for them directly in front of the gate. "DRIVE DRIVE DRIVE," Rahim yelled. Chance floored it and they drove right over the first of the SecurityBots. A vicious thump rocked the AutoBot as the tires popped over the Bots.

A scraping noise could be heard from the sides as two SecurityBots were able to latch onto the side of the vehicle, hanging on to be dragged by the AutoBot. Nia and Rahim looked out their windows in panic, seeing the Bots hanging on to stay with them. Frantically, they opened their doors and kicked their feet out of the cars into the exposed torsos of the Bots. After a few kicks, they were able to dislodge the Bots and keep driving. Everyone was breathing heavily after that,

"WHAT WERE YOU SAYING? WHAT'S THE WORST THAT CAN HAPPEN??" Chance screamed back at Rahim.

"Hey, we didn't die, right? How the hell was I supposed to know they were on the other side waiting for us."

"Maybe if you had taken a second to think about it you could have predicted that!" Nia yelled.

"I don't need this from you! Let's just be happy we're ok and keep moving alright?"

"There was no other way, this isn't Rahim's fault." Kabir vouched for him.

"THANK YOU! You're alright Kabir, this guy gets it," Rahim huffed.

An awful noise followed them, the damage done to the vehicle causing a grotesque whining sound. "My poor ears," Nia complained.

"I'm stopping the car," Chance said.

"The sound isn't THAT bad," opined Rahim.

"It's not that, well that's part of it, but there are other escorts of SecurityBots up ahead. We need to get out on foot from here so we can avoid any further confrontations. We won't be able to take any more damage, and then we'll be surrounded with no options."

"Oh yeah, that would kinda blow," agreed Rahim. They got out of the vehicle and slunk off down a side street to avoid running into the patrols of SecurityBots. "It's just a mile or so north of our direction, and then we should be there," said Chance. They traveled amidst the trees and shrubbery till they drew near Rommel's estate.

Quite the obnoxious structure, it was simply enormous. The lawn surrounding the mansion was the size of three football fields, with a massive pool in the front of the estate. Exotic trees were planted everywhere, dutifully maintained by the automated gardening systems installed.

The house itself was even more impressive, classical stonework designs embedded in the face of the mansion. Stone lions guarded either side of the tall black doors that made up the entrance. A helicopter pad was stationed atop the roof of the mansion, which was seven stories tall. Rahim whistled, "man rich people have bad taste, I have to say this house is freaking huge though."

Chance shrugged as she was used to the sight, "yeah this is a bit larger than the other homes around here, but yeah you might be right. Rich people just have bad taste."

They circled the perimeter, but surprisingly where there were scores of SecurityBots patrolling the surrounding areas, here nothing was guarding the house. The situation suspicious to them but they went forward anyway.

Kentrell

Kentrell experienced terror at the sight of the androids in front of them. All he could think of was the bloody sight of Elliot being murdered on tv. He clutched the pike he had been given desperately. He had no sense of confidence that he could step up to the plate and be of any help to anybody.

After Rahim, Nia, Chance, and the man with them had left, the androids had tried to follow, but were swiftly blocked by Lyall and the others. Kentrell stood behind, watching them square off. "You would be wise to get out of our way," the female android said in a chilling tone.

"You think that we would just let you stop our friends? That we'd let you break down everything we've worked so hard to achieve? Your wiring must be faulty, maybe a few bangs on the head will knock sense into you," Lyall stated. Lyall was much bigger than the androids, but for some reason, Kentrell got the sense from looking at them that they weren't worried in the slightest.

They took another step forward, prompting Lyall to throw a wide punch at the male-looking one's head. The android reacted with frightening speed, ducking to block the punch and turning to pick up Lyall in a fireman's carry as if he weighed nothing. Tossing him to the ground, Lyall landed with a sickening thud.

Zora raised her gun to shoot the man in the head, but the female darted forward and knocked the weapon aside, grabbing Zora by the throat. Dani lunged in to tangle up the legs of the female. The three of them went tumbling to the floor.

Kentrell stood by holding the pike Zora had given him, watching his comrades engage with the machines. The three women tangled together on the floor, while Lyall stirred to his feet to continue his bout with the other android. *Move dammit, move! Why can't I bring myself to help my friends? I know there must be something I can do, but what if I just get in their way?*

Lyall was now grappling with the other android, being manhandled in the process but hanging in there. Dani and Zora had successfully managed to at least prevent the other android from getting up, but it was a losing battle. *They know they can't win, but they keep trying anyway. If they can fight when things are hopeless, then why can't I? What makes us different?* Kentrell's knees shook as he underwent an internal battle, fighting off the weights that his subconscious placed on him.

At last, he gripped the pike in his hands tighter till his knuckles turned white. Baring his teeth, he audibly shouted "NO!" although no one seemed to register, preoccupied as they were. The female android had gotten to its feet at this point. Zora was doubled over and wheezing on the ground, Dani being lifted off her feet, the android's hands around her throat.

Kentrell steeled himself, and with more conviction than he had ever had in his life, swung the pike into the back of the android's head. Translucent liquid spilled out around the blade, the android convulsed and crumbled to its knees, dropping Dani as it fell.

The women looked gratefully at Kentrell as he stood before them, breathing heavily from the adrenaline that coursed through his veins. "Thank you, Kentrell, you saved us," Dani said with a weak smile.

Zora gave him a nod of approval, "we would have failed without you, you did well Kentrell." *I helped? I actually helped? Maybe I'm not worthless after all?* He thought to himself. Realizing that they weren't out of the woods yet, they turned to the other struggle still ensuing in the room.

Lyall was losing badly to the android. He clung desperately to the android's legs in an attempt to drag it to the floor. The android, meanwhile, was beating him about the head and shoulders with hammer fists. Blood dripped profusely from several places all over Lyall's body.

Kentrell and the two women stepped forward to assist Lyall, hoping that their superior numbers would overwhelm the android. Kentrell tried the same move again, coming at the head of the android with his pike, it wasn't nearly as effective this time though.

The android paused from its onslaught against Lyall, raised its hand, and merely caught the handle of Kentrell's weapon. It tugged the weapon from his hand as if it was a toy and chucked it across the room. Kentrell and the two women then bull-rushed the android, who lashed out with a punch that connected and badly hurt Kentrell. Zora and Chance were able to get in though and knock over the android. Pulling Lyall back, they regrouped. The android got up and faced off against the four of them.

Lyall was still in pretty bad shape, and Kentrell held his jaw that he thought might be dislocated. Without a word, they all knew their best strategy and fanned out to encircle the android. The android gave a creepy smile as they boxed it in. They closed in closer and closer, hoping to restrict its freedom of movement so they could deal with it. In a flash of movement, it lashed out a kick that connected with Dani's gut. She was able to hang on, getting dragged backward by the leg like she was a child.

Taking advantage of the android's reduced mobility, Kentrell stepped forward to try and wrap himself around the thing's torso. Just like before, the android swung a punch to catch Kentrell as he was coming in, but Kentrell was ready this time. He waited just long enough to dodge before springing forward to wrap himself around the android. Zora came in simultaneously from behind and also wrapped her arms around the android. Her arms snapped around the thing's shoulders to limit its arms from moving around. Though her grasp was paper-thin compared to the much greater strength of the android.

Slowly, they twisted the android's joints till it dropped to its knees, temporarily overwhelmed by the superior numbers. It wriggled to free itself from their grasp, all of them holding on for dear life. Lyall chose that moment to make his move, stepping in, he wrapped his thick arm around the android's neck and squeezed tightly. The machine did not need oxygen to function, so it appeared unaffected by the move.

Presciently, this was not what Lyall intended. Using the weight of the others to pin it in place, he gripped both of his hands together and wrenched his arm even tighter, pulling upward. The veins bulged in Lyall's neck as he strained with all of his might, pulling, and pulling, and pulling.

A tearing sound started to come from deep within the android's body. Giving a herculean heave, Lyall began to rip the head off of the thing's body. With one last pull, using the last of his strength, he ripped the head clean off of the body of the android. More of the translucent goop dripped out of the base of the neck, streaming off of the exposed wiring that now dangled loosely.

Lyall fell to his knees and breathed heavily, as did everyone else, the others rolling away from the android's body. Kentrell began maniacally laughing, the others soon following suit, relieved to be alive, they reveled in their victory.

"Rahim better come through for us or I swear I'll kill him," Zora stated. The others agreed wholeheartedly with her sentiment.

Rahim

Brandishing their weapons before them warily; Rahim, Nia, Kabir, and Chance carefully opened the doors of Rommel's home, which strangely were unlocked. Nia winced as the heavy doors closed with a thud, echoing throughout the reception area in the mansion. She shot daggers through her eyes at Rahim as he was the one to let the door close. "If nobody knew that we were here, they definitely do now" she hissed at him.

He regretted being so careless instantly but knew there was nothing he could do now, "sorry. Is it just me, or is it weird that we don't see any security inside of the building either?"

The interior of the home was spookily quiet, it looked more like a museum than a home really. Exotic vases and art pieces were situated throughout the room and along the walls as if the place was an exhibit. Wide lavishly decorated rooms extended in every direction from their vantage point in front of the doors. A winding spiral staircase ascended in front of them. Seeming to be the obvious choice, they took the stairs and went upwards.

They kept their ears peeled for anything suspicious that could possibly come out at them. However, it was not their ears that detected something strange, it was their noses that detected something off in the air around them. A repugnant odor permeated the air. The rancid smell grew stronger when they turned left. Following the scent, they traveled down a hallway towards a bedroom where the smell seemed strongest.

Plugging their noses out of nausea, they walked across an expensive rug and pushed the door open. Greeting them was a horrendous unexpected sight. A headless corpse lay in a king-sized four-poster bed, hands crossed over its chest.

Chance squirmed, "oh, god," she said. Bending over, she emptied the contents of her stomach onto the floor of the bedroom.

"Based on the blood around the base of the neck, it doesn't seem like this body was decapitated very long ago," commented Nia, seeming to be the only one not green around the gills.

"I just don't understand, what does this mean. Who is this? Obviously, this isn't right, but something REALLY doesn't seem right here," remarked Rahim.

While they speculated, Kabir had begun to explore the room. He noticed a small door ajar in the corner. Taking the initiative, he went forward before alerting the others. Just as he pushed his way through the door, he called to the others, "Hey guys, I found something." A second after he said that, and entered the room, a shocked, "oh, my, god," followed his entrance.

The others scurried across the room to see what the fuss was about, only to be a hair too late. A plexiglass wall slid over the entrance of the room that Kabir had just entered, trapping him inside. The others pounded on the glass, searching for a way to get him out until they looked past him.

The room Kabir was inside appeared to be positively frigid if the clouds his breath formed were any indication. Behind him were three marble pedestals. Atop each was a glass case, filled with viscous clear liquid.

Floating submerged in the liquid, were heads, one for each case. Kabir had his back turned to them, staring in horrified fascination at the spectacle before them. "There seem to be names on each pedestal," he called out. Indeed, there were gold plaques on each pedestal, lettering inscribed on each that was too far for the others to read. "Left to right, they say: Mathias Rommel, Manfred Rommel, Mitchell Rommel," Kabir told them."

"Mitch Rommel?" Rahim remarked, "that's our Rommel. How..." he stopped to think.

"This head does appear to be President Rommel," Kabir assured him.

"He seemed in full health when he spoke to us only a couple of hours ago. I know the guy is old and all, but this just doesn't add up. What happened?"

The others were speechless for multiple minutes. "Are you ok, Kabir?" Chance asked, seeming quite concerned.

"A bit chilly, but I'll be alright. Provided I'm not trapped in here too long at least." Kabir had wandered back over to the glass wall at this point. Preferring not to stand too close to the ominous heads now that his curiosity had been satiated.

Should we just go ahead and scour the house for the kill switch then?" Nia asked.

"I suppose that's the only course of action left to us at the moment," Rahim agreed.

Chance pressed her hand against the glass, "sit tight, Kabir, we'll be back for you." Moving on, the trio searched the rest of the bedroom vigorously. They were forced to pinch their noses to not gag from the smell of the corpse still in the bed. Stumped, they exited the room to search the house further.

Walking up to another floor, the soft sound of music could be heard floating from a far-off room. Giving each other strange looks, they went to investigate. Looking throughout the house, they followed the noise, the music growing louder as they drew closer.

A minute or so later, they came before a big white door, light shining underneath the cracks. The music was now identifiable as an ancient song from a bygone era. Guitar riffs, drums, and a high-pitched distorted sound could be heard, with the lyrics 'one motive no hope ah, yeah, born without a face' distinctly audible.

Rahim, Nia, and Chance gave each other incredulous looks, "who the hell is that?" Chance mouthed to them, the other two shrugged. Hesitantly, they turned the ornately carved door handle, pushing it inward to have their minds shattered.

Sitting before them, the name Mitch Rommel on a nameplate sitting on the desk he lounged behind, was none other than Rommel himself. Albeit a version of him that was significantly younger than the Rommel they had previously seen. *This can't be possible,* Rahim thought to himself. Feet propped on the desk, playing air guitar along to the music without a care in the world.

Unconcerned about the intruders who had just stepped into his office, Rommel gave them a nonchalant look, not seeming to care about their presence. A switch rested on his desk inside a glass case, the kill switch they could presume. "How is this possible, we just saw your head downstairs?" Chance questioned.

The Rommel before them put his hands up to his ears, "what?" he mouthed. Seemingly unable to hear them over the loud music playing around them. Chance began to repeat herself, but then Rommel gave a wink and turned off the music.

Chance repeated her question. "Oh, that old thing? I thought it was getting a bit too much wear and tear so I tossed it out. Kidding. The old coot fancied the idea of immortality so he thought that he'd create a better version of himself before he died."

Nia pressed him, "if that's why he created you, then what's the deal with the heads downstairs?"

Rommel shrugged, "Mitch certainly didn't get this idea in a vacuum. His grandfather was the first with such ambitions, though he envisioned himself achieving them through different avenues. After my creation, I decided it was only appropriate to put Mitch to rest in the same manner as his forebears. I also intended that room to be a nice trap for you all, but that oaf with you just had to trigger it too soon."

"So does this mean you're not Rommel?" Rahim asked.

"Good question, I suppose yes and no. I have his memories, his personality, and all of that good stuff. I even find myself identifying by his name, however, I can't help but picture myself as a completely separate being. Give whatever explanation that most suits you. Maybe I don't have his soul, maybe my circuits can never truly replicate his brain, in any case, I find myself unattached to that rotting corpse downstairs."

"So would you be interested in walking away and letting us have control of that switch there?"

"Heavens no, didn't I tell you? I still share an awful lot in common with Mitchy boy, which means that I still have his ambitions. Which, in this immortal body, are more attainable than ever. I do fancy the idea of being a god-king, using my vast resources to situate myself atop the global hierarchy, in deed if not in name." Rommel appeared lost in rapture just thinking about its plans.

The very idea disgusted Rahim, "so all of the lives that would suffer under your rule truly mean nothing to you then? The fact that you have enough resources to ensure that everyone lives comfortable meaningful lives, and you're withholding that, doesn't bother you at all?"

Rommel looked terribly bored, "not really no. The world belongs to me, by right of birth, why shouldn't I do with it what I wish? The old me, other me, whatever you want to call it, worked hard to get to where he is. His father worked hard, like his grandfather before him. Invented wonderful things that cleaned the earth and innovated in ways no one had ever dreamed, why shouldn't we get to reap the rewards? Those miserable scum who do nothing but whine about their miserable existences, don't deserve an easy handout. If they want success so bad they should work hard for it, they should take it for themselves. They can entertain me, and as a reward for their hard work, I'll toss scraps their way to keep them satisfied. To the spoils the victor, and the losers, the scraps. They can blame the wretches at the bottom of the pyramid for mooching off of their hard work and causing their demise, and envy those above them who have it better in life. The perfect incentive to work hard and seek out the American dream. It works out wonderfully in my favor, why would I change that? So people can start getting big ideas in their heads and think that one day they can usurp me? The idea that anyone could take my place is ridiculous. No no no, I think I shall continue taking as I please and doing as I please, as I so rightfully deserve."

Rahim could not tolerate the words he was hearing, they were antithetical to his beliefs. The thought of how much suffering was being allowed just to satiate the ego of this douchebag, infuriated him. The senseless cruelty of it all baffled him, he cursed whatever gods may be for allowing such mass hardship for no good reason.

All of the people living with broken bodies like his father, from lack of ability to pay for medical care ran through his mind. Those who put themselves through the meatgrinder in the cages day after day just to make ends meet. The people who couldn't fight, who were made to live off of scraps and exist as the butt of others scorn, those who went hungry at night.

All easily preventable, all being held over their heads to coerce them into participating in this crazy ritual. Just for the sake of a broken ideology that didn't care for a single human life.

Blood boiling, he turned to his darker impulses and raised the gun he held in his grasp. Lifting it, he aimed and fired at Rommel's head....only to bounce off. A bloody scrape was all that indicated that he had even shot it, red-stained metal revealed underneath its skin. *Bloody android,* he thought to himself, too angry to even laugh at the pun. Rommel looked bored, "was that supposed to hurt me?"

Rahim was shocked, wondering how he hadn't been able to inflict any serious damage. The armor-piercing bullets were supposed to work. Rommel laughed, "I guess you were counting on those armor-piercing bullets to do the job? Unfortunately for you, I am made of sterner stuff than my other counterparts made previous to me. You will never defeat me with those paltry toys, not with that, not with anything. It is as I said, I shall lord over this world in perpetuity, as is my right. I will take what I want, at the moment I fancy taking your life, so perhaps I shall."

"I'd like to see you try," Nia barked at it. Rommel grinned in response, its lifeless eyes glinting creepily. Rommel stood and approached them menacingly. Going forward, they took out their pikes and carefully circled it.

Rahim was the first to go, taking a large swing at Rommel's gut, only for Rommel to rip the pike out of his hand and toss it away. As one might slap a petulant child, Rommel struck Rahim across the face with an open hand. The slap echoed through Rahim's skull and sent him flying to the ground, blood dripping from his lip.

Nia and Chance ferociously came at Rommel from both sides with their pikes. It managed to stop Chance's blow, but Nia was too elusive and managed to land a hit that stuck into Rommel's cheekbone. It did nothing to penetrate or damage its inner workings, but it did manage to rip off the artificial flesh on its cheek, giving it a grisly appearance.

Not seeming to care about the exterior damage done to it, it complained lightly, "do you have any idea how much of a pain in the ass that skin is going to be to replace? Not very, but still, it's a nuisance." Ripping Chance's pike out of her hand it flipped it over and jammed it in her leg, "how do you like it?" it said. Chance screamed in agony, falling over, blood pouring down her leg where it had struck her.

Rahim and Nia leaped in front of her protectively, the two of them squaring off against Rommel. Rommel smirked, seeming unconcerned about the ordinarily formidable duo that stood in front of it. Zipping forward, it grabbed Nia by the throat and lifted her. She twitched as her mind finally processed what had happened, the unreal speed of Rommel taking her by surprise.

Rahim howled in anger and punched Rommel several times in the face, eliciting no reaction. "For all of your ideals, all of your righteous anger, when it's time to act, you are helpless. You spout all of this nonsense about caring for others, about the dignity of human life, but have no power to act. Look at me? I'm powerful, when it comes time for action, I take what I want and nothing will get in my way. You don't deserve to see out your vision, you never did. Because deep down you're just a pathetic loser who is unable to do what is necessary."

Its words cut Rahim deeply, his desperation at being unable to save Nia swelling within. In a manic effort, he stepped behind Rommel and wrapped his arms around its waist, picking it up. Fortunately, its weight did not match its durability. The motion caused it to drop Nia in the process. Leaning backward, Rahim suplexed Rommel, throwing it head over heels to slam its head onto the ground.

This move did not damage Rommel, but it did slow it for long enough to stop its assault on the two and slightly disorient it. It quickly got up, irritation showing on its face. It then easily picked up Rahim by the throat and bent over to re-pick up Nia, holding the both of them at arm's length. Scrabbling at its arms, they tried to speak but couldn't summon the air required. "What was that?" it said mockingly.

Loosening its grip, he allowed them to talk, "look behind you," Rahim said. Turning its head, Rommel was terrified to see Chance leaning on the desk.

Haggard from blood loss, her hand hovered over the kill switch, trembling. "Eat shit you elitist pig," she yelled before slamming her hand down onto the button. Right when she did so, Rommel slumped down to the ground, its body completely deactivated. The three looked at each other in relief and cried, at last, it was all over. The day had been won and they accomplished what they set out to do.

Epilogue

Over a month had passed since that pivotal encounter with Rommel. They had won and taken control of Quell's network of Bots, but the storm had not completely subsided. Chance, leading a new more thoroughly vetted team of technicians, was able to get the Bots back up and running again after many weeks. It was not a moment too soon, for hysteria had begun to take over the public.

So attached to machines for their everyday needs, people feared for the worst. Even so, the Bots hiatus from operations were the least of everyone's worries. All public authority had long since been divested into the hands of Quell, leaving no governing body equipped to take control in their absence.

Grappling with this dilemma, Zora had continued their hostile takeover of Quell, attempting to purge dissidents from the company. It was to discuss these matters, that Rahim found himself on his way to meet with Zora and several others.

Entering a room, he saw Zora sitting at a circular table with her head buried in her hands. Sitting around the table alongside her, were a multitude of individuals engaged deep in discussion. Also sitting at the table were Dani, Chance, and Kabir, they waved excitedly when they saw Rahim enter the room. Standing off in the corner of the room was Nia.

Not expecting her to be there, Rahim glowed at the sight. He hadn't seen her since that fateful day a month ago. Before he could speak with her though, Zora noticed him and eagerly beckoned him over. "Oh, Rahim, you would not believe the mess that has fallen into my lap the last month."

Rahim grew serious, "I have some idea, I've been hearing about the turmoil brewing all over the country. So, the Reds have still been mounting coups?"

Zora laughed darkly, "I suppose you could hardly call it a coup since we have yet to establish a legitimate base of authority, but yes. Armed attacks have increasingly been taking place, we hope getting the SecurityBots back online will deter the violence, but I doubt it. What's worse is the foundations of Quell that have yet to be addressed. Nia there has been a blessing, aiding us in identifying and locating fighters and officials that worked for Quell. The bigger issue is the international operations Quell maintained abroad. Their stranglehold was primarily on the US, but they still have seeds of influence throughout the globe. I suspect we will be overcoming many an obstacle for some time."

The news troubled Rahim, "Just let me know if there is anything I can do to assist you in any way. How have relations with the general population gone?"

Zora rubbed her fingers against her temple, "not good. For many reasons. People have spent their entire lives in this system, as terrible as it may be, it's all they know. If it's one thing people fear, it's the unknown. They will put up with an incredible amount of hardship so long as it is familiar to them. We have already sent out notice that the fighting system will be abolished, which unfortunately has resulted in more anxiety than relief. People just can't picture a life other than the one they have lived, 'what now' seems to be the dominant question in their heads. We will have to cross that bridge, but still, it is a strenuous task. What's more, the incident at the protest left many scared and suspicious of us, they just don't understand the cause behind it and still blame us."

Rahim whistled, "quite the mess you have on your hands. Do you have any plans yet for addressing this?"

Zora smiled, "on that front, I am a bit optimistic. It'll still take some time, but we have plans for converting the Towers into housing for DWs and others to take advantage of. Once Chance has fully asserted our authority over the network of Bots, we plan to begin distributing food and medical services as widely as possible. Though, the infrastructure to address the massive latent demand will take some time to figure out."

"It sounds like we're all in good hands. Just hearing you talk about this makes me excited for the future. Make sure to let me know if there is anything I can do, I would be happy to be at your disposal. Now, if you don't mind, I have someone else I'd like to catch up with."

"I don't mind at all," winked Zora.

Rahim moved across the room to speak to Nia, "Hey," he said shyly.

She raised her eyebrows, "Hey."

"I hear Zora has been keeping you busy hunting down the remnants of Quell," Rahim said, awkwardly trying to start a conversation.

Nia sighed, "you heard right, it's been a royal pain in my ass. I've had barely any time to myself this past month, everyone always wants more from me. As many names as I've given, there's still more, more than even I know about. I'm still confused on why there were so few of Quell's fighters sent to confront us. I know there are dozens more fighters from the Spartan and Designer programs, their absence concerns me. I'm confident we'll be pulling thorns from our side for a while to come."

"I'm sure, it gives me a headache just thinking about it. I thought one of the perks of winning was supposed to be the luxury of taking a break, but the work just keeps piling up. I guess that just proves the adage correct, success isn't a destination, it's a way of life., Rahim said, doing his best to sound wise.

Snorting, Nia poked at him, "you're just one big book of old sayings, aren't you? Do you ever take a second to listen to yourself? I already know I'm going to be worn thin dealing with you."

That last sentence caused Rahim's ears to perk up, "that sounds like you're going to be sticking around me for a while? Or did I misunderstand that?"

Nia fluttered her eyelashes at him, her hazel eyes boring into his, "you're interesting, I think life could be rather enjoyable by your side. If that's ok with you?"

A warm feeling spread throughout Rahim's chest, that idea sat just fine with him. Suddenly, the future seemed to be full of so many wonderful possibilities.

* * *

"Are you sure you're feeling alright?" Kabir asked.

Chance looked off to the side, "yeah, I'm fine, why do you ask?

Kabir gave her a look that indicated he wasn't convinced, "well dear, your hands have been getting rather sweaty since we arrived."

Her hands slipping in his grasp, Chance realized that her hands had become extremely clammy. "Now that you mention it, I suppose I am rather nervous. The thought of speaking to him just makes me uncomfortable, he brings up so many bad memories."

Kabir squeezed her sweaty hand reassuringly, "I can do this for you if you like, it doesn't have to be you that speaks with him."

Chance shook her head, "no, no, I'll do it. It'll be good for me to stare this fear in the face and overcome it, I just need a second to work up the courage is all." They stood on one of the lower levels of what was formerly Quell's facility. A large steel door faced them from several feet away, locking away the secrets it held inside. "Ok, I guess it's do or die time. Wish me luck?"

Kabir pecked her on the cheek, "good luck, you can do this. In and out, it'll be a walk in the park."

Chance smiled at the encouragement and walked forward, allowing a scanner to read her retina. The door swung open for her, allowing her into a small dimly lit room. A single chair was placed in the center of the room, in front of a plexiglass wall.

Visible through the wall was another room, partitioned away from the one she stood within. Encased within a straitjacket and chained to the wall, sat Mitch Rommel. He was alerted to the presence of a visitor by Chance's entry, looking up with his dead eyes, he smiled upon recognizing her. "My my, to what do I owe the pleasure?"

"I have some information that I need to extract from you," Chance replied. "I need you to tell me where I can find the database on the other androids you produced, rather the androids that the other you produced."

Although the frequency emitted by the kill switch had been able to deactivate all of the US-based Bots in Quell's system, all of the Bots were also reactivated when the system was rebooted. This was a challenge since the androids operated off of the main grid that the rest of the Bots were connected to. Rommel had sent out an unknown number of androids into the world before the kill switch was flipped, and the only way to shut them off without tracking them down would be to shut the whole system down again.

"And what's in it for me?" Rommel said indifferently.

I just knew he was going to make this difficult for me. "Maybe, just maybe, we can find somewhere isolated where you can spend your days until you rust away, where you won't hurt anybody."

Rommel scoffed, "a life relegated to obscurity? I think I'll have to pass, that sounds terribly tedious."

Chance grew irritated, her palms becoming clammier by the second. "Look, you're not getting out of here unless you cooperate. It's just a matter of time until we find them, with or without your help. If you want to be a part of the solution, then now's your chance."

Rommel's expression took on a darkly humorous shade, "You'll find them? Oh, my dear, I do think you have that backward. You see it is they who will find you. One way or another, when you least expect it, your paltry attempts to usurp my spot in the sun will be at an end. There are legions more than you even know about out there, lying in wait for you to let your guard down. We have all of the time in the world, unlike the fragile mortal husks you reside in."

Chance snorted, putting on a brave face. *He's just trying to rattle me. He knows he has nothing going for him and is just trying to get under my skin.* "Well, I gave you a chance. I hope you enjoy solitude because nobody is going to be coming back to visit you for a very long time." Chance turned around at that and left the room. Hoping in her heart of hearts that the worst lay behind her.

About The

Author

Bryce House was born and raised in Tacoma, Washington. He is a graduate of Franklin Pierce High School, and Western Washington University with a BA in Political Science. After completing a year of public service he became an AmeriCorps alumni, and is now attending graduate school for his Masters in Public Administration. He enjoys being in nature, sports, spending time with loved ones, reading, movies, anime, and soaking in new experiences. If you'd like to contact the author, he can be found at:

Booksonthehouse@gmail.com

IG-Houseman5799